Your Love is Enough

THE MORE THAN ENOUGH SERIES

Book 2

DONNA R. MADDEN

Also By Donna R. Madden

More Than Enough series
More Than Enough
Your Love is Enough
You Are Enough

Orlinda Valley series.
No One But You
No Love Like Yours
No Place Like Home
No Heart Like Yours

Book Club Novellas
Sand, Sea, and Shenanigans

This book is dedicated to everyone
who has stood by me and supported me.
Choosing only one person is getting
just to darn hard.

Your
Love is
Enough

Chapter 1

Stacey wrapped her coat tight around her and ran through the parking lot of The Pizza Place, the best pizza restaurant in town, on a chilly February afternoon. She swore winter was getting longer and longer and colder and colder. There was leftover snow, now black from the car exhaust, on the side of the parking lot. Typical winter weather in Tennessee—nice one day, snow the next. Now it's muddy and cold. Luckily, snow usually doesn't last long, but the chill in the air this year was freeze your lungs awful. It might be time to move farther south. Tugging on the door, she stepped inside and welcomed the warmth of the restaurant as it seeped into her chilled bones.

"Hey, Stace!"

She looked around and smiled as she walked to the table filled with her friends, shedding her coat as she went. They came here every Sunday after church. Most of them usually meet at church first. Stacey, though, joins them here. She works hard, and when she has Sundays off, sleeping in and waking slowly, was her idea of resting, not waking up early and heading to church.

After exchanging rounds of hugs, she settled into the only available seat at the table. "Well, look at this. I have the most handsome guy as my lunch date." She ruffled Grant's curls and planted a peck on his cheek.

Grant was the one-year-old son of her friend Elizabeth, and he held out his crust of pizza, wanting to share it with her. She looked at the slobbery wet crust and raised a brow. "Grant, you go ahead. I'll get my own. Thank you, though, for sharing."

He stuck the piece of crust in his mouth and babbled something while spit ran down his chin. Stacey chuckled and wiped his chin with a napkin.

"You know he likes you, Stace. He doesn't share his food." Elizabeth replied.

"But when he does share, it's always with the girls. I'm training him right." Brady, Elizabeth's fiancé—and Grant's dad—answered. Elizabeth elbowed him.

"I was starting to think you weren't gonna show up," said Kristen, her best friend, as she handed Stacey a plate with a slice of pizza.

Stacey shrugged. "You know, a long couple of days working, and I was a bit lazy this morning. I needed my rest." She avoided eye contact as she took a large bite of the cheesy goodness. Kristen, her oldest friend, could always see right through her, and she didn't want to talk about the real reason she was late this morning—a gorgeous blond with the most amazing smoky gray eyes she had ever seen, Tristan.

It had been a while since she and Tristan had talked. Stacey met him last summer when the girls had a get-a-way weekend for themselves and spent the weekend shopping and hiking in the mountains. They ended their day at a restaurant, and Tristan was there with a friend. The guys started talking to the girls, and Tristan and Stacey hit it off.

They talked a lot on the phone since then, but Stacey never let them go out again. She didn't do relationships. That ship had sailed. Her job as a labor and delivery nurse was her life. She worked hard to get where she was, and at times, it was emotionally demanding. She needed to make sure she was one hundred percent ready for whatever her work days threw at her, and the emotions that went with relationships always seemed to get in the way, especially when the relationship failed—which seemed to be inevitable. She was over relationships and had decided a while ago that guys were just not worth it. If she were meant to be with someone, it would happen without thought.

But then came Tristan, and Tristan didn't quit.

It was back in September when they had been talking for a couple of months, and he started asking her out. She kept saying no. She wasn't interested. He finally took the hint, and their talks turned into just occasional texting. But then she ran into him a couple of weeks ago when she and Kristen were shopping at a local outlet mall. He was with Adler, his friend from the mountains, and the four of them ate lunch together. He asked if he could call her again, and they've been talking ever since.

Fingers snapped in front of her face.

Stacey shook her head. She had been daydreaming. *Get focused.* "I'm sorry. What was that?"

Kristen shot a look across the table at Elizabeth.

Elizabeth raised her eyes and smirked. "Something, or maybe someone, has her attention."

"Yeah, I noticed. I wonder if it's a good-looking blond, with smoky gray eyes." Kristen's voice swooned as she said smoky gray, imitating Stacey's voice whenever she talked about the guy who she insisted she wasn't interested in. "First, she was late. Now she's here, but not here."

Stacey's face grew warm. "Whatever. You two are ridiculous. Tristan and I are just friends." She noticed the skeptical expressions on her friends' faces. "He might be interested in me, but remember, I…"

"Don't do relationships." The entire table finished for her.

She looked around, and her jaw dropped. It was really annoying that they always felt the need to mock her. They don't understand that she doesn't need a guy to make her feel whole.

She brushed away all of them and went back to eating.

Jacob, Stacey's brother and Kristen's boyfriend, leaned over the table. "Sorry for always barging in, Stace, but this guy appeared out of nowhere—again—and we know you've been talking."

Her mouth fell open. "How—?"

He held up his hand. "We hear you in your room, or you get a text and walk away."

Stacey rolled her eyes.

Elizabeth agreed. "It's been a while since you've been on a date. Your last relationship didn't end well, and we know you think you have a terrible history with guys, but you deserve to be happy, and Tristan seems really interested." Her shoulders rose to her ears. "Next time he asks you out, just say yes."

Stacey looked around the table at her favorite people. They wanted only the best for her, and they all knew that relationships aren't always easy. Jacob and Kristen have been on again, off again, more times than she could count. Elizabeth and Brady had some issues they had to figure out to get to where they are now.

Stacey sighed. "Fine. The next time he asks, I'll say yes. Does that make y'all happy?"

Her brother smirked. "It will only if you promise."

Stacey glanced at the ceiling. "Fine, I promise." Shit. That's going to be sooner rather than later. Just this morning, Tristan said his goal was to get her to finally say yes.

Her phone pinged right at that moment. She glanced at it. It was Tristan. Seriously? Her heart beat faster.

Seemed like she had to make good on that promise.

Chapter 2

Tristan was leaning against a light pole in front of the movie theater. Stacey would recognize him anywhere. What was it about a man leaning that made them look so hot? Much hotter in person than in the screenshots she stole as they FaceTimed. His dirty-blond hair was long enough to blow in the light breeze on this perfect February night. His gray t-shirt looked snug and stretched across his broad shoulders and muscular chest, accentuating his honed and well-chiseled abs. Even from this far away, she could see that his jeans were tight and fit perfectly in all the right places.

She made that promise at The Pizza Place a week ago, and later that night, he asked her for this date. After a long reminder that she didn't do dates, she sucked at them—well, at relationships in general—he finally agreed to call it a meeting of friends.

So, here they are, and it was just a meeting. *It's just a meeting.* Maybe if she keeps telling herself that, the fluttering that's going on in her stomach will stop.

She puffed out a breath and tucked her long, light brown hair behind her ears, then wiped her sweaty palms on the butt of her tight jeans. As she got closer to the corner, she looked across the street at Tristan and really studied him. His blond hair almost covered his eyes when it blew in his face. His eyes were large and curious. Her gaze traveled down, taking in his well-proportioned features. Then back up.

He was studying her as well. She felt the intense heat of his gaze radiating all the way across the blacktop. The fluttering in her stomach ceased and turned to a brick, causing a sick feeling to take its place.

A smile blazed across his face, showing off the perfect white teeth she remembered and that sexy little crease in his right cheek. Not a dimple, but a crease.

This is crazy, but God, he's so hot. Her nerves took over, and her confidence faltered. Why was she here? She forced a smile onto her face. Relax. It's just a meeting with a guy. It's not a date. Nothing big.

"Hey there, gorgeous." Tristan leaned in. Was he going to kiss her right away? Yes, they kissed that one quick night at the bar, but then she was drunk. It needed to be avoided. For now, anyway. She turned her head and stood on her toes to wrap him in a quick hug and avoid the awkwardness said kiss would have caused.

He squeezed her tight. Her heart skipped a beat—damn heart.

"You ready?" He waved the tickets in front of her.

Her heart, which a minute ago had skipped a beat, now failed to beat at all. She glared at him. "I told you I was going to pay for my own. This isn't a date."

"Yeah, I know. It's a 'meeting.'" His fingers made air quotes. "And I told you I'm old school."

Her eyes went wide, and her neck heated. She didn't want a guy to think she was weak and needy. She was a nurse, for God's sake, and didn't need anyone to do for her.

She breathed in deeply and blew it out. "Fine. I'll get the popcorn and drinks." She walked ahead of him and reached the door first.

He threw his hands up and smirked but reached around her to grab the door anyway and winked. Stacey's knees went weak.

The movie was entertaining, and the company was even better. They both laughed at the same places and got a little uncomfortable during the sex scene. Tristan's comments helped to ease the tension. Maybe it was just her who felt uncomfortable. Oh well.

They walked next to each other as they headed to the parking lot. She fidgeted slightly and wiped her palms on her butt again. Her nerves were shot. She wasn't sure she was ready for the kiss that was sure to come.

Stacey had avoided touching him all night, sat far enough away in her seat so he wouldn't put his arm around her, and tried to keep her hand out of the popcorn bucket when his went in. Her stomach, though, was a traitor and flopped when their fingers accidentally touched.

Finally, they approached her car, a black Nissan Rogue. She pointed. "This one's mine." She stopped and pressed the button on the handle, which unlocked the door.

Tristan's eyes roamed her face. "Is everything okay?"

She could feel him trying to scratch at the surface and figure out what was going on in her brain. She gave him a small nod and a slight smile.

"Well, good. I had a great time. I enjoyed being with you." He brushed his fingers from her ear to her chin and held her face tight, stopping her from fidgeting—she inhaled quickly.

She stood still and slowly passed her eyes up until they latched onto his. Her breath caught in her throat. They were so close; his breath fanned her face.

She licked her lips as Tristan's mouth drew closer to hers. Her heart leaped in her chest. Why was she having such a difficult time with the thought of kissing him? He was very easy on the eyes, and she could look at him all day. They've had great conversations on the phone for the past month, and even before that. He's smart and successful, good looking, independent, and a gentleman. He's almost perfect.

That's the problem. Perfect men don't exist—at least not for her. Stacey closed her eyes and took a deep breath. Calm down. Breathe. Suddenly, something warm and soft pressed against her lips. Her eyes popped open. *What the hell?* His lips were on hers, and his eyes were closed. She placed her hand on his chest and pushed him back. Her lips felt empty without his. Wow!

"What's wrong? You look like you've seen a ghost, or am I that bad at kissing?" Tristan teased.

Stacey shook her head. *Don't act like you're a saint.* She put some space between them and opened her car door. "I really had a great time, and hope we can do it again, but I need you to understand. I don't do relationships."

Tristan lowered his chin to his chest and grabbed her arm, gently pulling her back to him, and smirked. "That's not the first time you've told me that, and here I am. I'm not here for a one-night stand. I like you, Stacey—I really do, and I'm willing to wait and take things as slowly as necessary. If taking six months to get here hasn't shown you that, I don't know what will."

He locked his gaze onto hers and lifted his brows. "But now that I finally got you to go out with me for this *meeting,* I'm really not ready to let you go. How about coffee? The bookstore has a cute coffee shop. We can grab a coffee and dessert—I'll let you pay—and we can talk."

Stacey's heart finally calmed, and her breathing slowed. She really didn't want to let him go yet, either. "Yeah, okay. I'd really like that."

"Good." He closed her door and took her hand.

Two coffees and one enormous slice of cheesecake ordered; they found a quiet table.

"So, I know you're a nurse." Tristan took a bite of cheesecake. "You love taking care of people, but you hate people taking care of you. You're fiercely independent and not one to ask for help. Your brother and your BFF Kristen are the two most important people in your family, and you will do anything for those you call your friends. How's that for a summary of Stacey Lynn Kempt? Did I forget anything?"

His stunning smoky gray eyes were one hundred percent focused on her. He really was amazing. Maybe perfect wasn't a bad thing. "You remembered my middle name. I think I told you it only once."

He reached across the table and engulfed her small, delicate hand in his large one. "You did. I make it a habit to remember names. It's important to my job and when I want to get to know people."

His thumb made circles on her palm, causing sparks of electricity to seep deep into her skin.

She drank her coffee, engulfed in the silence. It would be easy to let him in. It would hurt like hell when things didn't work out, and he walked away.

She pulled her hand from his and surrounded her coffee cup in a death-like grip. "I'm impressed. I'm a nurse, and if I didn't have a chart with my patients' names on it, I wouldn't remember them. It's something I've always struggled with."

Small talk continued, and it came easily. They laughed about the movie and the unbelievable personalities of the protagonist and his future love interest. They talked about books and their favorite authors.

The cheesecake was down to graham cracker crumbs, and her coffee was empty. She checked her phone—nine o'clock. She needed to get home. Morning came early. "I've had a great time, but I really need to go." She pushed her chair out and grabbed the empty cups and plate and threw them away before he was even standing.

He joined her at the door and insisted on her going first, then grabbed her hand as they walked back to their cars.

It was crazy, but here she was again, anticipating his goodnight kiss. This time, though, it wasn't nerves that filled her, but excitement. She may not be about relationships, but all the things that come with relationships—kissing, playing around, sex—weren't off the table. And it's been a while. Okay, if she was truthful, it's been a long while. She hasn't made it past date number two with most guys before she's over it. This one, though, was different. She could tell already. That's probably why she'd been avoiding this meeting.

As soon as they reached her car, she again pushed the button to unlock it, but didn't open the door. Instead, she turned toward him and grabbed his shirt, pulling him to her.

His hands grasped the side of her head, his fingers weaved into her hair, and their eyes held each other in an intense gaze.

Stacey felt a connection, like an electric pulse entering her body. Her heart picked up speed, and her knees grew weak. His gaze radiated into her, heating her up from the inside out. Then finally, their lips met. It was soft and gentle at first as their tongues took some time discovering each other. Then, a hunger exploded inside her, and the kiss changed. It became hot, like him. Filled with passion and desire. It was a kiss that could lead to other things if they were in another place. She moaned as it became deeper and sank her fingers into his hair. She was sure that if he weren't holding her, her knees would have given out.

Finally, they separated, and she didn't bother to hide the desire in her eyes or the fact that she had a hard time catching her breath.

He brushed his finger across her cheek, held her face, and smiled that smile that made the crease appear.

She reached up to brush it, softly caressing his cheek. Their eyes locked together, searching deep within each other's souls. He brushed his lips against hers again. A much softer and sweeter kiss. She couldn't move away if she wanted to, but nothing in her wanted to.

All too soon, their lips parted, and Stacey felt like she was stranded in the middle of an ocean, and it took her a minute to get her bearings and catch her breath.

Tristan's hands traveled down her arms, and his fingers interlaced with hers. "This was a great night. Thank you."

"Thank you for what?" Her fingers heated where their skin touched.

"For finally saying yes and letting me take you out. I started to think I was wasting my time. Adler thought I was. Honestly, after waiting this long, I was thinking he was right and almost didn't ask again."

Stacey jolted, and she froze as those words soaked into her brain. Her stupid trust issues and stubborn emotions almost made this amazing night never happen. "I'm glad you asked, and I'm glad I said yes." She was, and she had a great night. He was different. She could feel it.

The crease reappeared when he smiled. "Can I call you tomorrow? Maybe take you to dinner?"

"I work the next couple of days." Noticing how his face fell, she added, "But I'll be free Wednesday."

"Perfect. Let's plan for Wednesday. I don't want to wait longer than that to see you." He smiled his handsome smile, and the streetlights glittered in his eyes. "I'll call you." He gave her another quick kiss and walked toward his car.

Stacey watched him go and enjoyed the perfection of his rear in his tight jeans and the sculpted way his shirt fit over his shoulders and back. Mm. He was yummy.

CHAPTER 3

S tacey lived with her brother in the house they bought after their parents passed away five years ago. It was a single-story brick ranch in an older yet well-kept subdivision in a small town north of Nashville. Her driveway was at the side of the house, and she followed the walkway leading the short distance to their backyard and deck. She climbed the few steps onto their deck, picked at the dead petals on one of the flowers in a pot, and walked into her house.

She entered the kitchen, probably her favorite room, as she loved to cook; though she didn't get too often, but she loved to eat even more. She grabbed a Diet Coke from the fridge, walked into the living room, and fell into the soft chair beside the couch.

The television was on, and Kristen was there as usual, with her head in Jacob's lap and spread out on the couch. She had her own place but had temporarily moved in with her and Jacob right before Christmas. Her mom moved to Florida and left her house to Kristen as a Christmas present. Kristen was having it updated before she officially called it her own.

Jacob slouched with his feet on the table in front of him, his fingers combing through Kristen's hair. "Hey, sis," Jacob greeted her, pausing the television. "So, how'd the date go?" He sat up taller, disturbing Kristen. She sat up and leaned against him.

Stacey shrugged and kept her eyes glued to the screen in front of her. "It was nice."

A pillow slammed into the side of her head, catching her off guard. She spun toward the assailant. "Hey!" She threw the pillow back at Kristen.

Kristen sat on the edge of the couch, her elbows on her knees, leaning as close to Stacey as she could, and blocked the pillow before it could hit her face. "Nice? Really? That's all you can say? You were out past your work-night curfew of eight. It's almost." Kristen checked her phone. "Holy shit, Jake. It must be serious. It's after ten!"

"No way!" Jacob wrapped his arm around Kristen, pulling her closer so he could see the time on her phone.

He glanced at Stacey. "Damn, sis. She's right. You were out way past your work-night curfew."

Kristen cocked her head until Stacey's eyes met hers, then raised her brow. "So? We need more. Was it worth the wait? Spill it." They both sat at the edge of the couch.

Stacey let out a sigh, and her eyes gleamed as she thought about the feel of his lips on hers. "Okay. It was amazing and *so* worth the wait." She leaned back. Her head was on the back of the chair, and her eyes were on the ceiling. "We had so much fun. He's smart, sexy, funny, sexy, successful, sexy..." Her eyes met Kristen's "... handsome. Did I say sexy?"

Kristen nodded.

"Oh, and an amazing kisser."

Kristen squealed and gave Stacey a playful slap. "Yeah, girl! That's what I'm talking about."

Jacob grabbed Kristen by her shoulders and pushed her back against the couch. "That's enough. My turn." He moved to the edge and got in Kristen's way so Stacey would be able to pay attention to him. "She's my sister. Let me interrogate her for a while."

Kristen laughed and sat back up next to him, placing an arm on his leg. "Fine."

"So, sis, if he's so awesome, when are we gonna meet him?"

"Well, nothing like getting right to the point, little brother. It's been one date. Nothing to write home about." Stacey took a deep drink of her diet cola.

"You've been talking to him for months."

"Over six months," Kristen corrected.

Jacob looked at Kristen and gave her a thumbs up. "Six months. You had a great date, and you seem to be attracted to him. We'd like to meet him."

Stacey turned her head slightly but peered out of the corner of her eye. "It wasn't a date. It was a meeting."

Kristen just rolled her eyes. "Semantics. Your brother deserves to meet him." She glanced at Jacob. "I already have."

Stacey sighed. "I know. I'm just not ready yet. My history with guys hasn't been good, and I don't want anyone getting too comfortable around you for me to dump him, eventually. Or him dump me."

Jacob shook his head. "Way to be positive, sis, and why do you think it will end with you getting dumped?"

Stacey sat up tall and glared at Jacob. "You heard how I described him."

Jacob sat up and glared right back. "Yeah, I did. You think he's sexy, and he seems just about perfect."

She jumped in quickly. "Exactly. Perfect. That's what's wrong. He's too perfect. Everyone who is that perfect has a flaw somewhere. Carl, the guy I dated in college. He was good looking, had money and a good career lined up. Everyone thought he was an amazing catch, and that included every girl. He turned out to be a rich, selfish jerk, and a number one asshole of a cheater. Steven last year. That didn't last long. He wanted me barefoot and pregnant while he slept around and did whatever he damn well pleased."

"God, sis. You're ridiculous. Listen to yourself. You're giving him shit because he's about perfect. Then comparing him automatically with your past shit relationships. Not all guys are selfish assholes. You just seem to pick the wrong ones."

"Some of us are pretty near perfect, though." Kristen brushed her blonde hair over her shoulder and winked at Stacey.

Jacob glared at her.

"Kidding, Jakey." She purred.

He rolled his eyes and pulled Kristen closer, kissing her on her head. "Anyway, sis. What if he's *the* one, you chase him off, and I never meet him?"

"The one, really?" Stacey got up and walked toward the kitchen. Her soda was empty, and she needed something to do. Jacob and Kristen followed. Not a surprise. "We've only been talking for a few months."

"Wrong, six months," Jacob intervened.

Stacey gave another eye roll. "This was our first official date. I don't think I'd be able to tell if he's 'the one' after just one date." She leaned against the counter, a bottle of water in her hand. *But he was amazing and easy to talk to, and it was a lot of fun.*

Kristen stood next to her. "So, are you going to see him again?"

Stacey tilted her head and smiled a sneaky smile at her friend. "Yes. He wants to take me to dinner on Wednesday night. He said he wanted to see me tomorrow, but since I have to work the next two days, I told him I couldn't. He didn't want to wait until the weekend. So, Wednesday night it is."

"Well, look at you. Maybe not serious yet, but it looks promising. And he's hot, and as you have pointed out—sexy." Kristen hip-bumped Stacey, making her tip her head back with laughter.

"Hot is definitely one way to describe him, but sexy! His ass in his jeans!" Stacey placed her arm around her friend. "I'd describe him as more of an Adonis." She waved her other hand in front of her face to cool herself off.

Jacob looked back and forth between the two girls. "Whatever. I really don't want to hear this. Don't you need to go to work in the morning? Maybe you should go take a shower and cool off."

"You're right, Jacob. I do need to cool off. Thinking about Tristan, his lips on mine and that sexy body of his is making my blood boil and causing me to get warm in certain places." Stacey panted and Kristen continued to fan her arms.

"TMI, sis." Jacob caught Kristen's hands in his. "You know we could take this into the bedroom and get your temperature up and get you warm in certain places."

Kristen moved closer to him and wrapped her arms around his waist. "Oh yeah? Do you think you're capable of making certain places on my body warm? And if so, how do you plan on doing that?" She gazed into his eyes.

Jacob placed his lips on hers, kissing her deeply. Kristen let go of his hands and grabbed his shirt to pull him close.

"Hey you two. I'm still here." Stacey said as she leaned against the counter. It was about time Kristen and Jacob were together. They had liked each other for so long, and watching her brother and best friend happy filled her with joy. It was so much better this way than when they were playing games with each other's feelings.

Jacob broke away from Kristen. "Sorry, sis." His expression became mischievous as he swept Kristen up into his arms. "Come on. Let me finish this in private."

Kristen's breath caught, and a smile crawled across her face. "And just like that, I'm warm in a certain place," she whispered hoarsely.

"Have fun you two." Stacey left them and hopped in the shower.

CHAPTER 4

*S*tacey *watched as a semi-truck crossed the median on the crowded interstate and collided with the car in front of her. The impact started a chain reaction of noise and cacophony and burned twisted metal. She heard a woman's soft voice calling their names. "Jacob, Stacey, my loves. Take care of each other." Blue eyes, the color of crystals, were in front of her, hands gently touching her face...*

Stacey's eyes flitted slowly open. She had been dreaming.

Five a.m. glowed at her, urging her to get up as if she hadn't just relived her parents' death. She touched her cheek, where seconds ago, she'd felt the gentle hand of her mom. Even though she could still feel the light touch of her hand, the only thing that really existed was the wetness from her tears falling from her eyes.

Stacey had replayed the accident that had taken the lives of ten people in her head over and over again throughout the years. Only two of those people mattered to her and Jacob. They'd lost their parents in that crash. They were coming home from an anniversary trip, yet never made it.

This dream always reminded Stacey of her responsibility to take care of Jacob and make sure he was happy. After the accident, she didn't do that. She focused only on herself and her dream job as Jacob mourned. She worked long hours because she wanted to be the best. The harder she worked, the better the hole in her heart felt. The harder she worked, the more time she spent away from the house and away from Jacob, giving him time to make poor decisions. The harder she worked, the softer the hole in heart felt. Stacey was thankful Jacob had Chad and Kristen because she wasn't there for him like she should have been. She's spent a lot of time in the past couple of years trying to make up for it. His feelings and needs have come before her own.

Pushing herself out of bed, she raked her hands over her face, trying to rub away the remains of the dream. She took a deep breath in and blew it out through her mouth, then twisted her body to the left, then to the right. Finally, she pushed herself up off her mattress and plodded to her bathroom, throwing herself into a shower. It's time to get ready for work.

The Labor and Delivery floor was busy today. There were three babies born during the night, and two families were expecting to go home. The small, intimate feel of the floor was one thing Stacey loved about working at County Hospital. She got to know her patients on a personal level, if she didn't already from living in the small town.

Stacey entered the break room to grab a cup of coffee before starting her shift. Karolyn, a red-haired firecracker, was sitting at the table texting and sipping on a can of Coke.

"Good morning, Karolyn." Stacey smiled.

Karolyn was the wife of an amazing husband, and the mom of two young boys. The nurses loved her husband because he often sent snacks and bagels to help them through their long shifts. Karolyn's always ready-to-go attitude helped to make the ward fun and upbeat. She looked up, with a frazzled expression already on her face.

"Wow, already a bad day? The shift hasn't even started yet." Stacey poured her coffee, added some creamer, and took the seat across from her co-worker.

"Oh, the boys are already giving my mom some issues. She's watching them today. Anyway," she turned her phone over. "Have you talked to anyone yet this morning?"

Stacey shook her head as she sipped from her mug, the warmth of the coffee feeling good as it ran down her throat. "Nope. Just got here. Haven't even seen anyone yet." The coffee was delicious, strong, and flavorful, helping her to focus on the now and forget about her dream.

"Well, we're having a mandatory meeting at the end of the shift. Rumor has it, they are making some cuts." Karolyn raised her eyes over her mug.

Stacey's eyes closed for a beat. "I've heard things being tossed through the rumor mills the past couple of nights. Do you know what's being cut?"

Karolyn shrugged. "Don't know. Just don't miss the meeting. I'm sure we'll find out." She patted Stacey on the shoulder. "Here's to a good day and healthy babies."

Stacey smiled and repeated the lines they all said to each other for good vibes. "A good day, and healthy babies."

Stacey's rounds started with checking in on a new mom who had given birth yesterday. Then she entered a room to check on another mom who had just had her baby in the middle of the night. When seeing the name, her face lit up. It was Leila. She didn't know her well, but she knew that she worked at The Main Street Boutique. Elizabeth, the assistant manager, talked a lot about her.

She knocked before she entered. "Good morning."

"Come in." Leila was a young woman, twenty-three years old, with long brown hair and brown eyes. She had her hair pulled back in a low ponytail, and her eyes had dark circles beneath them. She has probably had a hard night.

"Hi, Leila. I saw the lactation consultant leave and thought I'd come check on you."

She looked up from watching her baby nurse.

Stacey put a smile on her face. "How's nursing going?"

Leila placed her baby over her shoulder to burp. She shrugged. "I don't know. She falls asleep just as she starts eating..." She sighed. "It's difficult, and I'm tired."

Just then, there was a quick knock on the door. A pretty brunette with hazel eyes entered, all smiles. It was Elizabeth.

"Stace. You're here." Elizabeth entered and gave Stacey a quick hug before placing the balloon bouquet she carried on the table and hugged Leila. "Oh, she's adorable." Elizabeth placed her hand on the baby's soft head.

"Do you want to hold her?" Leila asked. Almost pleaded.

"Yes, please. I'd love to." Elizabeth took the baby and cradled her. She smiled and cooed at the little bundle in her arms. Then shot Leila a grimace. "It seems like she might need a change. Do you mind if I change her?"

Leila gave a tired laugh. "Please. Go right ahead. One thing my stepmom told me is to never say no to help with diaper changes."

Stacey got Elizabeth everything she needed. "She's one smart woman. You'll be changing plenty of diapers over the years. Is there anything else you need? Yogurt, water, tea?"

"No, thank you. I'm good for now."

"Just making sure. So tell me, Leila, how do you like working at the boutique? I hear that the assistant manager can be a real bear to work for." Stacey nudged Elizabeth, who was the assistant manager.

Elizabeth shot her a playful glare.

Leila watched as Elizabeth changed her daughter. "Elizabeth's been my lifeline these past few months. I don't know if she told you, but I met her at the pregnancy center. I take her new mom's class. She's been so helpful, and I really don't know if I would have been able to go through with being a single mom if it weren't for her." Elizabeth was surprised a year and a half ago with an unexpected pregnancy of her own. The Crisis Pregnancy Center helped her out, and now she volunteered her time with the women and girls who came in there.

"Oh, Leila, you're too generous. I just did what I needed to do." Elizabeth picked up the fussing bundle and placed her back in her mother's arms. The baby immediately started to root for something to eat.

Leila let out a sigh as the baby's cry turned to a wail. Her forehead creased. "She's hungry, and I can't do it. I don't know how to get her to latch on. The lactation consultant just left. She latched the baby on for me. As soon as she left, she fell asleep. Then you two came in...It's so hard." Tears streaked down her cheeks.

Stacey went to intervene, but Elizabeth stepped in. "Let me help. I remember all too well how stressful the first days of nursing can be. Grant and I had a major learning curve. I've got this, Stace. I had a great tutor when I had Grant." Elizabeth helped Leila hold the baby and gave her tips on how to get her to latch on.

Stacey smiled. "I'll come back in an hour to check on you two. Buzz the desk if you need anything." She walked out. There's no one better to help a new mom than Elizabeth. She felt the familiar emptiness that sometimes appeared when watching a newborn loved by their parents. She was almost thirty and pictured herself married by now and planning a family. She pushed those feelings away as she approached the next room. This family was getting ready to head home with their new addition.

She knocked on the mostly open door before entering. "Good morning."

The room was a bustle of activity. The new mom, Darcey, was dressed and sitting in the chair, eating some yogurt. An older lady was changing the baby and smiling at a man videoing the whole thing.

"Hey there, Stacey. We were hoping we'd get to see you before we left." Mark, Darcey's husband, greeted her.

"It's been a busy morning. But I wanted to stop in and see how things are going." She walked over to Darcey. "You look packed and ready to go."

"Oh, I am. I need to get home and get my life as a mom of two started. This hospital is too constricting." She stood up and took the baby from the older lady. "Stacey, this is my mom and dad. They're here from Pennsylvania."

Stacey shook the lady's hand. "Nice to meet you."

"You too." Her face glowed. "We're ready to spoil this little munchkin and help out as much as possible. We have a hotel room and plan on taking Markey with us for a getaway at the pool to give his mommy time to get to know this new guy."

"They're all so lucky to have you here," Stacey answered as she straightened up a little. The love filling the room was hard to ignore. It was easy to see the closeness of the family and the love the grandparents had for their grandsons.

A lump formed in her throat. Stacey smiled and excused herself, quickly explaining that the doctor should be there soon to discharge them, and swallowed down the lump. She kept walking until she got into the break room, where she poured herself a cup of coffee and fell into a chair with her head in her hands. A lone tear made its way down her face, and she wiped it away.

Seeing grandparents' love of grandchildren was always hard. Especially today. Her parents would have made amazing grandparents. Today was the fifth anniversary of their deaths. Be tough and breathe. Stacey drank her coffee and relaxed in the quiet for a bit before she got back to her work.

The rest of the day was pretty quiet and ordinary. No new moms were scheduled for births, so it was just helping the few that were there, and they spent time organizing and restocking. As she worked, she found her thoughts often wandered to her parents and everything they were going to miss. Stacey sighed deeply and moved her thoughts to tomorrow night. Seeing Tristan again. Just thinking about him sent fluttering butterflies into her stomach.

Thinking of holding his strong, firm hands, touching his hard, chiseled chest, and kissing his soft, warm lips made her become weak in the knees. *Be careful, Stacey. You need to guard your heart. You don't have time to pick up the pieces and put them back together when your heart breaks. You don't need a man. You have you.*

"Hey, let's get to that meeting." Karolyn poked her head into the break room.

Stacey jumped, coming out of her daydream. "Shit! I totally forgot."

She glanced at the clock on the wall behind the nurse's station. She couldn't believe her shift was over. She closed out the notes she was typing and stood up. "Okay, let's go."

They walked down the hall together toward the meeting room. "Bad day, huh?" Karolyn asked.

"Oh, you don't know the half of it."

They entered the room and took a seat. There were chairs set up in rows, and eight other nurses were already there, along with Nancy Trowder, the head nurse of Labor and Delivery, and another woman. Stacey didn't know her name, but she had seen her around. Her suit and heels gave her away as someone of importance. She shot a look at Karolyn as her stomach started flopping around like she was on a roller coaster.

Nancy stepped forward. "Thank you, everyone. I know it's difficult to stay a little later or come in a little earlier. You all work hard, and your time is important. We don't want to keep you longer than necessary. This is Doctor Elisha Hensley, the head of the hospital board. She is here to squash any rumors you may have been hearing and to let you know what is really going on. Doctor Hensley."

Elisha stepped forward with a smile plastered on her pretty features. She was tall and thin. She'd pulled her dark hair up on top of her head in a neat bun with wisps of hair framing her face and her bright brown eyes.

Dr. Hensley reminded Stacey of the lawyer who read her parents' will—one hundred percent business with no consideration of anyone's feelings. The flopping in Stacey's stomach now felt more like a fish out of water than a bad roller coaster ride.

Elisha squared her shoulders. "Hi, everyone. I'm going to get right to the point." She paused, her gaze passing across the room. "The board is well aware of the rumors that have been flying around about the hospital. Unfortunately, they aren't all rumors. As you know, the hospital has had to make deep cuts to deal with a money shortage and financial constraints. When looking at the daily running of the hospital, we look at each department, the need of the community to have that department, and the amount of use that department gets. Unfortunately, we have noticed that there has been a decline in the use of County's Labor and Delivery. With the larger hospitals increasing their L and D floors and putting more money into their women's centers, our patrons have been going to other places to have their babies. Because of all these issues, the hospital's administration has made the difficult decision to close the Labor and Delivery wing."

Nancy's gaze met Stacey's. She had been friends with Stacey's mom and helped get her the job after their accident. It was important for Stacey to stay as close to home as possible. But now Labor and Delivery was closing. Her stomach dropped. What did this mean for her job, for the career she had worked so hard to build? She glanced at Karolyn. Their eyes met. Karolyn reached over and squeezed Stacey's hand. She squeezed back. Karolyn needed this job to help her family. What was she going to do?

Elisha continued. "I know this will come as a shock to you, and I want you to understand that this decision was not taken lightly. The administration recognizes the impact this will have on each of you, as well as the community. The floor will be used at full capacity for the rest of this month. We'll work hard to transfer you either throughout County or into other hospitals. Nancy and I will be scheduling meetings over the next couple of weeks to discuss with each of you individually what you are looking for to further your careers."

Hands shot up all across the room, and a murmur rose through the crowd of nurses. Dr. Hensley raised her hand to hush all the noise. "I know you each have many questions and concerns. Here's a packet with paperwork and questionnaires for you to fill out. Like I said, we will be scheduling meetings with each of you to discuss this further at a later date."

Nancy passed the folders around the room and avoided eye contact with the nurses.

"Email addresses and contact information are right there. Please use this if you have questions that can't wait until your meeting. Thank you." Dr. Hensley nodded to Nancy and made a quick exit.

The room erupted.

Nancy tried her best to calm the questioners, but she was failing miserably. Stacey's shoulders dropped. She'll be out of a job by the end of the month. She and Karolyn quickly left the room.

"Well, this was a great ending to a shitty day." Stacey flipped through the folder as she and Karolyn waited for the elevator. The door opened; they got in, joined by a few other nurses. The conversation was filled with shock and questions no one could answer.

Karolyn giggled, and Stacey shot her a look. "What's so funny?"

She shook her head as the elevator doors opened. "Nothing. Just you and your favorite word. 'Shit.' It makes me laugh at how much you say it in a day."

"Shit? I don't say it a lot." Stacey exited the crowded elevator and walked with Karolyn the rest of the way in silence to their cars.

Once inside the safety of her car, she slumped into the driver's seat and laid her hands on the wheel and her head in her hands. "I can't believe they're closing Labor and Delivery. At least one month to look for a new job and prepare to move on, maybe more, but who knows?" She turned the key in the ignition. "I gotta look for a new job. Shit." She stopped and stared off into nothing. "Maybe I do say that a lot. Who knew?"

CHAPTER 5

Stacey sat in her car in her driveway and stared at the other two cars parked there. Even though she loved Kristen like a sister, she sometimes wished she could walk into a quiet house with no one who would need to talk to her. This was one of those nights. She just wanted to grab something to eat and pick up a book and forget about the day.

Stacey trudged slowly, her steps and heart heavy, through the back door and entered the cozy kitchen, where Jacob and Kristen sat at the table eating. Her quiet night wasn't going to happen. "Hey, y'all. It smells amazing in here. I'm starving. Is there anything left over?"

"Of course, there's plenty. I wouldn't forget you, sis." Jacob went to the stove and filled a plate with spaghetti noodles and meatballs with tomato sauce and placed a couple of slices of garlic bread on the side. He set the plate on the table in front of Stacey as he fixed a salad with ranch dressing.

She sent him a small smile.

Kristen sat next to her and filled a wine glass. Stacey took a huge mouthful, letting the fruity and subtly dry flavor fill her mouth. She closed her eyes and swallowed before she took a quicker sip, then got back to her meal. She felt the prying eyes of her two favorite people on her. She glanced up at Kristen and shoved her fork filled with noodles, sauce, and a piece of meatball in her mouth.

"So, how was your day?" Kristen asked.

Stacey chewed for a bit. *What are you, my mom?* Her eyes filled with tears. "Great, thanks. How was yours?" Sarcasm oozed from her words. She stuffed her mouth full of food, trying to avoid a large conversation about a topic she didn't want to discuss.

Kristen placed her hands on the table and fidgeted with the ring on her finger. "Are you sure? You seem a little off."

"Gee, thanks, *Mom,* for the words of encouragement." Stacey's frustration boiled over, and she spat out the words. She locked her gaze onto Kristen's and refused to look away.

"Hey, sis." Jacob reached across the table and placed his hand on her arm.

"If things were good, I don't think you'd be jumping on Kristen for asking a simple question."

Ugh. She couldn't stand it when they ganged up on her. "Look, just because you two are a couple now doesn't mean you have the right to team up against me." She turned to Kristen. "You're still my best friend. Remember the times you've been a bitch to someone over the years? I've been the only one on your side. Especially when the drama flew between you two." Stacey pushed her plate away. She was no longer hungry.

She looked at her brother and her best friend. They both held the same look on their faces. Concern and love. She did a double take, her attention jumping back and forth between them until she could hold their gazes no longer.

She dropped her head into her hands. "I'm sorry. Today was a real shit of a day." She looked up at Jacob. "It always is—his couple was taking their baby home, and her mom and dad were in the room and just talking about how excited they were about having their new grandson, and all the things they were going to help them with, and .... It...." Her voice caught as grief tore from her.

Jacob jumped up out of his seat and wrapped his arms around her, pulling her to his chest. The tears she had been holding all day finally exploded free.

Jacob held her tight. "I know, Stace. Today's always a shitty day. For me, too. I can't believe they've been gone for five years." Tears fell from his eyes also as he held his sister.

"I miss them both so much, Jake." Stacey sniffled and accepted the napkin Kristen offered her. "I had that dream again. I woke up and could feel Mom's hand on my face. It's been so long since I've had that dream, and it all came back again. All day, I've felt her. I've missed her so much."

"I miss them, too, but I know they're proud of where we are. Me working with a tech company, you working as a nurse at County."

Stacey jerked away from Jacob and shoved away from the table. She paced the small kitchen before she leaned against the counter. "Yeah, well, that's something else that happened today to make it even shittier. The hospital is making some cuts, and guess what department is getting the ax?" She shook her head as her eyes met first Jacob's, then Kristen's. "Yep, Labor and Delivery. It seems as if not as many people are using our services since the bigger hospitals have large fancy facilities with perfect rooms."

Her sight became blurry, but she continued. "We all knew we had empty beds often and had fewer nurses on the schedule at a time than we used to a few years ago, but it just made the care of our patients that much better. Moms always raved about how amazing it was to have a baby at County. But it's a business after all, and all that doesn't matter." Stacey's voice broke.

Kristen jumped up and ran to her, placing her arms on her friend's shoulders. "I'm so sorry. You love working there. How could they?"

"Money's pretty important when it comes to running a hospital. It's easy when you just see everything as dollar signs." Stacey shrugged and pursed her lips.

"Sis, what are you going to do?"

Stacey squeezed Kristen's hands and looked at her brother. "They gave us a folder of information, and they're going to have meetings with each of us over the next few weeks. We have at least this month, but eventually I guess I'll be looking for another job. Luckily, they're everywhere. I just loved working in the small setting of County. It's just another addition to the shittiest date on the calendar."

She picked up the folder and started reading over the papers in it. "All this junk is what they want us to look at before our meetings. I guess I'll go hop online and fill out the questionnaire. They want it done before they meet with us. No time like the present." She placed her plate in the sink. "I'm going to hop in the shower, then get to that questionnaire on my laptop in bed. Good night, y'all." She gave Kristen a hug.

"Thanks for dinner." She hugged Jacob.

"Good night, sis." Jacob held on a little longer and squeezed a little harder. She tapped his back and went to the shower.

Her phone vibrating interrupted her as she worked on the questionnaire. She was answering questions about what she liked, where would she like to work and dumb questions like that.

She glanced and saw Tristan's name. Her face lit up, and her heart skipped a beat. "Well, looks like the day's getting a little better." She smiled and laid her computer on her bed and said hello to Tristan.

CHAPTER 6

The next morning, Stacey walked into Main Street Boutique, the cutest clothing store in their small town, to buy something new for her date with Tristan. She also hoped to see Elizabeth.

The bell chimed as Stacey opened the door. The boutique, as usual, was bustling with activity. Customers mingled about, checking out the many items on the shelves and racks, and the fruity scents of candles, and the color of the decorations and displays that filled every corner, grabbed Stacey's attention.

"Good morning, Stacey." Elizabeth greeted her.

"Hey, Liz. What brings you up front?" Elizabeth hasn't worked in the front of the store for a while, as her job as assistant manager now entails working on the online store and purchasing items.

Elizabeth held up a finger, gesturing for Stacey to wait as she assisted another customer, then gave Stacey a hug. "I'm helping Mrs. Stanzel get time off because Leila is in the hospital with her sweet baby girl."

"It's been a while since I've been in." Stacey looked around at the shelves of figurines, candles, and warmers. She started looking through the clothes. "You've really broadened the clothing choices. This stuff is great."

"Thanks. With the online store, our merchandise has been selling quickly, so I'm able to add more styles to the inventory. I'm glad you like it." Elizabeth went to check out some customers.

Stacey continued her browsing and found a lot of cute outfits. She decided on a cute jumper that she could wear with a pair of sandals, a couple of pairs of pants, and some tops. Finally, her arms were full, and she was ready to go.

"Wow. Let me help you with that." Elizabeth emptied her friend's arms.

"Thanks." Stacey felt as if a thousand pounds had been taken from her. She followed Elizabeth to the register. The bell on the door rang again as the last customer left, and Stacey stepped up to the counter.

"Are you getting all this?" asked Elizabeth.

"Yep, I think so. I've got a date tonight, and I'm not sure what to wear."

Elizabeth's eyes became wide as saucers. "A date, huh! Is it with Tristan? Are you finally done having phone sex and decided it's worth your time to get to know him face-to-face?"

Warmth crept up her neck and onto her cheeks. "Phone sex? Really?"

"Well, you are getting a little red," Elizabeth joked. "Seriously though, I've known you for over a year and have yet to see you date a guy for more than a few weekends. The fact that you two have been talking this long says something."

Elizabeth was right. She hadn't dated anyone seriously since college, and Carl had messed with her heart badly. He said he loved her and bought her lots of gifts but had been messing around behind her back. When she finally got the nerve to confront him about it, he accused her of not trusting him, dumped her hard, and spread lies about her in the process. She was humiliated and embarrassed. Since then, she dealt with trust issues, causing her to date different guys on and off, but whenever things seemed to get serious, she would dump him and move on or hold him at arm's length, causing him to get bored and find someone else. Last summer, she started dating Steven, and after just a few weeks, she caught him out with someone else. That was it. She'd had enough.

Tristan, though. He's so sweet and handsome and seems totally different. A smile slowly filled her face. "Yes. It's Tristan."

"Awesome. Finally, going on a date. I guess you listened to us after all." Elizabeth pushed into her friend's shoulder. "It's about time you really put yourself out there. A guy would be lucky to have you."

She couldn't deny there was some truth in what Elizabeth said, but Stacey wrote it off as- if the guy was 'the one,' she wouldn't want to throw him to the side. There would be something connecting them she couldn't explain. Stacey peeked from the corners of her eyes. "Actually, it's our second date. We went to the movies. So, yes. I listened."

"What? And you didn't tell me?"

"I've been working and didn't think about it when I saw you at the hospital."

Elizabeth bagged Stacey's purchases. "Well, look at you, with date number two."

A smile was glued to Stacey's face.

"And with that smile, maybe it'll last a while."

Stacey laughed. "Do you always become a poet when talking about couples?"

"Not usually, but maybe it's a hidden talent." Elizabeth wiggled her eyebrow.

"Look, I know it's early, and there's no one else here, but I'd love to grab a sandwich and have some girl time. Can you get away?" Stacey was hoping the answer was yes. Elizabeth was always a good ear to talk to.

She nodded. "Actually, now's a great time. Mrs. Stanzel will be in any minute. She said she'd pop in to give me my lunch break."

At that time, Barbara Stanzel, the owner of the boutique, walked through the door. Barbara was a petite lady, all of five-feet-one, with dark hair, which she wore short. She was sweet and well liked in the community and at the church she attended. "Good morning, everyone." She smiled at Stacey. "Oh, and good morning, Stacey. I hope you're finding everything you need."

Stacey nodded. "Yes, ma'am. More than what I need, but I can't say no to any of them, so I guess I'm taking them all."

"Well, you can talk to my sales department manager. She has amazing taste when it comes to which fashions to carry."

"Yes, she does, but I wouldn't be upset if your sales department manager would stop buying such cute outfits. I'm going to go broke."

Barbara laughed. "You can always come to work here, Stacey, if you no longer want to work at the hospital. I give a small discount." Barbara retreated into the back of the store.

Stacey placed her hands on the counter and puffed air out of her lungs, blowing a piece of hair from her face. If Barbara only realized how powerful her words were. A job here would be simpler than the politics and selfishness of a hospital. *I just hope another hospital has the* small-town *feel that County does. That's what was best about County.*

Stacey paid her large bill. "I'll order for us at the sandwich shop and meet you at the table under the tree, so you don't need to go very far."

"That would be great. Thanks."

Stacey put her bags in her car and then walked across the parking lot to the sandwich shop. Main Street Deli was the best place in town to get soup, sandwiches, and salads. The bread was baked fresh daily, and the soups were to die for.

Walking in the door caused Stacey's senses to go on high alert. Garlic, Italian seasoning, fresh-baked bread, lots of smells accosted her senses and made her mouth water. She looked at the board with the daily specials, decided on roast beef on rye for both her and Elizabeth, and the homemade chips the deli was famous for.

Once she had their order, she went to the picnic table under the tree by the boutique. It looked over a grassy area just outside of downtown. There was a gazebo in the clearing, and an older couple sat there enjoying the day.

She opened the sandwich, took a bite, and savored the flavors. She ate slowly while waiting for Elizabeth and watched the streets of the small downtown.

She loved this town and didn't think twice about moving here after their parent's death. She and Jacob grew up a short distance away in the neighboring town, but after the accident, they needed a change. As soon as she could, Stacey put their childhood home up for sale and purchased the one they're in now, next to Elizabeth's parents. She chose this town for this purpose. It's safe, it's welcoming, and it's full of happy memories.

Her parents used to bring her and Jacob to the Christmas parade every year. Jacob played Little League at the baseball field at the park, and she and her mom frequented the small square and the cute stores that adorn the store spaces. Even now, on a Wednesday afternoon, there was a lively number of people supporting the small retailers, and sitting under this tree eating her sandwich was perfect. Peace settled over Stacey, and her stress melted away.

Elizabeth joined her at the table. "Thanks, Stace. I'm starving. By the time I got Grant up and ate breakfast, I was running late." She unwrapped her sandwich. "Brady and I chose a date for the wedding last night."

Stacey was dragged back to the present and almost dropped her sandwich. She slapped her hands flat on the table. "Seriously!" Her eyes popped at her friend's news. "When? I hope I'm invited."

Elizabeth laughed, took a large bite of her sandwich, and spoke with her mouth full. "Of course, you're invited. It's going to be on May eleventh. My dad's birthday."

Stacey's heart swelled. Elizabeth lost her dad a few months ago. He had an unexpected heart attack when the girls were out of town the weekend she met Tristan.

"Elizabeth, he would love that. What a great way to make him a part of your special day." Stacey noticed Elizabeth's eyes fill with tears. She reached across the table and squeezed her hand.

Elizabeth gave her a small smile. "Thanks, Stace. It's also going to be at our house. Just a small ceremony for close friends and family in our backyard, with dinner and dancing under a tent. That's what he wanted us to do when we first talked about getting married."

The excitement of Elizabeth's news almost made Stacey forget about hers.

Elizabeth wiped her hand through the air. "Wait, you didn't invite me to lunch to hear about my wedding plans. What's going on between you and Tristan? How'd things go yesterday?"

Stacey's face scrunched up. *What does she know about yesterday?*

Elizabeth continued. "I talked to Jacob. I know it was the anniversary of your parents' accident. How are you?"

Stacey fidgeted with the paper that covered her sandwich. "Honestly, it wasn't the best day." Stacey told her about waking up with the dream, how it seemed that all the patients had loving parents and grandparents supporting them, and then losing her job.

Stacey could see the sympathy getting ready to spew from Elizabeth's mouth and didn't really want anyone to feel bad for her again. She heard it yesterday from Jacob and Kristen, and then on the phone from Tristan when she told him about losing her job.

"But...I'm going to see Tristan tonight. We're going out to dinner." Stacey stared off into the distance, not really focusing on anything. "Elizabeth, he's different. Most guys just want to talk about themselves or throw money at me and brag about their wealth and that I don't need to worry about anything. They'll take care of me. They're so pushy and arrogant and into themselves. Tristan's not like that. Well, he did buy our tickets for the movies." *Typical man.* "But he listens to what I have to say. He also doesn't get offended if I ask to pay for something." She stopped and made eye contact with Elizabeth. "Now, don't get me wrong. I have nothing against a guy buying me presents and doing things for me, but I want them to know I don't need them. I want them." She stopped. "I've never gotten to the wanting part, though. Does that make sense?"

Elizabeth smiled, and her voice became soft. "Yes, it does. That's what I wanted, and I was a single mom trying to work things out with my baby's daddy. There's a difference between needing someone and wanting someone. When a relationship exists because two people want to be with each other, then the need to be together grows from that. That's love."

Stacey's breathing calmed. "My mom told me something like that once. That's the kind of love she and my dad had. They wanted to be together so much that their need for each other grew into two babies."

A picture of Tristan and her cuddling a baby together flashed through her mind. She blinked quickly and shook her head. "Okay, enough of that. As long as Tristan doesn't throw around money or lie and cheat, it'll all be good. I just want to have fun, be myself, and see where things go."

"I agree," said Elizabeth. "That would be a great way for a relationship to start. No need to jump the gun and go right for the family."

Stacey stopped eating as a chuckle escaped from her chest. "That's from the one person who had a baby first and a relationship second."

Elizabeth shrugged. "Yeah, well, whatever. I hope you have a great time on your date."

Chapter 7

Tristan took her to Nashville.

Even though she grew up just forty minutes from the city, she didn't venture here often. She was a small-town girl who preferred the quiet and openness of the country to the closed-in feeling she always got when she was surrounded by tall buildings and lots of noise.

Their dinner was delicious, though. They had sushi and hibachi. It was a fun night, and the company made it even better.

They talked about nothing exciting, but the conversation never got awkward. Once they finished eating, he wanted to take her dancing, so they hit one of the bars on Broadway.

Tristan was a superb dancer and even taught Stacey how to two-step. He was a natural on the dance floor, and she found herself laughing and forgetting about her crappy week. It wasn't hard, wrapped in his arms and watching his eyes gleaming with laughter.

All that dancing made them hot, and they needed some fresh air. She followed him up steps, and he pulled her through a door and out onto the rooftop of the bar overlooking the city. It was a beautiful, clear night. The sound of music spilled from the bars up and down Broadway, and laughter filled the air.

Wednesday nights downtown were crowded but not as crazy as the weekends are. Because of this, they were able to get through dinner and into the bar without a problem.

Stacey wandered to the railing and looked out at the view. The Cumberland River, off in the distance, was calm, and the lights of the city reflected off the still water. She leaned against the railing and closed her eyes. It was peaceful there, even with the muted sounds of music and laughter. They were high enough that it all seemed far enough away not to matter. She took a deep breath and felt the weight of the week float away.

Tristan intertwined his fingers with hers. "A penny for your thoughts."

Stacey sent him a smile and glanced at his handsome figure. She gave his hand a slight squeeze and moved closer to him. "I've had a blast tonight. Dinner was delicious, and I've never danced so much. Thanks."

"That's one of my favorite places to eat down here. Not fancy, but delicious. And you know, that's the second time you've told me that you don't go dancing often. I don't know why. You're a great dancer."

Stacey thought back to the other time they danced. It was the night they met. Once they started talking, Tristan asked her to dance, and they danced until the girls needed to go.

Thinking about their first meeting sent a grin across her face. "Honestly, I usually don't like to dance. I guess I just never had the right partner."

His hand released hers and made its way to her face. He caressed her jawline. Her breath caught as their eyes met. "I guess not. It looks like you do now."

They held each other's gaze for a moment more. All the stress she kept bottled up from the week seemed to melt away. Then their lips met. This wasn't the first time they had kissed. They kissed the first night they met at the bar. They kissed on their first date, but this wasn't a goodnight kiss. This was a kiss they both wanted. Just because.

This kiss had Stacey's stomach doing somersaults and made her pulse race. Her hand went behind his neck, and she pulled herself closer. They were so close together she could feel the heat of their bodies through their clothes, and again, there was a force that shot through her veins and traveled throughout her body.

His hands slid up her back, pressing her into him even more, and their tongues continued the dance their bodies had started earlier. She liked how his body felt against hers. His hard muscles against her soft curves. Their mouths continued tasting and devouring each other.

Her insides warmed and throbbed.

The door to the roof banged against the wall, and they jerked apart. They were no longer alone on the rooftop.

Catching their breath, Stacey laid her head on his muscular chest. She could feel the effect she had on him as his heartbeat thundered against her cheek.

Having control of her body and breathing, she gazed into his eyes. His eyes could change from a soft gray, like clouds covering the sky right before rain starts to fall, but now they were darker, stronger, like thick stormy gray rain clouds.

"Thank you for a wonderful time tonight. This week has been horrible, and I really needed this." She turned, looking back across the city to the river. "To be honest, I wasn't sure if I wanted to come tonight. If this would be something I needed to go into any further."

Tristan rubbed her arms and forced her to face him. "Hey!" He stooped so his eyes met hers. "I don't know what's wrong, but I'm a good listener." His hands moved to her face, and he held her there.

Stacey searched the depths for something to enable her to walk away from him now. She didn't want him to feel sorry for her or to try to fix her problems. She didn't want to be dragged into a relationship just to be dumped later.

But the more she searched, the more she could find only peace and safety. She pulled her gaze from his and pressed her lips together. She breathed in deep, calming her nerves, but the smell of his aftershave and cologne invaded her senses. She placed her hands on his arms and felt a smile crawl across her lips, and she relaxed. "It's been a really bad week."

She held his attention for a bit, then leaned in and lightly pressed her lips against his. "I may not have wanted to come at first, but I'm glad I did. You helped take my mind off everything." Her voice was soft.

Tristan smiled, flashing a set of perfect teeth. "Good. I'm glad you decided not to cancel on me. I don't know what it is with you, with us, but I really like you, Stacey. And I've had a great time tonight." He led her to the other side of the rooftop.

The brick gave way to a plexiglass wall, and they sat on a bench. The view here was all river. It was breathtaking.

Stacey laid her head on his shoulder. "This view is amazing." They sat in silence. She watched as a boat sailed slowly across the calm water with soft sounds of music floating up from it.

As she sat, she thought back to her week—the sadness she felt re-living her parent's death and the effects of her soon to be layoff at work.

Tristan reached over and brushed a tear from her cheek. She sat up, shocked. She didn't even realize she had started crying. Embarrassed, she wiped her face with her hands.

"I told you I'm a good listener."

Stacey took a small, shuddering breath. "I know. It's just that this past Monday was the fifth anniversary of something that changed my and my brother's world."

She turned to him. There was a man full of compassion and understanding standing right there in front of her, and seeing him gave her courage. "Do you really want to know?"

He didn't waver. "If you want to share, I want to listen."

He can't be this perfect. Where's the flaw?

Her heart skipped a beat. She could tell he was serious, and she felt a peace flow over her, and started to open up to him. "It's the anniversary of my parent's death."

Tristan's eyes grew wide, but he didn't say any of the usual things she'd grown tired of hearing, like:

"Oh, honey. How sad."

"Oh, I'm so sorry for your loss."

"Oh, how awful."

He just sat there and let her continue.

"They were killed coming home from their thirtieth anniversary weekend. Jacob and I had talked to them that morning and were expecting them home. We rushed around cleaning, making sure everything looked perfect. We even baked a cake so we could celebrate with them."

Stacey's voice caught in her throat, and she cleared it.

"Our grandmother, Mom's mom, stayed with us that weekend. We were both in college, but she insisted, and we didn't mind. We loved having her around, and being spoiled by her was always a plus." She glanced at him. "It was a good thing she was there. I don't know what I would have done if she hadn't been there. When I answered the door, two cops stood on our porch. They told us about the accident. I was in shock. Jacob became angry. He jumped at them." She brushed away tears that fell as she laughed at the memory of Jacob jumping at the cops, only saved by their grandmother holding him back.

She took a big breath. "Anyway, that was five years ago. Then, to make Monday worse, I found out that I have to find another job by the end of the month. So, yeah. That's been my week so far." She shrugged, took a deep breath, and stood up to stretch her legs.

Tristan stood and leaned next to her. "Wow. I can't say much about losing a job, as I work for the family business, but I know what it's like losing your parents."

Stacey's head flicked quickly toward him. There's no way. "You do?"

He nodded. "I never knew my dad. He died when I was a baby. My mom and I moved into the guest house on my aunt and uncle's property soon after. Adler, the guy I was with when we met in the mountains and again at the mall, isn't just my best friend. He's my cousin and like a brother. We grew up together. Anyway, my mom ended up with cancer and passed away when I was in middle school, sixth grade, to be exact. My aunt and uncle took me in. They raised me like their own and gave me everything I needed." He shrugged. "So, yeah, I understand what it's like losing your parents, and it sucks. It worse than sucks, but honestly, I haven't found the right word yet that quite fits it. To lose your job on the anniversary of your parents' death would double suck."

Just the way he said, "double suck" and the look on his face, his lips puckered, and his brow raised, was adorable, childlike, and just plain funny. She couldn't help the laugh that escaped. It was as if all the pent-up frustration had to come out and finally did.

"What's so funny?" He turned to her. She howled with laughter.

He arched his brow and cracked a smile. Then his smile turned to a chuckle until he, too, was laughing.

Stacey heard him laugh and laughed harder until her side hurt, and she had a hard time catching her breath. She bent over and wrapped her arm around her middle, focusing on trying to breathe.

Finally, she calmed down enough to talk. "Tristan, what the heck…" She had to take in a big breath. "…It isn't funny." She wiped at the tears falling down her cheeks.

"I…know… it's….not….sorry." He spoke between breaths.

Their eyes made contact. They both paused, able to take a big breath before they lost it again.

Stacey held up a hand and closed her eyes. She breathed in through her nose and blew it out her mouth. "Okay." Once she regained her composure, she opened her eyes.

Tristan's were closed tight. He had his arms on the wall in front of him and was focusing on his breathing. The moon shone on his features, and amusement creased the skin around his eyes.

He was even more handsome here now. God, he was perfect. His looks, his personality, absolutely everything. Stacey's heart seemed to stop.

She ducked under his arms and straightened between them. Standing on her toes, she intertwined her fingers behind his neck.

His eyes shot open, and a grin spread across his face, making his crease appear.

She caressed the crease with her thumb. "Thank you."

He wrapped his arms around her and gazed at her. "For what?"

"For understanding and making me laugh. That helped. And it sucks about your parents too."

They held each other's gaze. No one moved; no one talked.

Stacey's heart relaxed for the first time this week as a quiet understanding passed between them.

Then he kissed her. A sweet, light kiss. A kiss between two people who now had a deeper understanding of each other. An understanding that only those who experienced the same grief could share, filled with a need and longing.

When it ended, their foreheads touched, and Stacey breathed. This felt right. She relaxed with him in her arms, and her heart started beating again. Maybe for the first time.

Stacey laid in bed long after she got home. Thinking over their date made her heart race, and their goodnight kiss was even better. It was warm and sensual. Sweet. Her fingers went to her lips. He didn't ask to come inside; they just made out in front of the door. Something changed after he told her about his parents. It was like they shared something that very few people do, and because of that, they suddenly had a new connection.

Her stomach twitched at the memory.

There was a soft knock on her bedroom door. "Hey, Stace. You still awake?"

"Yeah, come in."

Kristen entered Stacey's room and crawled under the covers. "Hey, bestie. You came in late and alone. Again." She sat with her arms crossed on top of the covers, gazing around the room.

Stacey laughed and nudged her shoulder. "Yeah, so? Not everyone needs to hop right under the sheets with a guy after just a couple of dates."

Kristen's eyes grew wide. "What're you talking about? There's only been one guy I've ever jumped under the sheets with after a few dates or alcohol. And anyway, it seems to have worked. Now we're a thing."

Stacey's eyes rolled toward the ceiling.

"But you, on the other hand, seem to keep all guys out of your bed and keep them from meeting your friends." She clapped her hand over Stacey's mouth and caught her gaze. "Do not say I've already met him. That didn't count. I didn't know there was going to be anything between the two of you like this. Now, with feelings and things, it is totally different."

"Whatever! I don't understand why you're both pushing this so much. It's only been two dates. You met the last guy I went out with, and we know how that went. You knew the one in college. That was the mess that started all the messes. I'm just making sure this is actually something." Stacey fidgeted with a thread on her comforter as she avoided Kristen's glare.

"So, do you at least want there to be something? How are things going? I know he looks hot, so physical attraction can't be an issue."

Stacey shook her head and answered under her breath. "No. Attraction's not an issue; getting along isn't an issue; having things to talk about isn't an issue. Nothing's an issue." Her shoulders met her ears. "He's just about perfect. Which is the issue."

"Come on!" Kristen's voice came out much louder than she meant. She put her finger over her mouth in a gesture of quiet. She whispered and smiled, holding back a laugh. "How can perfection be an issue?"

Stacey deflated, the high from her date dropping as fast as a lead balloon. "No one's perfect."

Kristen raised a brow.

Stacey smirked. "Not even you, honey. No matter what you may think."

Kristen splayed her hand across her chest, and her mouth dropped in mock surprise.

"Seriously, though. There has to be something, and I don't think I'll be okay when it comes out. My heart will break. I really like him already." Her voice broke. "I'm scared."

Kristen put her arm around Stacey and pulled her in.

Stacey rested her head on Kristen's shoulder. She was glad she was here.

"Stace, it's okay to be scared. It's not okay to push him away just because. Tell me, what could be one thing that would make him not so perfect? What's the deal breaker?" asked Kristen.

That's easy. Stacey chewed on her bottom lip. Memories of how it felt when she was lied to and caught first Carl, then Steven cheating. Her heart couldn't take that again. "Lying. I can't stand liars. If he lies to me, I wouldn't be able to trust him again. And of course, cheating. Trust is hard to gain and easy to break—instant deal breakers."

Kristen pursed her lips. "Makes sense. But those are huge. What's something that would knock him down a few rungs on the perfection scale?"

"Expecting me to stay at home after we're married because he wants to make all the money. Or not allowing me to go half-in on meal bills. Or buying my love. God, I hate that. Money can't buy happiness. I hate those rich guys who think they can just buy me." Stacey shivered.

"Yeah, money, presents, flowers. Awful, awful things. How dare men!"

Stacey pushed her hard enough that she almost fell out of the bed. "Anyway, I'm waiting for the shoe to drop—you know—no one's that perfect. But then, whenever I think there might be a flaw, he gets even more perfect."

Kristen sat back up and re-situated her pillows behind her head. "I didn't know more perfect was even a possibility. How does someone become more perfect?"

Stacey stared across the room. "Well, I started crying, then ended up telling him about my parents."

Kristen went still. "Wow, that's a big step."

"Yeah, and he totally understood. His dad died when he was a baby, and his mom died when he was in middle school." She locked eyes with her. "See. More perfect, and I'm ready to put myself out there, but I don't want to get hurt. My heart's been hurt too much."

Kristen slipped her arm back around Stacey and squeezed. "Sometimes, Stace, you just have to put yourself out there. Or at least give your best friend a chance to give her input. I'll let you know really quickly if I think he's worth it, and this time I'll make you listen or I'll chase him off for you."

Stacey's eyes closed, and tears squeezed from beneath her eyelids. "Thank you, Kristen. I'm lucky to have you on my side." She wrapped her hand around hers. "Thanks for being such an amazing friend."

Kristen returned the squeeze. "You're welcome. I wish everyone was so easy to sway to my amazingness. So many think I'm a bitch."

Stacey let out a snort as she tried to hold in her laughter. "I just don't know why people would think that, Kris. I really can't figure it out."

Kristen rolled her eyes and pushed her away. "Get on your side of the bed."

Stacey moved over and scooted under the covers. "Why're you sleeping here tonight? Did you piss off Jacob, and he kicked you out?"

Kristen's eyes were closed, and her voice was sleepy. "No. I already had my way with him. He was exhausted and fell asleep. I heard you come home and knew you were alone and thought you might need to talk." She pulled on the blanket, wrapping herself in it like a burrito. "Just being an amazing non-bitchy friend."

Stacey smiled and closed her eyes. She felt at peace and filled with happiness. "Yes, you are, Kristen, and thank you for that. I don't know what I'd ever do without you."

"Yeah, me either. But feel free to hand over any un-wanted gifts you might get from Mister Perfect. No need to throw them away."

CHAPTER 8

Tristan woke up and walked down the back steps that led to the kitchen. Stacey wasn't far from his mind. He opened the huge refrigerator door, took out the gallon of milk, and sat at the table, ready to eat a bowl of cereal.

He couldn't remember when he had felt this content and satisfied without having sex. Even though the dream he had last night put sex with Stacey at the top of his mind, he was willing to wait for her. He wasn't in a rush. He would rather spend time getting to know her. Interesting concept.

He looked out the window at the expansive backyard. Horses were already milling around the back pasture in the distance. Closer to the house, the maintenance crew was out working on the lawn, working in the garden, and cleaning the pool. He took a large bite of cereal. Stacey's soft brown hair and large golden-brown eyes entered his thoughts.

He remembered the exact moment Stacey walked into the Mexican restaurant in Gatlinburg. It was as if the entire atmosphere of the restaurant changed. He looked up from his conversation with Adler and saw her laughing with her friends. He watched as she walked across the restaurant and sat down. She sat facing him, and when their eyes met, there was an instant connection that drew him to her.

"Earth to Tristan."

He felt a hand on his back, and jerked back to reality, spilling milk from his spoon. His aunt was there.

"Good morning, you thoughtful person. I'm surprised to see you in the main house this morning," said Aunt Elie.

Tristan smiled. Aunt Elie's dark hair, which was usually up in a messy bun, spilled around her shoulders. She wore yoga pants and a t-shirt. She was always relaxed when at home and not at her job running the hospital. He didn't know much about what she did or what hospital she worked at, but she worked hard, and was a smart, independent woman who loved her son and nephew.

"Good morning, Aunt Elie." He shoved another spoonful of cereal into his mouth. "If you really want to know, Adler had a—he curled his fingers—'guest' again last night. And I didn't want to deal with all that, so I slept in my old room. It worked out because you always keep the best cereal here for Uncle Don, and your milk is never sour because someone didn't close it. So, I'm also having the best breakfast ever before I head into the office. A win—win for me."

Elie took her toast from the toaster and a hard-boiled egg from the refrigerator. She grabbed a couple of bananas before she sat down to join him at the table, pushing a banana at him. "Well, if you insist on eating that ridiculous cereal, at least have a banana, so I can feel like my sis wouldn't think I brought you up eating junk food all the time."

"I'll do anything so she won't think you're starving her only son and making him malnourished." Tristan picked up the banana and nodded in thanks as he peeled and ate it. He loved the fact that even after all these years, they talked about his mom as if she were still there. It helped him keep her memory fresh in his mind, which seemed to be fading a little more each day.

"I wish the Adler issue were so easy to fix. Think I could throw a banana at that one and make it better?"

Tristan shot his eyes to the ceiling. "I don't think it's that easy. That guy's a mess."

At that time, the back door slammed shut, and it sounded as if one of the horses from the fields was stomping through the house.

"Looks like said mess has arrived." Tristan cleared his area and took his bowl to the sink.

Adler entered the kitchen wearing shorts that were once sweatpants, and Birkenstocks. His dark, unruly hair was sticking up all over, like he just rolled out of bed, but knowing Adler, that's how he fixed it. "What mess are you both talking about, and where were you last night?" He shot a look at Tristan. "Did you spend the night with that hot chick you've been seeing?" Adler opened the fridge, took out the milk, and drank right from the jug.

Tristan just smirked and rolled his eyes. He leaned against the counter and watched his cousin.

"Hey, mannerless. Please act like your parents taught you something." Elie grabbed the milk from his hands and put it back in the fridge. "If you're going to steal my food, drink from a cup."

Adler's hands went up. "Hey, freeloader there gets to eat, and I get forced out of my own refrigerator?" This was the typical go-between with Adler and his mom.

She pulled his face down to make eye contact with her son. "Just remember which one of you is not only the chosen one , but also the responsible one. I still wonder where I went wrong with you." She placed a loud kiss on his cheek and patted it in.

The chosen one and the responsible one were two terms that were always directed at Tristan from sixth grade on when he moved in with the family. It was a good thing Adler had a big head and way too much attitude, or else he would have always held it against Tristan, but instead, it made them closer. Adler had always made sure Tristan was with him because he could do anything as long as Tristan was there to keep him straight and out of trouble.

Adler laid his arms around his mother's shoulders. "Oh, Momma, he may be the chosen one, but I'm your gift from God. Just remember that." He gave her a loud kiss on her cheek. "I love you, Momma."

She shook her head. "Love you too, stinker, but…" She walked away and leaned on the counter next to Tristan. This is how they usually showed a united front. When they agreed on something and needed to stand up together to Adler. "… It would be so nice if you would stop bringing random women home. When are you going to realize you are a prize for one person and not a cheap gift for many?"

Adler grabbed a Pop-Tart from the pantry and turned to Tristan. "Really? You told her I had someone over?"

"I was here when she got up. I had to give her a reason for sleeping here, and drinking her milk. You know me—the truth is always the best way."

Adler threw a piece of his breakfast at Tristan, who backed away.

"No food fights in my kitchen," Elie yelled.

Adler popped the last bit into his mouth and held up his empty hands. "Anyway," he said with his mouth full. "It wasn't someone new over last night; it was that brunette from the benefit we did last week, all legs, curvy body. I've been seeing her for the past couple of days."

Tristan nodded. "That's right. Wasn't her name Becca?"

Adler pointed. "See, she's not some random girl. You remember her."

"Yeah, but her name's Missy, not Becca." Tristan slapped Adler's finger away. "Come on, show them some respect. At least remember her name."

Elie shook her head at her son. "One day, a woman will grab your heart, and I can't wait for that to happen."

"Whatever. How are things going with that girl you're seeing? Has that hot friend of hers dumped her cheating boyfriend yet?"

"You've been seeing someone, Tristan?" Elie asked.

"Yeah, he has been. We met them when we went to the mountains. If they aren't together, they're talking on the phone. Seems interesting, yet he's home every night after their dates. She's playing hard to get."

Tristan shot daggers at Adler and opened his mouth for a comeback. Elie held her hand up. "All right, I've heard enough. It sounds like she's a strong girl who's waiting for the right guy. You, mister." She poked Adler in the chest. "Need to take a few pointers from Tristan. It wouldn't hurt. You're not getting any younger, and I'd love to be a grandma one day."

She kissed them both on their heads. "Enjoy your day, boys. I'm going into my office. I have work to get done."

"You know, Mom, you should stop calling us boys. We are thirty—I think that puts us in the men category." Adler pointed at his mom.

"Men live on their own and don't mooch off their parents."

"Whatever, Mom. Hey, where's Dad?" Adler asked.

"He's already headed to the ranch. He had a big meeting and said something about you two working late. So, get your butts in gear. Love you both."

"Love you back, Aunt Elie."

"Love you back more, Momma." Adler shot Tristan a look, and Tristan pushed him out of the way.

They always played around with who could get her affection the most. Like Tristan said to Stacey, he was treated like a son, and Adler, his brother. They fought and argued like brothers, also. He wouldn't want it any other way.

"It's time to get ready for work. Race you to the house." Tristan was out the door before he finished his sentence. Adler caught up.

Everything to these two was friendly competition and a race. Even before Tristan showed up permanently, they acted like brothers. Adler was born in February; Tristan in June. They were in the same grade at school and played the same sports; they competed at everything but cheated at nothing.

They were neck and neck as they crossed the line.

Yes, a line in the concrete was what they always raced to. It was right in front of the oversize two-car garage attached to the guest house.

Guest house was just a term.

The guest house on the property was a two-bedroom, two-and-a half bath, one thousand square foot pool house. Tristan lived here with his mom until she passed away, then he moved into the main house.

The boys moved to the guest house after college. They paid rent and lived here. It was great. They usually drove to work together and lived on the hundreds of acres, which had horse fields in the front and a cattle ranch way in the back.

That's where they worked.

Adler's grandfather was a rancher. He owned hundreds of acres in Tennessee and even more in Texas. Adler's father owned it now, and the boys helped with the day-to-day operations of the ranches and learned about the business.

"Tie," Adler said, catching his breath.

They both bent over, breathing hard, their faces turned toward each other.

"Fuck," responded Tristan. Ties need to be broken. There needs to be a winner. "This is the second time this week our race has ended in a tie. Someone has to win."

Adler stood up, linking his fingers behind his head. "We played rock, paper, scissors when we were kids. That always worked."

Tristan's eyes rolled hard. "We aren't kids, Warfield. We're adults."

"I hear ya, Calhoun. Are you too mature for kid fun? You'll be a boring dad. I'll make sure to tell...." He looked up at the sky.

Tristan shoved into Adler as he walked by. "Her name's Stacey. And that's a bit premature. There's no talk of kids."

Adler pushed past Tristan to get into the house first. "I guess not. There's got to be sex before kids." He pushed into the house. "There, I won. Got inside first." He punched Tristan's shoulder and ran off to his room.

Tristan sighed and shook his head. Bringing up Stacey made him think of her, so he sent her a good morning text. He was already looking forward to seeing her again.

CHAPTER 9

Stacey left the room and went to the nurses' station to fill out her paperwork, making sure it was all completed before her shift was over. She glanced at the clock over the desk.

Shit. She had fifteen minutes before her meeting.

It had not even been a week, and her number had already come up. Dr. Hensley and Nancy had only spoken with one other nurse in Labor and Delivery. She was a part-time nurse, who they offered to give impeccable references to for any other job she wanted to apply for. What could it mean that she was being called as the first full-time RN?

Karolyn sat in the chair next to her. Stacey gave her a small smile as she finished typing her reports, then turned toward her with a sigh. "I have my meeting in a bit."

Karolyn lifted her lip and scrunched her nose. "I'm sure it'll all be good."

Stacey chuckled at the look on her face. "Yeah. You look so sure of that."

"Seriously, I'm sure it'll be fine." Karolyn placed her hand on Stacey's shoulders.

She stood and took a deep breath. "Well, I guess we'll find out." She waved as she headed for Nancy's office.

"Hi, Stacey. Come on in." Nancy met her as she was walking down the hall; she had water in her hand and stepped aside as Stacey followed her inside.

Stacey gave her a small smile. She tried to encourage herself as she entered. Be positive, and positive things will come.

"Take a seat and get comfortable. I'm sure Dr. Hensley will be here soon." There were three oversized chairs facing each other in the middle of a well-decorated office. Stacey took a seat, and Nancy sat in the chair next to her. "How is Jacob? I haven't seen him lately."

"He's good. Working hard and focused on getting a promotion," Stacey answered while squeezing her fingers nervously.

"Good. How are you doing with this news? I know it couldn't have come on a worse day for you. It was the fifth anniversary, wasn't it?"

Stacey nodded and noted tears glistening in Nancy's eyes.

"I miss your mom. There's not a Sunday that goes by that I don't miss her alto voice next to me in the church choir. You know, Stacey, I haven't seen you in church for quite a while."

How could she tell her that she held God responsible for her parents' death? Jacob had been trying to get her to go with him to church for years. He finally wore Kristen down, and she attended with him on most Sundays, leaving Stacey to drive alone to meet everyone at The Pizza Place afterward for their weekly lunch. Maybe one day, but she doubted it.

Luckily, she didn't have to answer as Dr. Hensley entered the office. "Hi, everyone. Sorry I'm a little late." She got comfortable in the last chair in the circle, across from Stacey. Again, she wore a suit skirt, black, with a white button-up underneath. She had her hair in the same bun, pulled neatly back, with just a few hairs strategically out of place. She was pretty, yet frightening. Stacey couldn't be sure if she was really that intimidating or if it was just the situation. She swallowed hard to calm her nerves and gave what she hoped was a positive and sincere smile.

"Hi, Stacey. Let's get right to it. I understand that the closure comes as a shock, but as Ms. Trowder has said, we will do all we can to give you anything you need to help you find a new position. Your time here has been wonderful, and as your record shows, you're a great nurse, and any hospital, or even department, would be honored to have you. I've read the questionnaire you submitted online. You want to stay in Labor and Delivery but want one of the smaller hospitals." She shuffled some papers. And pulled one out of a folder and passed it to Stacey. "Here is a list of the Labor and Delivery openings within the city." She also gave a copy to Nancy.

Stacey read the list. All these were great hospitals, but they were in the city. She really wanted to stay in a small town. She glanced around the room, her eyes pausing on pictures of Nancy's family on a shelf behind the desk to stall for time.

"So, is there a hospital on there that you'd be interested in working at?" Nancy asked.

Stacey focused on the woman in front of her. "These are all great hospitals, and I'm sure they would be amazing to work for, but is there any in one of the towns close by? How about Tri -City Hospital or North Star?" Those are two hospitals in neighboring towns. Both were larger hospitals than County, but still had a small-town feel.

Dr. Hensley's unfeeling dark eyes focused on her. "Ms. Kempt. You are one of the best nurses in this department; that is why we are talking with you first. We want to make sure you get first pick.

The best pick. All those hospitals are great hospitals, which you should be honored to work at. The smaller hospitals aren't on the list because I feel they don't have the facilities you need to allow you to bloom and grow as a nurse. You should be shooting higher. Some place that will give you lots of space to move up in your career." Dr. Hensley paused.

Stacey held the gaze of the devil woman across from her. She really had some nerve. *Move up in my career? Is this lady serious? Does she think there is no place to move up in a smaller hospital?*

Dr. Hensley continued. "Please think hard about your choice and let us know by the end of the week."

"Ummm, it's Thursday." Interrupted Stacey.

"Yes, please let us know by the end of your shift on Sunday." Dr. Hensley stood, ending the meeting.

"I have Sunday and Monday off."

"Well then, that gives you extra time. We need your decision by Tuesday. Thank you for your time, but I've got to go."

Sighing, Stacey stood and shook the woman's hand, then, turning to her boss, she pushed her shoulders back and nodded to Nancy. "Thank you for giving me the first choice. I appreciate the thoughtfulness. I'll see you with a decision on Tuesday." Her lips pushed up slightly at the corners. She turned and walked out of the room with as much confidence as she could muster.

Stacey was fuming. That woman was rude. How dare she act all high-and-mighty. She might have doctor in front of her name, but she wasn't a medical doctor. What did she know about actual medical care? She acted as if small hospitals weren't worth her time, and Stacey was wasting it.

She needed a jolt of caffeine and entered the staff room, storming past Karolyn, who was putting on her coat. Stacey banged cups and spoons as she prepared her drink.

Karolyn froze. "I guess your meeting went well."

Stacey's eyes went wide. "Sorry. I just can't believe that woman." She filled Karolyn in on the meeting. "She is the coldest bitch I've ever met."

"It's okay, I promise. What do you say we go get crazy drunk?" Karolyn said as she buttoned her coat.

Stacey remembered the text she received earlier. "I can't. It seems as if I have a visitor who's going to meet me at my house tonight." She glanced at her phone. He'd be there in about fifteen minutes. "Maybe another time."

"Of course. The night my kids and hubby are at their grandma's, and I get to do something fun, I've got to go home, anyway. Oh well. I guess it's a Hallmark movie night for me."

"I haven't watched any Hallmark movies in a while," Stacey answered as they entered the garage.

"I'll give you a summary, but if you're meeting that hot guy you've been seeing lately, I'll say okay. Just tell me all about everything later." The girls hugged and went their own ways to their cars.

CHAPTER 10

S tacey was jamming to the radio on her short ride home, to keep her mind off her meeting, but it wasn't working. Why is it that every song seemed to work against you when you need to get your mind off something? Every song was about being stabbed in the back, starting over, a bitch who ruined your life. Anything that kept her seeing that long-legged, dark-haired, bun-wearing, condescending woman, who sat in front of her acting like small town hospitals were beneath her. Stacey's blood boiled.

She froze when she pulled into her driveway. Her night just got better because Tristan was already here, and damn he looked good.

He leaned against his black truck with his powerful arms crossed across a sexy, muscular chest. He smiled that deep smile, showing off the crease in his cheek when their eyes met. *Damn, why does he have to look so good? It makes this whole—non-relationship thing—much harder to pull off.*

Stacey turned off her car and grabbed a quick glimpse in her rearview mirror. Just don't act like you're excited to see him. Play it cool.

She bent down as if she were looking for something, but quickly put on some lip color and fluffed her hair a bit. She grabbed her purse and sat up as her door opened. "Shit!"

Those amazing thighs and that chiseled chest were right in front of her.

"Sorry. I didn't mean to scare you." Tristan put his hand out.

She took it. "No, not a big deal. You just scared the living shit out of me."

He chuckled softly as he closed her door and followed her as she walked to the back deck. "If you weren't so worried about your hair or lips, you would have noticed me walking toward you."

She stopped and turned—big mistake.

He caught up and cupped the side of her face. "I don't know why you were so concerned about putting anything on those lips. I'm just going to kiss it off."

Her objection was interrupted by his mouth on hers. She tried not to give in to the kiss, but failed miserably. Her hand brushed against his neck as her tongue entered his delicious mouth. So much for playing it cool.

"See. Gone." The crease in his cheek appeared.

Her insides melted.

"How was your day?" Tristan's eyes sparkled. She was sure that her surprise was the cause.

Stacey cleared her throat. "It was okay. Yours?"

"Amazing now." That smile filled his face.

Her heart fluttered. Damn body, always giving away too much. "Well, it looks like you're going to meet my brother and Kristen. They're both home." Her heart jumped again, but she was pretty sure it was just nerves this time. "Since you insisted on showing up here, I guess we can't avoid it."

Stacey walked into the kitchen with apprehension. There was no one there. Good. For now at least, there will be no interrogation.

She stepped aside and gestured widely with her hand for Tristan to follow. He did, and didn't take his eyes off her as he entered.

Her stomach was on that roller coaster again. She closed the door softly, and his hand brushed her arm.

"Is everything alright?" He bent his head low to look at her.

She shook her head. "Yep, it's all good." Stacey went to the refrigerator and found the container with leftovers. "I haven't had dinner yet. You want any? It's spaghetti and meatballs—Jacob's specialty."

She heated it up in the microwave. *Stacey, it's not a big deal if Jacob meets him. He'll love him. He's a great guy.* The roller coaster ride her stomach was on, sped up like they were going down a large hill into a loop. She needed a drink, and water wasn't going to be strong enough. She again went back to the fridge. "Want a beer?"

When Tristan nodded, she took out two beers and went to the table to eat. They sat in silence as they ate, and she watched him. Was she nervous for him to meet Jacob, or because they were alone in the house? She really liked him. He seemed amazing.

His gaze locked onto hers. The roller coaster came to an abrupt halt in her stomach, and her breath hitched. She was already in deep. That's what she was scared of.

She needed a distraction, but found it strange that there were no noises. "Did you see or hear anything when you got here?"

Tristan shook his head. "No. I wasn't here very long before you pulled in."

"Hmm, Oh well." She shrugged. "Jacob and Kristen are gonna miss out on meeting you. Guess they're in bed."

They finished eating, and she cleaned up as her nerves jumped around inside her. She could feel Tristan's eyes on her the entire time, but she found something else to keep herself busy. Between her encounter with Doctor Bitchy, and him actually inside her house, her anxiety ate away at her.

"Let's talk. Something's up with you. You are a fidgeting mess." Tristan lightly touched her shoulder. "What's up?"

She turned to him and froze. His eyes, his body. She shook her head, picked up her beer, and finished it in a couple of gulps. "Want another?" she asked.

"I'm good." He shook his head.

Stacey shrugged, got another for herself, and walked into the living room. She wanted to be comfortable. She sighed and fell hard onto the couch, almost sloshing beer onto the pillow next to her.

Tristan sat beside her and put his arm on the back of the couch. "Stacey, if my being here makes you feel uncomfortable, I can leave." His voice sounded flat to her ears, with a slice of irritation.

She needed to get a grip. She took another mouthful of beer and released a breath. "I'm sorry. Only part of this is you." Stacey watched a muscle in his jaw pulse. She needed to do a better job of managing her feelings. He may not be here long if she doesn't figure her shit out.

She placed her hand on his thigh. "Your being here isn't a bad thing." His thigh felt nice beneath her touch. Strong. Muscular... maybe they should have stayed in the kitchen. She moved her hand and finally put her beer on the table and leaned back to get comfortable. "Okay, this is ridiculous." She sat back up. "Yes, I'm a nervous wreck because you're here. Having a guy in my house is a step I didn't want to take. It can lead to things—great things, I'm sure—but still things I don't want to go to. Remember I..."

Tristan moved closer and ran his fingers through the ends of her hair. "I know. You don't do relationships. I got it."

Their eyes met. Her heart went squishy.

"Is that everything?" His left eyebrow raised.

She let out her breath. "No, it's not." Her fingers found their way to his leg again and played with a crease in his jeans. "I told you about Labor and Delivery closing. Well, I had my meeting today, and Doctor Condescending Bitch was not helpful at all."

"Nice name."

"Thank you. I made it up myself." Stacey's nerves relaxed, and a smile grew on her face.

"Did she do something, like say you weren't going to get support finding a job?"

"No. She said I was one of the strongest nurses in the department. That's why they met with me first. To give me the pick of any job I wanted."

He gasped. "Oh, my God. What a bitch!"

Stacey punched him playfully in the gut. "No, I was moved that she said that about me. It was just that she didn't want to listen when I said something about preferring one of the smaller, more local small hospitals. Like I should be above them. It was rude."

He pushed her hair behind her ear and played with her earring. "Maybe you're too big-hearted, and someone like her is just too snotty to understand you."

Stacey relaxed at his touch, and she stretched her neck. "Exactly. Rich people who think they are better than small-town people irritate me. Just because you have a big house, acres and acres of land, and can do what you want, doesn't mean you're better. You're usually less of a person."

Tristan's hand stopped. "Really, less of a person, just because they have money and stuff. How many rich people do you know?"

"I work at a hospital. I'm around rich shitheads all the time. They're annoying. I have no time for rich people who think they're better than those who work hard for what they have."

"How do you know rich people didn't work hard?"

She narrowed her eyes. "Why are you sticking up for them? They have the money. They can do it themselves."

He removed his hand from her neck. "I think you're being a little hard, is all. It's making you get little wrinkles right here." He rubbed her forehead, and their eyes locked.

His smoldering gaze stopped her breath.

"I don't want wrinkles." Her voice came out in a whisper.

His head moved back and forth slowly. "No, you don't. Let me help you relax." His hand brushed lightly across her forehead and down her cheek, resting on her chin. He rubbed his fingers over her lips.

Her lips separated as she gasped for breath.

Then their lips met.

His hand went to her neck again, but this time gripped hard and pulled her against him. She moaned as the kiss became more intense. Need took over, and she could no longer think. She wrapped her arms desperately around his body, clutching onto him, pulling him closer.

She was relaxed. Totally relaxed.

Someone cleared their throat, and another giggled.

Kristen and Jacob. Shit.

Stacey reluctantly pulled away and quickly got herself together, though not much space came between them. "I think you need to meet my brother and bestie," she whispered breathlessly.

He placed another kiss on her lips, soft and sweet, then pulled them up to stand.

Tristan shook hands with both of them. "Nice to meet you, Jacob. And Kristen, we sort of met before, but this time's official."

"Nice to meet you, officially." Kristen shook his hand and gave him a once-over.

Noticing this, Tristan put his arms out and walked slowly in a circle. "You approve, I hope."

Kristen nodded. "Yeah, looks good. And Stacey was right. You've got a nice ass."

Stacey's face was bright red. She covered it with her hands. "Oh. My. God!"

Jacob chuckled playfully and walked to her. "Since this is an interrogation, tell me, do you have a record we need to know about?" He slipped his arm around Stacey's shoulders. "How about any illegitimate children?"

"What the hell, Jacob!" She elbowed his side.

"Ouch! Stace." He stepped away, rubbing his side, and laughing. "Both important questions. I've gotta look out for you."

"You both wonder why I didn't want to bring him home. Please. Why didn't you keep ravaging each other in your room?"

Kristen gave her a hug. "What, and miss the total fun of embarrassing you? Nah, we don't get enough chances to do that. You're too focused and serious. Let us have our fun."

"Well, I'm glad you two came out here." Tristan sat back down on the couch with Stacey cuddled at his side. "I've heard a lot about you both, and it's great to meet you."

The four of them sat and talked. College and pro sports, music, camping, lots of different things, and the guys had a lot in common.

That's why Stacey had such an easy time talking with Tristan. He was a lot like her brother.

The guys started spitting out sports statistics and their picks of who would make it to the playoffs. The girls rolled their eyes, excused themselves, and went into the kitchen to get more beers.

"Girl, I think I just lost Jacob to your boyfriend."

Stacey placed the empty bottles in the trash and turned. "I told you, he's not my boyfriend."

Kristen waved her hands in the air. "I know, I know. You don't do relationships. Blah, blah, blah. Noted. But with how your lips were tied together when we walked in, I'm thinking you're re-thinking that, aren't you?" She leaned against the counter and crossed her arms. "Or are you still waiting for mister perfect to have a flaw, then you can dump him for being human?"

Stacey rolled her eyes and leaned across from her friend, taking the same stance. "I don't do that. Everyone's human. I know that."

"Do you?" Kristen caught her eye and held on. "Seems to me your goal is to keep yourself lonely and miserable forever. You know Jacob and I are fine. We don't need you mothering us." She placed her hands on Stacey's arms.

Stacey looked away. *I don't do that.*

"Hey, it's good. We're good. It's time for you to think of yourself. Tristan seems to really like you. Just try, and see where it goes. It might be worth it." Kristen waited until their eyes met. "Hey, forget the shitheads in your past." Stacey tried to look away, but Kristen grabbed her shoulders and held her in place. "I know they made it hard for you to trust guys. Your heart was torn out and stomped all over.

I've been there. I remember. But they aren't all like that, and it's about damn time you realized that. You've held Tristan at arm's length—well, farther than that—for how long, and he's still here. Give yourself permission to love someone again."

Tears fell down Stacey's cheeks. Kristin was an awesome friend. Stacey wrapped her arms around her neck and squeezed. "What would I do without you?" She sniffed.

"Probably live a long, lonely life as an old cat lady."

Stacey pulled away and wiped at her face. She handed two beers to Kristen and took two for her and Tristan. "I don't have any cats."

"Not yet. You're too young to be an old cat lady. Let's just hope it doesn't turn to that."

Stacey breathed in deep. She felt better, and Kristen was right. She needed to try to see where things went. They went back into the living room. The guys had moved on from football to the local minor league team. It seemed as if they were planning a night out.

"Tristan said his uncle has rented a club deck at the minor league game. We can go. Food and drinks included. How awesome would that be?"

Stacey stared at Tristan. Sounds expensive. *Rented a club deck, owns a company. How big is this company?*

Thankfully, Kristen was never one to beat around the bush. "Wow. Rich much?"

"It's work related," Tristan said as he put his arm around Stacey's shoulder and pulled her to his side. "Not a big deal. They do it at least once a season. It's not until the end of April. I'll find out the exact date and let y'all know."

The guys continue their talk about sports, which puts Kristen to sleep. She was passed out on Jacob's lap.

Stacey's mind kept going back to the game. Tristan mentioned it's not until the end of April. That's over a month away. He was already seeing them lasting that long. Her heart had that squishy sensation again. She liked it and leaned against his chest.

He and Jacob were getting along and had a lot in common. She was enjoying listening to them. It was important to her that her brother liked who she was dating. He tended to be overprotective, and she didn't blame him.

Her thoughts were interrupted by a loud snore coming from Kristen.

"Oh, my God." Stacey roared with laughter. "I've never heard her snore before."

Jacob shot her a look. "If she hears you laughing at her, you'll have to deal with her."

Stacey tried to compose herself. "I can't wait till tomorrow. I wish I had videoed it."

Jacob shook his head. "I guess I should get sleeping beauty to bed." He shook her a little.

She woke up and stretched. "Yeah, I'm beat. And I wasn't snoring, Stacey. I just breathe loud."

"You heard me? Oh my God, you were so snoring. It sounded like a chainsaw." Stacey imitated a chainsaw sound.

Kristen shot her a death look. "Tristan, it was great to see you again. Take care of our girl. I might kill her in her sleep."

Stacey wiggled her fingers in a wave. "Good night, chainsaw."

Kristen gave her the finger.

Stacey walked Tristan to his car. The night was clear and cool. The wind was light. "You cold?" he asked as he wrapped her in his arms.

"Just a little, but I'm sure you'll warm me up." If nothing else could, those eyes could. Her heart skipped a beat as their gazes collided and melted into each other. "Your eyes change colors. Sometimes they're so light gray, they're almost blue. Sometimes gray, sometimes—like now—they're really dark."

"Yeah, from what I've been told, I have my dad's eyes. My mom used to dress me in gray shirts for family pictures. It made the gray of my eyes pop."

He was wearing a gray shirt now. He usually did. "Is that why you wear a lot of grays? Because of your mom?"

He nodded.

Stacey smiled and pointed to the deck. "See all those potted flowers? My mom and I always filled pots with lots of colors. When she died, it's what helped me through the days and weeks. My grandmother came by all the time with flowers and dirt. We would plant different ones. It was my therapy."

"You don't talk about your grandmother much except in your memories of your parents. Why not?" They both were leaning on Tristan's truck.

"She had to go into a nursing home a few years ago. She passed away. I guess it's been almost three years. Jacob and I are all we have left." Her shoulders became heavy, but she pushed them back.

Again, she didn't want him to feel sorry for her.

"Anyway." She turned toward him and played with the collar of his shirt. "I think Jacob and Kristen both liked you."

"Good. I know that's important. Your brother's great." His hand went around her neck, and the corner of his mouth ticked up. "Where were we?"

His lips lowered to hers. They got right back to where they were when they were interrupted, and the kiss quickly became heated. Tristan pushed her against his truck door.

Stacey pulled his shirt from his pants and ran her hand over his abs. His skin was warm and soft. There were ridges where his six-pack was. She moaned as her hands rubbed along her body.

He pulled back, and his gaze burned into her. He put his hand under her top and slowly traveled it up her stomach.

Their gaze never faltered, but her breath quickened.

When he cupped her breast, she closed her eyes and tipped her head to the side. His mouth met her neck as he massaged her breasts.

"Tristan."

He moved his lips to her mouth, and he kissed her. Hard, and an all-male sound tore from his throat, and his kiss held a hunger she had never felt from him before. Their tongues tasted each other, and she felt her heart would explode as their mouths crushed and devoured, until his lips left hers and he was kissing down her neck.

Her blood pounded throughout her body. Heat radiated through her veins, and wetness pooled between her thighs.

They were in the driveway. This was crazy.

She pulled away as her breath heaved in and out of her lungs, as if she might never catch it again. She felt Tristan's excitement pressed up against her leg, hard. It felt good. It felt amazing. "Tristan."

"Hmmm?" His lips were on hers again. God, he tasted good.

He stopped and pulled away. Far away, and combed his hands through his hair. She stayed up against the truck, not trusting her legs to hold her full weight.

"Girl, wow." Their eyes connected. "I've gotta go. Now, or I'm not gonna leave at all tonight." He opened his door.

She touched his hand, and an electric shock warmed her entire body.

His fiery gaze burned through her. "Would you be offended if I don't kiss you again? If I do, I don't think I'll be able to stop."

The two of them, right here, right now, on the side of his truck, flashed through her mind. She took a large breath and pushed it out slowly. "I think that's a good idea."

He climbed into the truck and rolled down the window. Stacey stood back with her arms across her chest.

She could still feel his hands on her skin and his kisses on her neck. Maybe if she held her arms close, the feeling would never go away.

"I'll call you tomorrow." He waved and pulled out of the driveway.

Stacey watched him, then slowly walked up to the couch on the deck and fell onto it. "I can't go any further. That guy messed with my insides."

CHAPTER 11

Tristan had a hard time staying focused on the podcast he was listening to while he drove home. His mind kept wandering back to Stacey. She was amazing. He was glad they were finally getting to know each other after months of only talking on the phone. He hoped he could get through her hard exterior, which stood firmly against relationships. He needed to figure out why she was against them.

He pushed in the code to open the large black wrought-iron gates with a large W etched on each and pulled through them slowly.

The driveway meandered through wooded property, which, during the day, shaded the driveway and cast a secluded and serene feeling as you entered. After many twists and turns up the drive, the house came into view.

It was a sprawling mansion with an immense entrance onto the porch. The house was an 1800 plantation home, redone but kept up to date. The porch was never used, and neither was the front door. It was the side and back of the house, which had been added on to and modernized.

Tristan followed the road behind the huge four-car garage and to the rear of the property to the guest house, and he used that term loosely.

This house was perfect, lived in, and homey. The pool, which sat out the back door, included a waterfall filtering the water constantly.

He sat in his car and looked around the property. Stacey didn't hide how she felt about rich people. What will she think when she sees all this? The women Adler brought home are materialistic and only notice what they have. Adler says it doesn't bother him, but it bothered Tristan. He loved his aunt and uncle, and he's thankful they took him in, but sometimes he wished this money wasn't a part of his life. Finding the right woman would be so easier if he didn't have all this.

Getting out of his car, he walked to the gate, letting himself into the pool area. Steam from the heated water hovered in the air as he walked around it to lean on the brick wall at the rear.

Here, he looked out onto hilly pastures that went on as far as his eye could see, lit up by the full moon hanging low in the sky. How long could he avoid bringing Stacey here? And when he did, how could he get her to realize he wasn't this money; he just lived here. He worked hard but didn't want to be judged by his family's wealth.

"Beer for your thoughts." He turned to see Adler in swim trunks, standing next to him, a beer in each hand. "I was heading out for a midnight swim, saw you here, thought maybe you needed to talk. What's going on in your head?"

Tristan took the beer and gulped it, enjoying the coldness cooling off the inside of his body.

"Who says there's anything to talk about?" He tried his hardest to shrug off the worry from earlier, not really wanting to talk this out with the lady's man standing before him.

"Calhoun, I know you better than anyone, and you only stand here staring off into the darkness when your mind is wandering as far as your eyes are now. Did your lady leave you high and dry again? You know there are plenty of girls who'd gladly give you a stress reliever. Just say the word, and I'll get one to show up tonight. Missy's in my bed, and she's got some friends."

"Warfield, really? You're out here while some girl is in your bed? When are you going to show respect to women?"

Adler threw his hands up. "What are you talking about? She's not just some girl. She's the one I've been seeing for a while. And anyway, she's asleep. We wore each other out, but you know me. A dip in the pool is how I like to cool off." He downed his beer.

"It's February. A little chilly to swim."

"That's why the pool's heated, remember?" Adler took off and dove into the water with hardly a splash.

Tristan grabbed a couple more beers from the outdoor fridge, placed one on the edge and sat in a chair poolside. Adler swam to the edge, pulled himself up, and grabbed the beer. "Good thing you didn't show up an hour earlier. We were having some fun right here in the water. You would have had a show."

Tristan tipped back his beer. "Good to know. I'll make sure to honk as I come up the driveway from now on." Tristan felt eyes on him. He looked up and dipped his chin, waiting.

Adler placed his drink on the concrete. "You know what? That's the second time you've ignored my question about your date. What's her name again? Stacey?"

"Look at you. You can't remember the names of the girls you bring home and screw, but mine you can."

Adler glanced at the sky as if he were thinking about something. "Yeah, weird. Seriously, though." He got up and sat in the chair next to Tristan. "How are things going with you two? It's been a long while since you've spent this much time with a girl. Well, anytime with a girl." He pushed his cousin's arm. "Talk, Calhoun."

Tristan shook his head. "She's amazing. Beautiful. Smart. Fun." He glanced at Adler. "But not into relationships, so she keeps her space, but then—like tonight—she's wanting more and instigating things, and hot. I'm hoping it's something."

"Damn. That hot, but still home by yourself."

Tristan nodded.

"Seems as if there's something else."

"Yeah. She works at a hospital and can't stand rich people. She says they're heartless and materialistic and look down their noses at everyone else. There might have been more, but you get the main idea."

"Well, it's a good thing you don't know any rich people." Adler slapped his hand on Tristan's shoulder.

Tristan lifted his beer. "Right?"

Adler tapped his against Tristan's. "I'm gonna guess she knows nothing of all this."

Tristan shook his head.

"So, what are you going to do next Saturday? The company's yearly fundraiser. I thought you'd invite her."

A sigh escaped from Tristan as he laid his head on the back of the chair. "Yeah, I was planning on it. Thought it'd be fun. Now, not so sure."

Adler laughed. "Well. If you're hoping this goes somewhere, it's not like you'll be able to hide your family from her forever. *Warfield Meats* is a household name. How're you keeping that from her?"

Tristan shrugged and kept his eyes closed as his head rested. "She never asked your last name. I guess she thinks you're a Calhoun."

"So, you lied."

"It wasn't a lie. It never came up. We talk more about her than me."

"Leaving things out is almost the same as lying, you know."

Tristan didn't have to worry about answering that because just then, a petite woman with long blonde hair came out on the patio. Tristan noticed her first and nodded to Adler, who turned around.

She was wearing a see-through tank top, which barely covered her naked and perfect ass. "Hey." Her voice was groggy with sleep. "I was cold, and you weren't in bed. Come back and keep me warm."

"Okay, babe. Go back inside. I'll be there in a minute," Adler answered. She blew him a kiss as she turned around and sauntered back into the house. He stood up. "Well, gotta go."

"Yeah. Have fun."

Adler raised his beer as he turned toward the house.

"By the way, Warfield," Tristan called to Adler. "That's not Missy from last time. Missy's a brunette."

"Really?" He paused. "Interesting." Adler shrugged. "We'll try to keep down the noise. Don't want to bother you."

"How thoughtful."

"You're welcome."

Tristan watched as Adler entered the house. He drank his beer and sat staring at the sky. Thoughts of Stacey wouldn't leave his head. "How do I tell her about all this? Maybe I *should* just move."

CHAPTER 12

S unday morning Stacey felt hung over, though it was just exhaustion from working six days straight with only Wednesday off.

She sat with her head in her arms on the kitchen counter, with a mug of coffee beside her. "Oh, my God. I'm too tired to pick up my coffee. I should have brought home an IV to drink it." The house was quiet. Kristen and Jacob were at church and would be expecting her to meet them at The Pizza Place for lunch.

She grabbed her phone, and there was a text from Tristan. Her pulse sped up as she read his good morning message. She missed him, and it's only been two days. Thankfully, that streak will end this afternoon. He's coming over. Thank the Lord.

She froze. Wow! She never wanted to be around a guy this much. She really had feelings for him. Absentmindedly, she scrolled through their texts. He was such an amazing guy. He really cared about her and was so encouraging, even when she did not want things to go further. What made him keep pursuing?

His comment that he almost stopped because he thought he was wasting his time entered her mind, and her heart faltered. *Stacey, you've got a man who is caring, thoughtful, loving...wow, he is. Don't. Screw. It. Up.*

She answered him and glanced at the time. "Ten-thirty!" She dropped her head heavily back into her arms. "A shower. I need a shower. It'll wake me up." She pulled herself up and gulped down the hot liquid in her coffee cup before forcing herself into the shower.

She eyed her bed when she passed it, feeling a pull to hop back under the covers. *Do not touch that bed.*

She made it. It was noon, and she was in her car, driving the short distance to the town square to The Pizza Place. Jacob, Kristen, Elizabeth, and Brady were saving her a seat at a table.

"There she is." Elizabeth stood up and gave her a welcoming hug.

"Hey, everyone." Stacey took a seat, and a big sip of the Coke sitting waiting for her. "Where's Jessica and Chad?" Jessica and Chad are total opposites but made a perfect couple. Chad was Jacob's best friend and the jokester of the group. His girlfriend, Jessica, was the sweetest, tiniest thing you'd ever lay eyes on.

"They were going to eat with Grams. She hasn't been feeling well, so they took her lunch." Jacob explained. "But they're looking forward to your birthday party Friday night."

Stacey put her elbow on the table and laid her head in her hand and groaned. "I thought I told you we weren't doing that!"

"What!" Elizabeth and Kristen squealed simultaneously.

Her other hand went to her head. "Can you two please keep it down? My head is banging like there's a little man in there with a hammer." She took another long drag of her Coke. *Come on caffeine. Do your thing.*

"Sis, you know we've got to do something for your birthday. There's no getting out of it."

"Yeah, isn't it your thirtieth?" asked Brady. Stacey shot him a look that she hoped would burn him.

"Oh, man, you said the big, bad word." Jacob lowered his voice to a whisper. "Thirty. We don't say that. We say twenty-nine and holding."

"Damn straight we do." Kristen intervened. "No one turns thirty. We hold at twenty-nine."

Brady took a bite of pizza. "You're thirty, Kristen? Jacob, you got yourself a cougar."

Kristen's eyes bulged, and her hands gestured. "Damn, Brady! What do you not understand about not saying the three-oh number? Elizabeth, do something about him. Quick."

Elizabeth made eye contact with Jacob and placed her arm around Brady's shoulder. "It's a good thing we're still young guys. We have plenty of time until we're holding."

Jacob wrapped his arms around Kristen. "Elizabeth's right. The only thing I need to worry about holding on to is you, babe." They started kissing.

Stacey looked up. "Blah. Come on. All of you. Stop being mushy. It's gross."

Kristen pulled away from Jacob. "Really? This is from the one we walked in on almost doing it right on the couch."

"What?" Elizabeth's eyes went wide. "With Tristan? She finally invited him in?" She asked Kristen.

"Yeah, and I'm surprised he actually left with how their hands were all over each other."

Elizabeth squealed.

Stacey reached for a piece of pizza. "You know, I liked you two better when you didn't talk. Our lunches were much quieter."

"Yeah, well, you worked hard to get us to be friends. Now look at us. Almost besties." Elizabeth said across the table.

Kristen rolled her eyes. "I wouldn't take it that far, but you're not as bad as you once were."

"Kristen," Jacob said.

Kristen rubbed her hand against his cheek. "Just kidding. She knows we're buds."

"Anyway," said Jacob. "Everyone be at the house by six Friday night and prepare to get hammered. My sister only turns thir—"

Stacey shot him daggers.

"Holds at twenty-nine-for-the-first-time, once."

Once Stacey got home, she changed into her cutoff sweat shorts and laid on the couch with a bottle of water set to watch a bunch of chick-flicks. Jacob and Kristen were out and promised to bring her back dinner. Tristan would be here soon. She yawned. Man, she was exhausted. Forget the TV. Hopefully, she could get a nap in before he showed up. She closed her eyes.

She was on the corner of Main Street, by the deli and the coffee shop. It was raining, and she was sipping a coffee, though it smelled oddly like pizza. Warmth spread over her face until something covered her mouth. It was light... warm...

Her eyes fluttered open, and she jumped. Tristan backed away and sat on the edge of the couch. "What, the...." Her vision finally focused.

"It's just me." Tristan raised his arms in surrender as a smirk crossed his lips. Jacob and Kristen rolled with laughter.

"Shit." She spat and sat up catching her breath, glaring at Tristan. "You scared the hell out of me. What the hell?" She pressed her hand against her chest to calm her galloping heart. "You gave me a heart attack. Feel." She grabbed Tristan's hand and pulled it to her chest.

The heat that radiated from his palm through her shirt was like electricity, and her mouth went dry.

Tristan calmed his laughter. "I'm sorry." He leaned in close. "You looked so peaceful sleeping. I couldn't help it." Their lips were almost touching, but he didn't kiss her. "I'm sorry." The crease in his cheek appeared.

Stacey studied his features, and her hand touched his cheek. Heat radiated through her palm, causing her to melt like chocolate on a hot day. Her heart returned to a relaxed tempo. Waking up to him was something she could get used to. "Okay," she whispered and closed her lips on his. Mmm. His kiss was amazing. It was like a birthday and Christmas present wrapped up in a small, gentle package. Perfection.

Stacey rubbed the sleep from her face. "What time is it? I just laid down. And didn't we have pizza for lunch?"

Jacob opened the box. The tomato and garlic smell of deliciousness filled the room.

The fact that she had just had pizza no longer bothered her. It smelled amazing. Her stomach growled.

"It's seven-thirty," Jacob said.

Stacey's eyes popped. "What? No way." She turned to Tristan.

Tristan nodded as he grabbed a slice of pizza and took a big bite. "Wow. This is amazing. Good call, Jacob."

Jacob nodded in acknowledgment. His mouth was full.

"I tried calling to let you know I was on my way, but you never answered. You were sleeping and looked like an angel." He winked at her.

Her heart skipped a beat.

He glanced at his phone. "And yep, it's seven-thirty." He turned his phone towards her.

"Wow. I slept all day. Now I'll never sleep tonight." She glanced at Tristan. Heat radiated throughout her body. "Guess I'll have to find something else to keep me occupied."

Tristan swallowed hard. "Don't tease me. That's not nice."

"Who says I'm teasing?" Tingling traveled from her head to her feet.

"Okay, you two. Enough. Your brother's in the room." Jacob stood up. "Who could use a beer? I could use a beer."

He looked at Tristan and then Stacey. "Do either of you want a beer?"

Tristan chuckled. "Sure, bring us both one."

Jacob gave him a thumbs up and left, returning quickly with a beer for everyone.

Stacey ate in silence, observing her favorite people. Kristen and Jacob were so comfortable together. A small smile played on her lips. Friends and lovers. It was sweet how easily they reacted to each other and finished each other's thoughts. She covered a yawn. *Wake up already.* Her eyes wandered to Tristan, who talked with Jacob and Kristen easily. It felt right having him here and interacting with them.

Her gaze traveled over him. He wore shorts and a gray t-shirt tonight, which was untucked, and his hair was messed up like he had his windows open on his drive over. She reached over to run her fingers through his hair, flattening it out. He turned toward her, his eyes smiling. Had she only known him for a handful of months? It seemed so much longer. She put her plate down and leaned into him. He wrapped his arm around her, and a sigh escaped from her lips. She was content.

The four of them decided to watch a movie, and the guys quickly agreed on the newest horror movie they could find. Stacey and Kristen adamantly opposed that decision, and a small—yet playful—argument broke out. The girls lost and squished together in the middle of the couch, and Stacey grabbed the closest blanket.

Tristan watched as the girls wrapped the blanket tightly around themselves. His eyebrows shot up in amusement. "You two know we're here, right? Stacey, you can move toward me. I'll keep you safe."

Stacey shot a quick look at him and whispered. "You don't understand what it takes to stay safe during a horror movie. Kristen does."

"Yeah, if you want us to watch, we can't trust you guys to help us. You're guys." Kristen agreed as she hid her face under the blanket but kept one eye out, so she didn't miss anything.

Jacob leaned back. "Ignore them. It's like they're one person sometimes. They do their own thing. You've gotta get used to it."

Tristan gave him a thumbs up and chuckled as he got comfortable in the corner.

Two hours later, the movie was over, and the guys were cleaning up because the girls needed a potty break and had to go together. You never know what might jump out of the shower. When the girls came back to the living room, everything was cleaned up, and the TV was off.

"I see you made it out of the bathroom safe." Tristan pulled Stacey to him.

Kristen clutched Jacob. "Yes, we did. It's been fun, but we need to go, or I'll never get to sleep before him." She pulled him toward his room.

"Who said anything about sleeping? I'll get your mind off the movie, and the monsters under the bed." He followed her. "Good night, you two. It was fun." He raised a hand in a wave.

Tristan wrapped his arms around Stacey. "Those two are great together."

She smiled. "Yeah, they are. I'm glad they're finally happy. They deserve it."

He brushed the hair from her face. "What about you? You deserve to be happy, too."

Her smile faded. "You're right." Her hands got sweaty. She pulled away from him. "And I am." She wiped them on her shorts and sat on the couch.

Tristan blew out a breath. "There you go closing up again."

"What do you mean?" She wrapped her arms around her body. "I'm not closing up."

Tristan reached over and unwrapped her arms, clasping her hands in his. "Jacob told me you never put yourself first and spend way too much time worrying about him and Kristen."

Her head snapped toward him. "Not true—anymore."

"Then tell me what you want? Put yourself first. Be selfish, Stacey. Do you even have selfishness in you?" He challenged her.

What is he talking about? Her pulse sped.

"Stace. I don't understand. We talked for so many months before I could finally convince you to go out with me. We've gone out on two dates." He pulled her face to look at him.

She caught his eyes, and her pulse skipped.

"The dates were amazing. We had a great time. You are amazing."

He knows they weren't dates. She furrowed her brow. "Those weren't..."

He placed a finger on her lips. "They were dates. They were amazing dates." He cupped her face in both his hands, keeping her from turning away.

She couldn't ignore the electricity between them. It was like a shock going into her heart, causing it to speed up. They were dates, and he was right. They were amazing. She wanted this. She wanted him. Why was it so hard when he was here? He wasn't like the others. He was one of the good ones, but still...

"I want a relationship, Stacey, with you. I know you don't do them. You've made that abundantly clear. But I want you to try. We might screw it up. But who cares? You're worth it. Make us worth it." His voice cracked.

"Tristan, I'm bad at relationships." There was that smile. That crease in his cheek. Her heart pounded.

"I'm bad with feelings." His eyes were smoldering. Her insides melted.

"Relationships never work."

He dipped his head closer.

Her pulse raced.

"Just because relationships haven't worked in the past, doesn't mean ours will be that way," Tristan said as he rubbed her leg.

His hand sent chills coursing through her. "How do you know about my past relationships?" Who has he been talking to? Her insides were so confused. It was difficult to ignore her feelings for him when a touch sent her body tingling and kept her from thinking straight.

"You. It doesn't take a PhD to know why a woman feels the way you do. That a guy treated you wrong. Unfortunately, too many guys are like my cousin. They treat a woman as if she's disposable, or they cheat. Not enough are like me."

She shook her head. Her feelings were tearing her heart back and forth. "Love doesn't last."

"Love can last, but you have to give it a try." He placed his hand on the back of her neck, pulling her a closer.

If he keeps on, she's going to need CPR. Her heart keeps stopping.

"Please give us a try." His gaze pleaded with hers.

He was so close she could feel his breath on her face. Fear gripped her heart as her eyes searched his for an answer.

Her breath caught in her throat. There was only one answer she could find.

He is every bit as good as he seemed. She closed the small space between their lips. As soon as their lips touched, a vibration filled her entire body. She grabbed his shirt and pulled herself closer, kissing him deeper. She ran one hand through his hair as her other traveled down his back. They kissed desperately and with a need which had her moaning with pleasure.

She stood up and pulled him with her. "Stay with me tonight."

He watched her. "Are you sure?" he asked as he stared heavily into her eyes.

"Yes. I want you to." A need filled her, and her pulse raced. "I want you." She did. She wanted him badly and closed her lips on his again. The kiss was slow and warm. Her tongue caressed his in a sweet embrace. Finally, she broke away and pulled him behind her until they were in her room.

Stacey stood with her back against the closed door and watched him. His chest moved as rapidly as hers. She grabbed his hands, and he pulled her until she could feel his heartbeat beneath her palm. She tugged his shirt, brought it above his head, and tossed it on the floor.

Her fingers caressed his skin, and her eyes traveled over his hard, sculpted pecs. Her thoughts were confirmed. His heart wasn't the only thing amazing about this man.

Her breath came faster. She placed a soft kiss on his abs, his skin warm beneath her lips. Her hands felt the ripples of his muscles and traveled up his chest. She leaned in and kissed him over his heart. A moan escaped him, and his heart thrashed beneath her lips. She traveled her lips across his chest and up his neck.

He whispered her name.

Every time his breathing increased, or a moan escaped, or when he said her name, a tingling sensation filled her body, and her need to feel him grew.

When her lips caught his, she nipped and kissed them. Her tongue mingled with his. Her body pulsed with desire. He made her feel wanted and special. He made her feel...loved.

She broke the kiss and stepped away from him and undressed. Her clothes suddenly became an unwanted barrier between them.

He did the same.

They stood there together, naked. His hands reached for hers, and his eyes taking in every part of her body until their gazes locked.

"Stacey." He breathed her name as one hand came and brushed her cheek.

She closed her eyes and breathed him in. A sense of calm took over her body, and her anxiety evaporated. He was different. This was worth trying. She pulled him toward the bed, and they continued to search and feel each other until their lips joined again.

Tristan laid her onto her back gently. His lips left hers and trailed kisses down her neck, across her collarbone, and finally to her breasts.

His name escaped her as his lips sent fireworks through her, and she fought for control. It had been forever since she had felt this way. Since her body tingled with need and desire. Since she let herself go.

His fingers traveled along her body and touched her in places she hadn't been touched for a long time. Tingling ignited and shot heat through her.

"Tristan, yes."

Again, his mouth found hers as his fingers continued igniting the flame of desire deep within her. She fought for a breath as her body went over a cliff and convulsed. She devoured his mouth and tongue. She needed him now. "Tristan, the drawer." She nudged him and moved closer to the edge of the bed and opened the drawer to show him a box of condoms. "Do condoms have an expiration date? They've been in there a while." She bit her lip, not sure whether she should laugh or be embarrassed.

A smile crept up along his face. "They do, but it's years."

"You might want to check."

He grabbed the box and kissed her lips. "They better still be good. I didn't come prepared for this." He read the box, and a wicked look crossed his face. "We're good."

Stacey leaned up, grabbed him around the neck and quickly got them back to where they were before.

Chapter 13

The movement of the mattress woke Stacey early the next morning. She slowly rolled over, and the view of Tristan sitting on the edge of the bed naked revived her sleepy body. "Good morning. Where are you going?" she mumbled and reached out to touch his bare back.

He turned and leaned down to kiss her. "I didn't want to wake you. It's seven-thirty. I was going to hop in the shower. I need to get to work."

She smiled sleepily. "Mmm. I need a shower."

He laughed. "As amazing as that sounds, I have got to get to work. I'm gonna be late. If you hop in with me, I will be late."

He kissed her again. "Can I come back later? I get off at five. I'll bring dinner."

"I'll be right here, waiting for you." She kissed his lower chest, as that was what was there, and continued, traveling her kisses down.

"Woman, please." He stood up and walked toward her bathroom.

Stacey sighed and rolled over. She was tempted to climb in the shower with him anyway, but knew he needed to go, so she wrapped the covers tightly around her and rolled over. She was soon dreaming of his amazing body and his kisses traveling over her.

"Hey. What brings you in here?" Elizabeth stopped stocking shelves at Main Street Boutique and greeted Stacey.

"Trust me, I shouldn't be, but I was out running errands, and thought I'd just look around." Stacey gave her a hug. "I need some pillar candles. Do you have any with a light rose or lavender scent?"

Elizabeth led her to the candle section. Stacey smelled a bunch of them and decided on four beige candles, which smelled amazing. She grabbed candle holders, gold with pearl. These will add a bit of romance to her room tonight.

She took her time getting to the checkout counter, picking up a light scented body spray on her way past. Stacey felt Elizabeth watching her.

"What are you planning?" asked Elizabeth inquisitively.

"Just a little romantic rendezvous. Nothing exciting."

"You're kidding!" Elizabeth's mouth dropped. "I thought you didn't do relationships."

Stacey rolled her eyes. "Who said anything about a relationship? You can be attracted to someone and have fun in bed without a relationship."

"Really?"

Stacey looked away. "Yeah, it is possible." *It might be possible, but not with Tristan.* She thought of the night before her, and her mouth ticked up.

"You're right. It is possible, but I've heard how you talk about him, and from what Kristen says..."

Stacey reached out and grabbed her arm. "You've talked to Kristen? When?"

Elizabeth chuckled and pulled gently from Stacey's grasp. "Yes, she stopped in earlier and told me all about the dinner date and movie night at your house last night." Stacey felt her neck warm.

"She also said something about an additional car in the driveway this morning."

There was now no warmth. She knew she had turned red.

Elizabeth laughed. "You know, from what I remember, he's a good-looking guy. He seems like he's sweet, and from what you've said, perfect. It's okay to like him. He seems to like you quite a bit."

A stupid grin filled Stacey's face. "True. He's all those things. And he wants a relationship. He said so last night."

"Girl! Great! What did you say?"

Stacey covered her face with her hands. "I tried to say yes, but instead, I asked him to stay the night." She peeked at Elizabeth through her fingers.

Elizabeth's face lit up. "It's a start."

Stacey straightened and bit her bottom lip.

Elizabeth put Stacey's purchases in a bag and told her the total. A customer walked in, so she lowered her voice to a whisper. "So, how was it?"

Stacey's face warmed, and her pulse sped up just thinking of last night. She beamed. "It was amazing. No, it was more than amazing. It was..."

"Life altering, and a relationship in the making?" Elizabeth filled in for her.

Stacey felt her face heat up, and a smile broke out across her face. "Yes, exactly."

Elizabeth let out a squeal that could wake the dead and ran around the counter to engulf her in a hug. "Here's your bags. You have another amazing night. You so deserve it. And remember, love isn't always bad." She squeezed her arms.

Stacey lifted her brows. "Thanks. I'll see you later."

CHAPTER 14

Stacey stood in her bedroom. The lights were dimmed, and the four pillar candles were ready to be lit; their rose and lavender scent filled the air with a light crispness.

She turned to her reflection in her full-length mirror and smirked. She was wearing a black lace bralette, double-layered crop top and a tiny and tight cut-off jean skirt, which sat low on her hips. She had her long brown hair pinned up in a messy bun, with some strands loose around her face, very little makeup and just a tiny bit of eyeshadow and mascara. She finished her look with colored lip gloss just as a knock sounded on the kitchen door.

She took a deep breath and paused before she opened it.

Tristan looked amazing. The t-shirt he wore was dark smoky gray and brought out his eyes. His hair was perfectly messed up, and his shirt was tucked into his tight jeans, which fit snugly in all the right places.

He was checking her out also, and she could tell he liked what he saw. The smoldering look he gave her made her weak in the knees, and she could feel her body warming. She swallowed down the lump in her throat. "Hey." She stepped sideways, giving him room to enter her kitchen.

The bags in his hands smelled amazingly like Chinese. "Hey, back." He walked right in, not even bothering to give her a hello kiss.

She closed the door as he laid the bags on the counter. "You..." She didn't get to finish her protest as he grabbed her and devoured her mouth.

This kiss was hotter and sexier than any before. Their lips pressed together as if they parted, they would be gone from each other forever.

Tristan backed away. "You were going to say something?"

"Yeah." She was disoriented and couldn't think. She shook her head. "Doesn't matter. I don't remember." She touched his cheek. "I've been thinking about you all day."

"Really?" He asked.

She nodded and placed another kiss on his lips. *This is where I belong. This is right.* Stacey's eyes fluttered open.

There was a gleam in his eyes. "I've missed you." His voice was hoarse. He separated enough to look at her. "When you opened the door in this, I couldn't..."

"Then don't." She stopped his words and devoured him, pulling his shirt from his jeans.

They didn't stop their hands from feeling and groping.

He pulled away again, and she thought she was going to die. "Where's your brother?"

Stacey tried to catch her breath. "He won't be here tonight. They're at Kristen's."

"So, no one's here but us?"

She nodded. "All night."

She felt his eyes rove from her head to her feet, then back again. His eyes burned into hers. "Then there's no rush. As much as I'd love to take you right here on the kitchen counter, I'd rather wait till I can enjoy every bit of you." He kissed her gently. Then grinned. "I'm starving. Let's eat while the food is still hot. Like you."

Her mouth dropped, and she studied the counter. "The counter sounds good to me."

He chuckled and handed her some chopsticks. She let out a loud breath.

They ate their Chinese food at the kitchen table. They sat next to each other and ate out of the many cardboard boxes filled with rice, noodles, dumplings, beef and broccoli, chicken and mixed vegetables. There was more food than the two of them could ever eat in one sitting.

Stacey's eyes kept flicking back to the counter. "I don't think I'm ever going to sit here again and not think about having sex with you on the counter. You put that in my mind. I can't get it out."

"Have you ever had sex on a kitchen counter?"

Stacey's eyes creased. "Umm, no. How about you?" Her stomach churned. Did she really want to know?

He winked at her. "I don't kiss and tell."

Her mouth dropped. "Seriously? Someone else's kitchen has gotten christened?" She felt her stomach drop. The thought of him with another girl, doing what she wants him to do to her, made her insides boil with... jealousy? Is that what she felt?

Tristan reached over and grabbed her hand, bringing her back to now. "Hey. You were lost somewhere." He squeezed her hand to get her attention. "I've never had sex on a kitchen counter before. Or in a kitchen on anything before. I promise."

Stacey shot him a look. She wasn't sure if she believed him, but the boiling in her stomach cooled a bit, and turned to mush. "You don't have to say that just to make me feel better. I know you've been with other people. It's not a big deal."

He laid down his chopsticks and took a big drink of water, not taking his eyes off her.

She watched him swallow.

Then he finally spoke. "Really? It wouldn't bother you if I said I've done another girl on her kitchen counter?" His eyes searched hers.

She tried her best to keep her face neutral, though she couldn't miss the acid starting to boil again deep in her gut. She couldn't talk, so just shook her head while taking a drink—a large drink to cool herself off.

"Well, honestly, I get crazy jealous at the thought of someone having you that way." He took another drink. "I'll be honest, though. When you opened the door, and I saw you covered in almost nothing, looking amazing like you do, something in me snapped, and keeping my hands off you and my lips from you was going to be difficult. I wanted you badly, and the counter looked like a great place to take you." He closed the space between them. "Thinking of you with someone else." He shook his head. "Jealousy is not an emotion I do well. I'm selfish, and I want you all to myself."

She froze. And stared at him. He wanted her as much as she wanted him. "I agree."

Their lips met.

"Better watch out, gorgeous. It sounds like you're starting to fall for me. Maybe a relationship is in your future."

"I can like you and not want a relationship, you know." She hoped those words sounded more believable than she felt.

"Not if I have anything to say about it." He wrapped his arms around her. "If I have my way, we will be in a relationship, and we'll have a lot of time to get creative."

"Hmm, doesn't sound so bad. We can start now. The table looks sturdy." Stacey felt the familiar warmth radiating throughout her body, and she kissed him with need. She traveled her kisses down his neck and felt his breath hitch. Her heart did a flip she hadn't felt before. She cleared her throat. "Is this what we're going to do all night?" She wouldn't complain if it was. Her bedroom was ready.

He stood up and started cleaning the table. "Nope. I have other plans. Go change into shorts and a t-shirt. I'm taking you to the club. We're going to play Pickleball."

CHAPTER 15

They drove up a long driveway surrounded on both sides by a golf course. Up ahead was a huge white plantation home with a large parking lot next to it. In the back there was a swimming pool, a couple of pavilions, tennis courts, and they pulled into a parking area of what looked like smaller tennis courts. Surrounded by fancy sports cars and people dressed in expensive clothes, with rackets slung over their shoulders, Stacey felt like a fish out of water.

"What are we doing here?" she asked.

Tristan glanced at her as he turned off his car. "It's just the club my uncle belongs to. I reserved a pickleball court and want to teach you. It's fun. I promise you'll love it."

"You're rich?" The last time she was at a country club was with Carl. That was a nightmare she really didn't want to relive, which included an ex-girlfriend and being treated as inferior. She took a deep breath to calm her nerves and wiped her hands on her shorts.

Tristan opened her door, pulled her out, and enclosed his arms around her waist. "I live with my aunt and uncle. They have money."

"How much money?"

Tristan sighed. "Really, does it matter? I'm not one of those stuck-up rich guys you insist on hating."

She looked into his eyes. No, there was not one thing about him that she hated. "I don't hate you, but why didn't you tell me you're rich?"

"Seriously? Because of this reason right here. Don't judge me because of my family's money." He raked his hands through his hair. "Fine, have you heard of Warfield Meats?"

Stacey's eyes almost popped out of their sockets. "The largest beef company in the country? Of course."

"Yeah, well, that's my uncle's company."

She had no words except. "Shit." She froze.

"Hey." He shook her a little to get her attention. "Breathe. See. This is why I didn't tell you."

"Sorry. Now I'm uncomfortable because I'm with a big shot's son." She tried her best to make light of being here with him, but she felt suddenly inadequate.

"Technically not his son, his nephew. But don't feel that way. You know me. Anyway, It's not a big deal. We aren't gonna talk to anyone. It's just you and me and the Pickleball court." He kissed her lightly and gave her that smile she couldn't resist.

She smiled back and wobbled her head. "Okay. Let's do this." She placed a peck on his cheek and let him lead her to the court.

The pickleball court reminded her of a tennis court, only smaller. In her hand she held a racket that was like a ping-pong paddle, just a little bit bigger. She swung it back and forth. "Okay, so what's this prickly-ball thing?"

Tristan laughed. "It's not Prickly-ball. It's pickleball. It's a combination of tennis, ping-pong, and badminton."

"Okay. I'm good at badminton. We used to play it in the backyard all the time with Mom and Dad." She was swinging the racket, getting the feel of it. "This racket is light. What's the rules?"

He gave a quick description of the parts of the court and some basic rules.

Stacey held her hands up, gesturing around her side of the court, and bounced on her toes, ready for action.

Tristan chuckled and got ready. "Okay, why don't we just make it simple and hit the ball back and forth to get used to it. Then we'll add a rule or two as we go."

"Sounds good." She gave him a thumbs-up.

They played, and she caught on quickly. It was fun. Much easier than tennis, but harder than it looked. They played for a while before they kept score.

She didn't have all the rules down, and it took her a bit to understand she had to stay out of the kitchen—the front part of the court—unless she was chasing a ball that bounced in there, but soon she had it down. Tristan won the first two games. Of course, she thought he cheated, but she came back and won game three.

They were taking a break, and Stacey was enjoying herself. "Now that we're tied…"

Tristan grabbed her water bottle. "Tied? Who's tied? I won two games to your one."

She snatched back her water bottle. "No. Game one was practice. We've each won one. We're tied."

He lifted an eyebrow. "Okay. Since you want to be tied, we'll have to break the tie with a wager."

She swallowed the water and gazed at him. She liked the idea of a wager. She could think of some interesting things they could bet on. A smile grew on her face. "What kind of wager?"

She hoped he would come up with something interesting—something they could do in bed or somewhere creative. The kitchen counter came to mind, and a smile met her eyes.

Tristan shot her a smoldering look that melted her every time. "Are you game for anything?"

The counter, maybe the shower. She looked around. Here? "Oh, yeah."

"Loser must service the winner any way they want for thirty minutes. Tonight."

Stacey shivered. She already had some ideas. That's an easy bet. If she wins or loses, it'll be fun. But she doesn't like to lose.

She shot her hand out. "You're on."

He winked at her. "Let's do this, gorgeous." He kissed her cheek. "You serve." and walked to his side of the court.

"Hey, Tristan," Stacey yelled across the court.

He stopped and turned. His brows lifted. "I like pickles. Large dill pickles. I like to suck all the juice off. Mmm." She licked her lips and served the ball.

He wasn't ready. Point Stacey.

She served again. He volleyed it back. She stepped into the area of the court called the kitchen. It's his serve.

"Remember, gorgeous. Stay out of the kitchen." He served.

"Why?" She returned it. "I'm thinking it could be my new favorite room."

He missed again. Point two Stacey.

"You're a cheater," he yelled across the court.

"You need to keep your mind on the game..." She served "...and out of the kitchen, Sexy."

Point three Stacey.

The game continued. The score was ten for Tristan, eleven for Stacey. She needed one more point to win. She served, and they volleyed for a while.

"Tristan." She hit the ball. "I could really..."

He hit it back.

She returned it. "Suck the juice off a large, stiff pickle."

He missed. She won.

They met at the net. "Too bad. I'll have to settle for a real pickle." She grabbed his shirt, pulled him to her, and kissed him over the net.

"You're a cheater," he whispered against her mouth.

She smiled wickedly. "Me? What did I do? I just talked about pickles and the kitchen. Seems to me you have a dirty mind."

He shook his head and pulled her up and over the low net and into his arms. Her legs wrapped around him as she squealed, but it was cut short as his mouth crushed hers. She held on, and her body warmed. She could feel how much the kiss affected him, and it was touching right where it needed to be.

"Hmm. Someone's pickle is hard." She backed up to see his eyes. "We need to go. We need to go. Now."

"I agree, gorgeous. I have a bet to settle."

CHAPTER 16

"What the hell?" Tristan pressed the brake hard as they pulled into the driveway, which had much more than Stacey's car in it.

Her jaw dropped down to her chest when she saw who all was at her house. Jacob, Kristen, Elizabeth, Brady, Jessica, and Chad were sitting on the patio, deep in conversation. They all looked over as Tristan and Stacey got out of the car.

Stacey grabbed his hands. "I guess you're going to meet everyone."

Tristan bent to look at her directly. "Why are they here? I thought you said no one was gonna be here tonight."

"That's what I thought." She stood on her tiptoes to see him better. "Don't you worry. You'll get a chance to pay me. I won't let you forget." Her lips closed on his, and his hands wrapped around her waist.

"Trust me. That's one thing I won't forget. That was a bet I totally loved losing." His eyes stayed on hers, and the crease in his cheek formed. "Now, introduce me to your friends."

They walked hand-in-hand onto the deck. Stacey quickly introduced him to Chad and Brady. "Jessica and Elizabeth, you've sort of met before."

"Hi, Tristan. Good to see you again," said Elizabeth.

"So," Stacey looked around at all her friends. "What the hell are y'all doing here? I thought we were going to be alone tonight." Stacey hoped they would get the hint.

Kristen looked up. "Yeah, well. We were at The Pizza Place talking about your party Friday night, and Grant got fussy. Elizabeth put him down. We didn't want to stay at her house and possibly wake him. Her mom said she'd watch him, so we came over here."

Tristan pulled Stacey onto the couch next to him. "Well, it's good to meet all of you. You said something about Stacey's birthday?"

Kristen filled him in on the party Friday night. He joined in the conversation as Stacey looked at her friends. Her mouth gaping.

They don't listen. She's told them time and time again she didn't want all the fuss, but here they are anyway, doing what they want, not paying any attention to her.

"You tell me what I need to do. Money isn't an object. Whatever you want for this girl will happen." Tristan responded.

Stacey looked at him. "No. No, you don't. I told you. I don't want a guy to buy things for me."

He stopped her. "I know, and you don't like to need anyone, and you don't want a relationship. But I do. I want all of those things."

Stacey's eyes got wide. What the hell? Him, too? "Does no one listen to me? Tristan, I.."

"No. I want you to listen to me. Like I said. I want all those things, but I want them with you. Your friends want to give you a party, and I want to help." He grabbed her arms. "We care about you, Stacey. Get used to it."

Stacey was speechless. He cared about her. He admitted it in front of all her friends. How did she feel about that? What could she say to that? How can she tell him no? He is the sweetest and kindest guy ever. He really is amazing.

"Yeah, Stace. We care about you. Get used to it." Jessica agreed, and everyone else piped in.

Stacey took a deep breath. "Okay, okay. Have a party for me. Fine. I only hold at twenty-nine for the first time once. Make sure it's a big one, and there's plenty to drink. I'm going to need it." She rolled her eyes at her friends. "Now, all of you need to get your asses off my property." She turned to Kristen and Jacob. "That includes you two. I have a bet to cash in on." She placed her hands on Tristan's face. "And I can't do that with all of you here."

They left, promising to see her Friday night, and Jacob said he'd be back tomorrow.

Tristan watched them go. "Good job getting them gone. Now it's time for me to pay up."

Stacey grabbed his hand and pulled him into the house. "Let's take a shower, and maybe I'll give you a tip."

A couple of hot showers later, they were in Stacey's bed cuddled together, her head on his chest and her eyes closed. She was enjoying the feel of his fingers as they traveled up and down her back.

"Stace?"

"Hmm?" she mumbled. She had no strength left to talk. He wore her out and paid his lost bet well.

"I haven't asked you yet, but my aunt and uncle are having a fundraiser picnic Saturday at the property. I'd love it if you came with me."

Fear engulfed her, and her breathing stopped. "Will I be meeting your family?"

He sat up, and she followed. "Yes. My uncle and aunt are the sponsors, so of course you'll meet them. My aunt's like my mom, so she'll love you. You already know Adler, sort of. He'll be there. The only other one is my cousin, but he's in Texas. That's my family. The rest will be employees of our company and some from where my aunt works and their families. It'll be fun. Horseback riding, food, swimming."

"Swimming in February?" Stacey interrupted.

"The pool's heated."

She pulled away.

"What's wrong?"

She stood up, wrapped her silk robe around her, and sat on her bed. *This is crazy. He's so out of my league.*

"Stacey? What?" His hand touched her back.

"Pickleball at the club. Horseback riding and a heated pool at the property." She turned to face him. "How rich are you?"

"Me? I'm not."

She stood up and walked away. "Come on, Tristan. You know what I mean."

He followed her. "Why? What's it matter?" He lowered his head so he could make eye contact with her.

Her heart skipped a beat. He was amazing. He didn't flaunt money. But it's just the concept. She looked away.

"Stacey. My uncle has money. And the property is where we live. Yes, we have horses, a heated pool, and a membership at a club. He owns hundreds of acres here and even more in Texas. It doesn't matter. It's not mine." He threw his hands in the air, palms up.

Stacey closed her eyes. *You need to make a decision. You need to realize how truly amazing he is and get past your trust issues or continue how you're acting, and you'll lose him.*

He grasped her arms lightly. She turned toward him. His eyes were soft and filled with emotion. His tender touch warmed her soul.

"Tell me. How did you feel about me, about us, before you knew all this? Be honest." Tristan asked.

His eyes—were pleading with hers for answers. He had a ridiculous effect on her that made her feel special and important. Her stomach fluttered. She sighed. "I care about you. I'm starting to find it hard to ignore us."

He squeezed her arms. "So, that shouldn't change. I'm crazy about you. You, Stacey. I..." He paused and swallowed. "I want to be here, and I want to wake up tomorrow morning and watch you get ready for work." His hands rubbed her arms. "Don't make it a big deal. Please."

She looked at him. In his eyes, and ran her hands through his hair. She leaned in and kissed him with a hunger, a need. She needed him. She needed this. "It's not a big deal. Sorry I acted that way. There's nothing I want more than for us to be together."

Their lips linked and came together like magnets. She lost herself in the kiss, in him. She felt how much he wanted to be with her, how much he cared.

"Tristan." Her words were lost as she melted into his gaze. Their kiss deepened until they were on the bed.

Their hands were exploring, and everywhere he touched, her skin turned to fire. He felt how much she needed him, how much she wanted him. Her body was tingling. Their kisses were devouring. Her heart was throbbing.

They rode the wave of satisfaction all the way to shore.

CHAPTER 17

S tacey sang under her breath as she rode the elevator up to Labor and Delivery. Thoughts of Tristan clouded her brain and left her giddy all over. She was ten minutes early and needed a quick caffeine jolt since her night was quite the active one. She filled a mug with coffee, added cream and sugar, and leaned against the counter.

She was on cloud nine.

She's in a relationship. Her. She hadn't fully admitted that to Tristan yet, but she could to herself, and she would make sure he knew soon. He made her feel important. Respected. Strong. She released a deep sigh of contentment as her lips turned upward.

Karolyn walked in with a few other nurses as everyone was ready to start their shift. She leaned next to Stacey. "So, why do you have that weird grin plastered on your face?"

Stacey glanced over her coffee mug. "What weird grin?"

"The one that makes you look like you had the most amazing sex of your life."

Stacey's face heated.

Karolyn let out a squeal. "Holy shit. It's because you did have the most amazing sex of your life, didn't you? You and that guy you're seeing."

Stacey's eyes went wide.

"Girl!" Karolyn put her coffee down and grabbed her shoulders. "Was it amazing? Hot? Kinky?"

Stacey dropped her jaw. "I'm not giving you details."

Karolyn flopped against the counter. "I need to know. I'm a mom. We get quickies between naptimes and what little time we have before a little body comes to share our bed. The kink is gone for a while. I need to hear that someone is having fun."

Stacey shot her a Cheshire-cat grin. "Let's just say. It was amazing. It was hot. The shower, the bed." Stacey paused. "Mostly, though, it was sweet and pretty unforgettable."

Karolyn sighed and leaned back against the counter. "Wow. You've got it bad. I want to hear all about him. Any guy who lights your face up like he has, is someone special, and you deserve special."

"It's a date. But not now. We have mommas needing to see us." Stacey and Karolyn left to start their rounds.

Stacey was having a great day. The moms and babies were in great spirits today, and time flew by.

"Hi, Stacey." Stacey looked up from behind the nurses' station and saw Nancy Trowder leaning on the desk.

"Hi, Nancy." Stacey finished up what she was typing and pushed out of the chair. The way the woman was standing put her on high alert. "What's going on?"

"Nothing. I wanted to catch you and ask you to come see me before you leave. We need to talk. It won't take long." She patted her hand on the desk twice and lifted her hand as she left.

"Okay. See you then."

Karolyn came past the desk then and raised her brows in question. Stacey shrugged and continued on with her shift.

The afternoon was long and not as satisfying as the morning. Moms were irritable, dads seemed on edge, and babies were whiny. It could have been the vibe Stacey was giving off also, as she was not one hundred percent focused. She kept thinking about what Nancy could possibly want. There were plenty of times when they just talked. Nancy's known Stacey most of her life, but with the changes going on now, she wasn't sure.

Stacey took a much-needed break at dinner to grab a bite and get some rest. She wasn't alone long before Karolyn joined her and wanted more details about her amazing time spent with Tristan.

"Girl, he sounds amazing. Remember, happiness is a gift, and we need to make sure that when we find someone who makes us happy and lights us up, that we cling on to them and see it as a blessing because they are." Karolyn paused. "You're glowing, Stace. Everyone can see that."

She was right. There was a difference in her, and it was a good thing. She felt herself flush.

Karolyn reached over and grasped her hand. "I know it's hard for you to put your heart out there, but remember, your parents would want you to be happy."

Stacey changed the subject and found out that Karolyn had had her meeting with Doctor Hensley over the weekend. They found her a job that required only day shifts and occasional weekends. She was able to put her family first and not have to worry about missing Saturday ball games.

Other nurses talked about what their plans were when the department closed. It seemed decisions were being made for everyone but Stacey. Soon, she was heading for Nancy's office.

She knocked and then let herself in.

Nancy sat behind her desk. She held her finger up and pointed to a chair. Stacey closed the door and sat down. Her heart leaped in her chest, and suddenly, her hands started sweating. She wiped her hands on her scrubs. She hated this nervous habit.

Nancy hung up the phone and smiled. "Thank you for coming." She walked around her desk and leaned against it.

Stacey nodded and gave what she hoped looked like a sincere, not creepy, smile.

"How are you doing?" asked Nancy.

Small talk? Do we really have time for small talk? "Good," answered Stacey.

"I'm glad. Have you thought any more about what you'd like to do?"

Stacey laughed under her breath. Honestly, she hadn't given it any thought all weekend. Her mind was in other places. "Unfortunately, no. But I told you and Doctor Hensley I'd like to work at Tri-City Hospital or North Star."

Nancy sat down in the chair opposite Stacey. "I know, and I've been making phone calls on your behalf. There are no positions available at either of those hospitals. I'm sorry. I really am."

Stacey could tell her words were true, but she couldn't hide the fact that hearing that was disheartening. She felt herself deflating a little. The big hospitals have great working atmospheres and more opportunities for upward growth but are so impersonal from a get-to-know-the-patient point of view. They're so busy, it's like they have a revolving door, and no time to become a part of the family.

"Mrs. Trowder, what do you think I should do? You know what I like. Where would be the best place for me? Honestly, I don't care what the *great doctor* says. But I'll listen to you." She couldn't keep the sarcasm out of her words.

Nancy chuckled. "I understand, Stacey, but honestly, without moving, there really isn't another hospital except the ones in the city. The rest would be a drive."

A loud knock on the door interrupted them, and Doctor Hensley entered. "Well, hello again, Stacey. Have you made a decision?"

Stacey's stomach suddenly felt heavy. How could just the presence of someone change the atmosphere of a room so drastically, and not in a good way? She studied the woman intently. She walked so straight that Stacey pictured her putting a rod in her ass to keep herself from bending over. Her skirt and blouse were impeccable. There wasn't a wrinkle to be seen, and even the strands of hair that were free from her tight bun had a purpose and a place.

"No." Stacey's tone was flat when she spoke. "I just asked Mrs. Trowder for advice. I really don't know what I should do."

The doctor placed her hands behind her back and stood even straighter. How was it possible? Stacey couldn't figure it out. But she did. "You have too much talent to waste at one of those small hospitals. Summit Woman's Center has an opening and would love to have you. Your pay would almost double, and you would have a pick of your schedule. I have a contact there who is interested in talking to you." She stopped, and her gaze bore into Stacey.

Stacey fidgeted in her seat.

"Ms. Kempt, all you need to do is let me know, and I will get you an interview before the week is out. You can be working there by the end of the month."

Stacey felt privileged that they would consider her working there. Summit Woman's Center was the best hospital to have a baby. She had been on their Labor and Delivery floor before. A friend of hers recently had her baby there. It was nice. It was fancy. It was large.

"Stacey, it's an amazing opportunity." Nancy broke into her thoughts.

She was right. It was an amazing opportunity. Stacey nodded.

Doctor Hensley clapped her hands. "Great. I'll get an interview set up for Friday. It's settled."

Stacey stood, and her eyes narrowed into slits. "I didn't agree to anything, and I can't Friday. It's my birthday, and I have the day off."

"Well, consider it a present. Happy birthday. I'll let Mrs. Trowder know what time your interview is. I'll make it early afternoon." She nodded and walked out of the office.

Stacey stood with her mouth open, watching her back as she left. Then pivoted to Nancy. "Is she always like that? She didn't even listen to me."

Nancy sighed. "Yep. That's Doctor Hensley." She walked back around her desk. "It's an amazing opportunity, Stacey. Your mom and dad would be proud of you if you took it." She started typing. "I'll let you know what time your interview is set up for. Go home, and I'll see you tomorrow."

Stacey let out a big breath. "See you tomorrow." *Looks like she has an interview already.*

CHAPTER 18

Adler was in the stable when Tristan finally found him. He was brushing one of the chestnut mares, Ginger.

Weird. Adler doesn't usually like manual labor, even something as simple as brushing a horse.

Talk about money going to his head. That's Adler. He's as shallow as it can get. But he's like a brother, and Tristan needed some bro time.

"What the hell are you doing with a horse brush in your hand?" He leaned against the stable with his arms crossed over his chest.

Adler shot him an eat-shit look. "It's called brushing out a horse. I do know how. I took her out for a ride. Needed to get some things off my chest." The stable hand, Jonathon, came and grabbed the reins from Adler and took the horse out to the pasture. Adler placed the brush in the basket, and the guys left.

"What do you have to get off your chest, and who are you?" Tristan had no clue what had gotten into his cousin, but getting things off his chest were weird words coming from Adler. They hopped onto the 4-wheeler. Neither spoke as they took the short ride back to the house.

"Mom sent a text saying she wanted us to eat in the main house if we were going to be home. Are you going?" Adler parked and got out as he talked.

"If you go, I'll go." Tristan knew when they were asked to dinner it was usually for something they had to band together for.

"So, you'll actually be home tonight? I figured you'd be with your new woman."

Tristan stopped and spun to face his cousin.

He looked pissed. He was pissed.

What did the ladies' man, who was never home, and always telling him to find himself someone, have against Tristan suddenly doing just that? "What's going on? You're pissed. Why?"

Adler pushed past him. "Not pissed." He stomped through the door into the kitchen.

Tristan followed. "Yeah, right." He got two beers from the fridge, popped the tops, and handed one to Adler, who leaned back against the counter, his long, muscular legs stretched in front of him. "You're pissed because I did what you said and finally found someone to spend time with."

Adler rolled his eyes, just like a child.

"Dude, you're acting like you're ten. Not thirty." Tristan leaned against the counter.

Adler gave him the middle finger. "I didn't tell you to find a full-time girlfriend, just someone to fill your bed."

Tristan laughed. "Seriously? You want me to hoe around, like you?" He shook his head. "Yeah, that's not me. You should know that by now."

Adler didn't bite when Tristan said he hoed around. There's something else wrong. He usually defended himself when that word was thrown out. "There's something else. What's wrong? Speak to me."

Adler finished his beer and slammed it on the counter. "I'm glad you and what's her name?" He looked at Tristan with his eyes wrinkled.

"Stacey."

"Yeah, Stacey. Are doing great. You deserve to have an amazing girlfriend."

"So do you, Adler," Tristan interjected.

He nodded. "Funny you say that. I agree."

He agreed? He agreed he deserved to have an amazing girl? Tristan walked to his cousin with concern and placed the back of his hand on Adler's forehead. "Nope. No fever."

Adler flicked his head away. "I'm not sick. I've got..." He stared off.

"I can't help you." Tristan shrugged. "If it's the brunette, her name's Missy. That blonde from the other night? You're on your own."

"Yeah, I'm not seeing Missy anymore. The blonde is Callie." Adler shot him one of his smiles that the girls fall all over. Lopsided, and all teeth.

"That makes-their-panties-wet smile doesn't work on me, you know." Tristan walked out the door. Adler followed.

"Didn't make your panties wet?" Adler asked and laughed.

"Can't say that it did. Not that I wear panties."

Adler laughed, then added. "Race-ya. GO!" He took off.

"Fuck." Tristan had some ground to make up, but he wasn't going to lose if he could help it.

Adler's parents had a cleaning service come in two days a week, usually Monday and Thursday, and on those same two days, they also had someone cook for them. Because of their cook, dinner at the main house was always delicious, which is why the guys went when they were asked. Tonight's dinner didn't disappoint.

Tristan never knew the fancy names of the dishes, but he didn't really care. Tonight's meal started with a creamy soup with chicken and veggies. The main course was a roast lamb with some sort of fancy scalloped potatoes and roasted Brussel sprouts. It was delicious. He made a mental note to take some leftovers for tomorrow night.

Even though the meal was fancy, they ate at the small kitchen table. It was only the four of them. Uncle Don was actually here in time for dinner. Most nights, he ate leftovers long after dinner was finished.

Uncle Don and Adler favored each other. Uncle Don was tall and built, with a lot of dark hair for his age. There were some grays sprinkled throughout, and his eyes were dark as night. Between the Greek ancestry of Uncle Don and the Italian side of his aunt, it was no wonderw here Adler got his dark hair, eyes, and complexion.

"So, what, or who, has your thoughts taken up?"

Tristan shook his head, realizing that his uncle was talking to him. "Excuse me?"

Uncle Don laughed his deep laugh. "You've been lost in your thoughts. I've noticed it at the office as well. Who's taking up your thoughts?"

"Hmm," said Elie. "Adler said something about a girl taking up all his time."

Lord, now his aunt's getting involved. He can't stand it when they get all focused on him. Hasn't Adler done anything stupid lately they can get stressed about? "Really? Y'all realize I'm no longer a teenager. My life isn't your business. I'm thirty and responsible for myself."

Aunt Elie and Uncle Don shared a look, and his aunt cracked a smile. "You're right, honey. None of our business. There's nothing wrong with me wanting you to be happy and settle down with a family."

"Yeah, one of you needs to settle down," Don agreed. "Elie feels like she may never get her chance to be a grandmother. And if she waits on Adler, we know we won't even get a wedding."

Adler rolled his eyes.

Another first. Maybe he really is ready for a relationship. Interesting. "Y'all didn't ask us here to pick on us about our love lives. What's up?" Tristan figured that changing the subject would be a good idea. Adler owes him one.

Uncle Don sat up tall and clasped his hands on the table. "You both know that the fundraiser is Saturday, and your attendance is not an option." He glared at each of them.

They both nodded. Like it's ever been an option.

"Good. This year, you are both going to be expected to play a larger role than ever before."

Tristan raised his brows in question at Adler. Adler just shrugged.

"Now that, as you've stated earlier, you are both thirty and responsible, you will be expected to add some of that responsibility to the day. You are both going to give horseback rides to the children."

Tristan's eyes went wide. He looked at Adler, whose reaction was worse. He looked scared to death.

Tristan sat forward. "You expect us to hang out with the kids, and give horseback rides?"

His aunt and uncle were nodding.

Adler's mouth was hanging open.

What the hell? "We tried that last year. Remember? It didn't go well." Memories of last year and kids running and screaming all around their property were coming back into his mind. Kids eating so much junk food that they puked in the pool; kids scaring the horses to death. Kids falling off the ATV.

Adler agreed. "You both realize we don't do kids? Right?"

"Uncle Don, are you crazy? Do you want to get sued? Do you want to lose the business?"

Adler jumped in. "Yeah. Don't do this, Dad. We need something to run when we get old."

Aunt Elie had her hand over her mouth, and Uncle Don was laughing at them so hard that tears were coming down his face. "Please, you two. This will be good for you. We have total faith in your abilities to take care of the children." He had to breathe. "Any way, Jonathon and Carla will be helping this year also, so they will make sure nothing major happens."

Jonathon and Carla are the main stable hands. That made Tristan feel better. He sighed a breath of relief. He saw Adler deflate a bit, also. Jonathon and Carla will do most of the work and make sure no one dies.

"Good. I'm glad that's taken care of. Make sure you're both here early. I don't want to be looking for you at all during the day." He stood up, ending the conversation. "I have some paperwork to finish. I'll be in my office." He kissed Ellie as he passed her. "Good night, boys."

They both said good night as he left the room.

Aunt Elie stood up. "Well, you two can clean the dishes. The cook already did all the big things, I'm sure. This." She gestured to the table. "It's all yours." She kissed them both on the head. "Love you both. Good night."

"Good night, Aunt Elie."

"Good night, Mom."

Well, then. That was not a discussion he was expecting.

Tristan pushed up from the table. "Let's get this done and get back to the house. You having anyone coming over tonight?" Tristan picked up plates and silverware and went into the kitchen.

Adler grabbed the glasses and soup bowls. "Nope. How about you?"

Tristan shook his head. "Not tonight. Stacey works in the morning. I'll see her again on Thursday. What do you say we double date? Dinner and dancing. Bring Missy or Callie or whoever."

Adler was rinsing the plates and putting them in the dishwasher. "Sounds good. I'll tell Callie."

Tristan pulled himself to sit on the counter. "You mean you'll ask her, right?"

Adler smirked. "No, I meant what I said. Remember. This is me." He put his arms out wide. "I tell them they're going out with me. They jump at the chance."

Tristan shook his head. "You're a dick."

Adler started the dishwasher. "Yep, and like the body part of the same name, I'm a big one."

CHAPTER 19

I t was Thursday morning. Stacey was looking forward to the next four days of rest and relaxation. She planned to take advantage of a long shower and a book. She had a nail appointment, and a massage scheduled for one o'clock and three o'clock and should get home with enough time to clean up and change for her date with Tristan.

She was looking forward to a night alone with him, but he told her last night that they would be doubling with Adler and some girl he's seeing. She's not excited about sharing her time with Tristan, but she needs to get to know Adler. He is like Tristan's brother. So, oh well. She'll deal with it. She'll have Thursday, Friday, and Saturday night, so that will more than make up for it.

Three nights with Tristan. She got chills just thinking about it.

She was enjoying her book and the quiet when her phone rang. It was Nancy telling her about an interview she had tomorrow afternoon at three at Summit Woman's Center, Labor and Delivery. She tried to complain about the time, explaining she had plans for her birthday. Nancy explained that Doctor Hensley insisted it was the only time, and it was important that she keep the appointment.

She agreed and hung up.

"It's all good, Stacey. Hensley might be a witch, but she pulled a lot of strings to get you an interview. Suck it up." She took a big breath and blew it out.

Just a short eight hours later, she had pretty nails and toes, less hair in all the right places, relaxed muscles, and a renewed spirit.

She dressed in a little black sleeveless dress, with a wrap to keep her arms warm if needed, and black sandals. She pinned her hair on top of her head, then applied minimal makeup and lipstick, and she had time to spare.

"Look at you!" Kristen, who was cutting up vegetables, said as she made catcalls when Stacey entered the kitchen. "Looks like someone has a hot date."

"Sis, you're looking good." Jacob looked up from his phone.

Stacey wiggled her eyebrows and picked a cucumber slice off the cutting board. "So, what do you two have planned tonight?"

Kristen shook her head. "Nothing. You know, some of us actually work five days a week and don't like going out on work nights."

Stacey grabbed another slice of cucumber. "Noted. Don't forget we'll be here tonight. We shouldn't be late. We're double dating with Adler."

Kristen's eyes got wide. "Really?"

Jacob jumped in. "Who's Adler?"

Kristen went back to cutting vegetables. "Adler's Tristan's friend..."

"Well, yes, and no. Adler's his best friend, but also his cousin." Stacey interrupted.

Kristen continued. "Oh, sorry. His cousin, who was with him when we were at the mountains. Adler hit on Elizabeth. I think they kissed." Jacob's eyebrows jumped an inch.

Stacey shook her head. "They didn't kiss. Tristan said that Adler tried, but Elizabeth turned her head."

"That makes more sense," said Jacob. "I'd be surprised if she did. I know it was a bad time, but she wouldn't have crossed that line."

Kristen spun toward him and jutted out her hip, the knife pointed at his chest. "Really? She didn't think twice about crossing that line with you. She kissed you. Why wouldn't she kiss a complete stranger?"

Jacob shot her a harsh look.

Stacey intervened. "Kristen. Don't go there. That's been dealt with a long time ago. Everything is good with you two and her and Brady. Let's not bring that up again." There was a knock on the door, and she glanced between Jacob and Kristen as her heart skipped. She pulled open the door, and Tristan stood there, looking handsome, and a tingle went through her body as a smile lit up her face.

"Hey," she breathed.

"Hey." He held a bouquet of black-eyed Susans. They were beautiful. "I don't know why, but they reminded me of your eyes. Brown with specks of gold."

She felt herself flush. "They're beautiful. Thank you." They kissed, and she let him in.

He greeted Jacob and Kristen while Stacey found a vase.

Adler was at the door. "Hey, sorry for barging in, but Callie needs to use the restroom."

He looked dashing in tight dark jeans, cowboy boots, and a red t-shirt. The blonde girl next to him wore a tiny white dress with a plunging neckline that showed voluptuous cleavage. Stacey raised an eyebrow at Kristen, who did the same.

Jacob put out his hand. "Jacob, Stacey's brother. I'm guessing you're Adler."

Adler shook his hand. "Yep. And this is Callie." He gestured to the girl next to him. "Bathroom?" Jacob pointed them in the right direction, and she smiled and left the group. She wasn't gone long, and they were able to head to dinner.

Before they got to the car, Tristan grabbed Stacey's arm, pulling her into his chest. "I am not sitting in that car and driving into the city without doing this first.

He brushed her cheek as he placed his lips lightly on hers. Her heart fluttered madly, and her hand went behind his neck, pulling him in closer.

They pulled apart but kept their foreheads together. Stacey breathed in deeply, inhaling him. "I missed you." Her eyes fluttered open.

His lips ticked up. "I missed you too, gorgeous."

She brushed her finger over the crease in his cheek that she loved.

"Let's go. We have reservations," Adler called from the truck.

He grabbed her hand and pulled her to the truck.

It was an elegant Italian restaurant, complete with tablecloths, opera music playing over the stereo, and the smell of fresh bread and garlic in the air. Stacey took the seat between Tristan and Callie. They ordered drinks and went back to the conversation Adler had started in the car about a YouTube video he watched. Callie acted interested in him. Stacey watched as she flirted with him and leaned in with a bubbly and slightly annoying shrill laugh.

But then the server came and took their orders.

He was very personable, and Callie started openly flirting with him. She actually reached out and held his arm while she asked him what he would suggest. Tristan and Stacey were both wide-eyed, and Tristan put his hand on Adler's shoulder to keep him from confronting the situation.

"What the hell was that about?" Adler's voice came out louder than necessary as soon as the server left.

She turned, watching the rear of the server as he walked away.

"Hey!" He grabbed her shoulder, pulling her body toward him. "You're here with me. Eyes back on the table, please." He snapped his fingers in front of her face.

Her hands came up with her palms flat. "I don't understand what your problem is. I can talk with whoever I want."

Adler's eyes went wide. "Not when you're on a date with me."

"Relax, Addie. We aren't married, you know." Callie ran her fingers through his hair. "I'll be in your bed tonight. That's what matters."

Stacey thought she was going to throw up. The girl was ridiculous.

Adler turned away. The stress level at the table was high.

"Thank God our food's here." Tristan had a look of relief on his face. "And with a different server."

Stacey chuckled, and Adler shot daggers.

The meal was good, and it was the quietest meal Stacey could remember. She and Tristan exchanged glances. Neither of them knew what to say to break the awkward silence. Adler stared at his plate as he ate. Never once looking up.

Callie ate a salad, or rather picked at her salad, as she didn't eat most of the vegetables that were in it. Finally, she pushed her plate away. "I'll be right back. I've got to...you know." Callie grabbed her purse and left the table.

Time ticked by, and her seat sat empty.

"What the hell's her hold up?" Adler threw his napkin on the table. "No one takes this long to use the bathroom."

She had been gone for at least fifteen minutes. That was a bit excessive.

"Bro, calm down," Tristan's voice was almost a whisper.

Stacey placed her napkin on the table and stood. "I'll go check on her. Make sure she's okay." She brushed Tristan's shoulder as she walked away.

This girl is crazy. I don't have a good feeling about this. Stacey pushed open the bathroom door.

The bathroom was empty. There was no one at the sinks, but one of the stalls was occupied, and she could hear some soft noises. Stacey was about to call out for Callie when she noticed her shoes under one of the stalls, but she wasn't alone.

Her stilettos had company. Black shoes. Men's shoes.

"Holy shit." Stacey breathed. Her hand went to her mouth.

The quiet, breathy sounds she heard at first, and didn't think anything about, quickly became louder and turned to panting.

They're doing it in the stall. Should she be grossed out or pissed? Not sure.

The panting became soft expressions of enjoyment.

Stacey had to press her hand over her mouth to hide her combination of a gasp and laughter.

Suddenly, expletives came from the stall, and the door flew open. Callie and their hot server spilled out, falling onto the floor—her dress up to her boobs and his pants down at his ankles.

A mom, who had just entered the bathroom with her daughter, screamed and turned the little girl around. The girl was looking at her phone and saw nothing, but whined that she had to go to the bathroom as her mom covered her eyes and yelled for the manager.

Stacey stood there, her mouth gaping open. All eyes locked on each other. The server looked scared to death. Callie looked shocked. Stacey shook her head and left as the manager came to see what the mom was fussing about.

Stacey flew back to the table and about fell into her seat, her hands over her mouth and her eyes wide. "Oh. My. God." She spoke into her palms.

Tristan placed his arm around her shoulders. "Stace. What's wrong? What happened?"

She tried to avoid Adler's stare, but couldn't. "She was having sex in the bathroom."

At that time, Callie came back and plopped back in her seat, like nothing had happened, brushing her hands through her hair.

"What?" Adler yelled and pushed up from the table. His nostrils flared as his face turned a bright shade of red. Stacey was scared of his blood pressure and Callie. He looked furious. Rightly so.

Just then, the server walked by the table, followed closely by his manager. The server said something to Adler that Stacey couldn't quite make out, but the words kick and ass were in there.

Adler lunged at him.

Adler was quick, but the server was ready. Adler's punch landed in the server's gut, and he threw a left hook that hit Adler in the jaw. Tristan grabbed Adler to hold him back. While someone came and pulled their server away.

In the ruckus, Callie's strawberry daiquiri spilled down the front of her white dress. She screamed, and the manager asked them to leave.

Tristan pulled Adler outside as Stacey gathered their phones and pulled Callie from the restaurant.

"She needs to find another way home." Adler bellowed when they were waiting by Tristan's truck. He got in her face. "You're not coming home with us, you fucking slut."

Stacey couldn't help laughing. Yes, their night was messed up, but the look of confusion on Callie's face was too much. It was like she didn't understand why Adler wanted nothing to do with her. Add in the red stain all over the front of her white dress. It was funny. If she didn't laugh, she'd probably cry.

Callie stalked away and called an Uber.

Kristen was sitting at the kitchen table with an extra-large bowl of ice cream when Stacey trudged into her house and slammed the door.

"Shit, what happened? Why are you home so early?" Kristen's face was filled with concern as Stacey grabbed a Diet Coke from the refrigerator and a spoon from the drawer, slamming everything harder than necessary.

"Adler's a dick, and the girl he had with him tonight is a whore and Tristan had to take Adler home." Stacey plopped in the chair next to Kristen, popped open her can of Diet Coke, and took a large spoonful of her friend's ice cream.

Kristen watched as Stacey attacked her bowl, then slid it over to Stacey. "Okay, then. Are you going to give me details, or do I have to dig it out of you?"

Stacey shook her head. "Tonight was a nightmare."

Kristen's face lit up. "What happened?"

Stacey started recalling the entire night to Kristen.

Kristen was listening with interest, and she held onto every word.

Stacey held up her hand. "Oh, wait. It gets better. You'll never believe where I found her."

"Where?" Kristen was an attentive audience.

"She was in one of the stalls with our server, and from the sounds I heard, he wasn't giving her toilet paper."

Kristen's hands shot to her mouth. "Holy shit! Seriously? Sex in a bathroom stall, on a date with another guy, and a hot one at that!"

"Can't make this shit up."

"No, you can't. That's awesome!"

Stacey continued to tell Kristen about the mother who walked in and called the manager, the fight at the table, and getting kicked out of the restaurant.

Kristen burst out laughing.

It was funny, and Stacey joined Kristen.

Kristen wiped at the tears that were spilling down her face. "I just see that girl falling out of the stall. Sex in a bathroom. WTF?"

Stacey lost it and felt so much better after a good laugh. Her night may not be ending like she wanted, but at least it was an unforgettable date.

Kristen finally got her laughter reined in. "Stacey, I'm sorry your night was ruined. I'm also sorry Adler was dating someone like her. How's he?"

Stacey shrugged and took some time to finish off Kristen's bowl of ice cream. "Not really sure. His jaw was sore by the time they dropped me off, and his eye was red and swollen. The guy's punch landed hard. I'm sure his ego was hurt more than his face. But he thinks he's hot shit, so I'm sure he'll be fine." Stacey yawned. "I've got to get to bed. I'm exhausted, and I have an interview tomorrow."

Stacey left Kristen in the kitchen.

CHAPTER 20

I t was her birthday, and even though it was already five thirty, and weekend traffic would probably take her over an hour to get home, she was on cloud nine.

That went pretty well. Stacey was walking through the parking garage after her interview at Summit Woman's Center. She was surprisingly happy with the Labor and Delivery floor. It is larger than she's used to, but everyone was so friendly. She could see herself working there.

Before she pulled out, she turned her phone notifications back on and noticed a missed call from Tristan. She called him back, putting him on her car speaker.

"Happy birthday again, gorgeous. How'd things go?"

She filled him in on the interview, and how well she thought it went. He was going to be at her house when she got there and asked if Adler could come by. He'd be alone as he was no longer seeing Callie. Shocker. She wasn't sure if she really wanted to deal with him, but Tristan assured her he'd behave. He needed something to do, so she agreed.

As she was stuck in Nashville rush hour traffic heading north, she found her mind wandering to Tristan. He was so different from anyone she had dated before. He truly cared about her, and he listened to what she had to say. He was proud of her for stepping out and giving this hospital a try. She thought of his smile only for her. His kisses only for her lips. His amazing talents in the bedroom and only for her body. She didn't want to share him and didn't want to be without him. He could leave, and she could get hurt, but he was worth the risk.

He was hers, and it was time for her to make it official and stop acting like she didn't care as much as she did. Her heart fluttered. It could happen. It would happen. What an awesome birthday this would be. All she had to do was say the word, and for once, her birthday would be perfect. Even this first year of twenty-nine and holding.

It was almost seven o'clock when she finally pulled in front of her house. The driveway was full. Her pulse raced as she turned off the car. All these people were here to celebrate her. That kind of attention always embarrassed her, which was why she didn't usually allow birthdays. She took a deep breath and jumped out of the car as Tristan walked with purpose across the lawn.

She smiled from ear to ear, and her heart turned to mush. He was the best looking birthday present ever. His faded jeans, always tight in the right places, a dark gray sweater, and his face was filled with a smile. She let him engulf her in his arms. Her feet lifted from the ground, and his lips immediately found hers.

She was lost for a second in all things Tristan. His kiss was soft and gentle, his taste sweet with a touch of mint, his body muscular and safe, his smell woodsy and masculine.

"Happy birthday, gorgeous." He brushed hair from her face, gathering in a ponytail with his hands at the base of her neck.

"Thank you." She kissed him again. A deeper, more intense kiss. Yeah, she wanted him. She wanted all of him. Her heart swelled. "Thank you for being here."

He pulled away, and that crease in his cheek showed itself. "Seriously, where else would I be? Here with you is where I belong." Another long kiss. "Let's go. Everyone's waiting on you."

The backyard looked amazing. There were gold and brown balloons hanging everywhere, with vases of black-eyed Susans sitting around as decorations. There were two grills going, tables filled with all kinds of food, and one just for dessert. She laughed when she saw the cake. "Stacey, first year holding at twenty-nine" written on it, and it was also edged with the yellow and brown, black-eyed Susans. It was amazing and perfect. Her eyes filled with joy as she met Tristan's. She had no words, but picked up a flower that was lying around the table.

"Like I told you before, the gold mixed with browns, remind me of your eyes. They are as beautiful and unique as you are."

Her heart skipped. "They're perfect. Everything's perfect." Stacey hugged him tight.

Soon, she was having a blast with her friends. The yard was filled with people. She was talking in a group with some of the girls and laughing with them as Elizabeth told a story about Grant's latest issues with nap time.

Suddenly, a loud roar filled the night.

Everyone turned their head, and there was no mistaking it. Adler had arrived. And he was noticed. He parked his motorcycle off to the side and turned it off. The night got quiet.

Stacey rolled her eyes as she noticed her friends were no longer lost in discussion, but lost in Adler.

"Damn. Who is that?"

Stacey turned, and her mouth dropped at Charity, one of her happily married friends.

Desiree, Charity's best friend, spoke what Stacey was thinking. "Stand down, girl. You have your handsome husband. You aren't on the market."

"Doesn't mean I can't look."

And an eyeful they got.

They watched intently as Adler swung his leg over the seat, his back to his groupies, took off his helmet, and ran his fingers through his dark hair.

Stacey almost gagged when some of the girls let out a distinctive sigh when he took off his well-worn leather jacket and threw it over the handlebars. She could see how he got the girls' attention. He was a good-looking guy. He wore tight jeans, cowboy boots, and a tight blue t-shirt, which showed off his muscular arms and his eagle tattoo on his left bicep.

He turned and searched the crowd. Stacey was sure he was looking for Tristan.

"Okay. Who *is* that?" Desiree asked as Adler sauntered over to Tristan.

"That's Tristan's cousin. Adler. And yes, before you ask, he's single, ladies."

"I call dibs." Desiree chimed in. "You need to introduce me, Stace."

Stacey caught Desiree's eyes. "You sure you want to go there?"

The pretty girl nodded, pushing her auburn hair behind her shoulder. "Oh, yeah. I'm sure. I'm definitely sure."

Stacey walked with her entourage toward Tristan and Adler.

She wrapped an arm around Tristan's waist and introduced him and Adler to the girls. She rolled her eyes as Desiree pushed in front and extended her hand to Adler. She didn't have the heart to tell Desiree that just last night Adler had sworn off women. Of course, he had just got punched, screwed over—literally—and wasn't in the mood. Who knew how long that would last.

"It's cake time!" Kristen announced. Everyone moved toward the cake and present table, but Stacey stayed put. Tristan yanked on her arm when he realized she wasn't moving on her own. Her eyes rolled, and her shoulders drooped, but she followed behind him reluctantly.

It was the worst-sounding rendition of Happy Birthday she ever heard. But she found herself enjoying it.

"Blow out the candles," Elizabeth said.

"And don't forget to make a wish." Kristen chimed in.

Stacey glanced next to her and met Tristan's gaze. Her insides warmed as a smile grew on both their faces. She knew what her wish was going to be. It was obvious. She pulled him closer to her side and blew out the candles.

All of them went out.

Chad's eyes perked up. "Dang, Stace. You're good at blowing."

He pounded Tristan on the back. "You're a lucky guy."

"Yes, yes, I am." His grin met his ears, and everyone laughed. What the heck! Stacey felt her face turn red and heat, and she elbowed him in the side.

Stacey sat watching the party as she ate her cake. The cake was delicious, all her friends here for her, and there were all these presents. It was too much.

"Hey gorgeous." Tristan sat down next to her. "What are you thinking about?"

Stacey melted into his smoky gaze. "Just how amazing tonight has been. Thank you."

"You're welcome." He brushed her hair off her shoulders. "And thank you for including Adler. I think he enjoyed himself. He's already left with a couple of phone numbers."

A chuckle escaped her throat. "Yeah, I was concerned when he first rode up that the girls would start a catfight for his attention."

"Well, there were no catfights, and I'm glad you're happy." He gave her a quick kiss and then joined the guys, and Stacey joined the girls who were left.

Stacey filled them in on how well her interview went.

"See, and you were concerned about Doctor...What did you call her?" Jessica asked.

She, Kristen, and Elizabeth looked at each other and laughed. "You wouldn't say the name even if you remembered it, Jess," Elizabeth said. "She called her Doctor Bitchy."

"That's right." Jessica nodded. "And no, I wouldn't have. But just think. If it weren't for her, you wouldn't have gotten that interview."

"True." Stacey nodded as Tristan, Jacob, and Chad joined them.

"What did we miss? I hear you making fun of my girl again." Chad wrapped his arms around Jessica.

Kristen spoke up. "We weren't making fun of her, just talking about a doctor Elizabeth's been dealing with at work. She calls her Doctor Bitchy, and Jessica wouldn't say her name."

Tristan wrapped his arm around Stacey. "Are you talking about that doctor or, as you say, not-doctor you've been dealing with at the hospital?"

She contained a smile. "Yes. I call her Doctor Bitchy because she walks around and conducts business like she's better than everyone else, but she isn't even a medical doctor. I'm not really sure what she has a doctorate in, but it could be bitchiness. Do they give doctorates in that?"

"Yeah, I don't think so," said Kristen. "What's her real name, anyway? Doctor what?"

"Dr. Elicia Hensley." Stacey felt Tristan's arms tighten around her and turned to face him. His face was blank. "Hey, what's wrong?" She placed her hand against his cheek, forcing his gaze onto hers.

He shook his head. "Nothing. Just tired." A small smile crept up his face, and he touched his lips to hers.

When the last of the group left, Stacey stood looking around at the mess. It was a long day, and she was exhausted. Ugg. There was so much to clean up. Looking across the yard at Tristan, Stacey could think of only one thing she wanted to do now, and it was to be in her bed with that handsome man over there.

Kristen pulled her into a hug. "Happy birthday, bestie."

Stacey pulled her eyes away from the Adonis across the yard. "Thank you so much for all this. It was amazing. The food was delicious, and the cake was the best. It was a great night."

Their arms stayed around each other as they watched their guys working together to take down tables and chairs. "Don't thank me. Tristan planned most of this. The flowers and color scheme were all him. He said these colors reminded him of your eyes." Kristen arranged herself to really look at Stacey. "He is so sweet. And he's crazy about you."

Yeah, she knew that. There was no doubt.

"You deserve him, Stace. You deserve to be happy with Tristan." She hip-bumped Stacey. "You know that, right?"

Stacey felt her hands sweat and wiped them on her pants. But she nodded. "I know." She watched him across the yard again. "I was thinking a lot about us on my drive here today." She met Kristen's eyes. "I really like him. Like, *really like him*. Maybe more than like?"

Kristen's face softened, and her arm squeezed Stacey's side. "Yay, for you. Finally, putting your feelings first."

"Yeah, I guess I am. I thought I'd tell him tonight. So, let's get this cleaned up."

Kristen stopped Stacey and called across the yard. "Tristan!"

He looked up.

"Take this woman inside and give her a proper present. Jacob and I will finish up out here."

"What?" Stacey's mouth dropped.

Kristen whispered. "You heard me. Go get yourself an amazing gift. I'm sure there's something he hasn't given you yet."

Tristan grabbed Stacey's hand. "I'm not gonna argue. Come on, gorgeous. Let's make this great day better."

Stacey's stomach flipped, and her heart melted.

CHAPTER 21

Tristan closed Stacey's bedroom door and led her to sit down in the chair by her window. He closed the blinds and pulled a duffel bag from under her bed.

"Tristan, what are you doing?"

Opening the bag, he pulled out a large box wrapped in pretty paper with a nice fancy bow. "I haven't given you anything yet. So, happy birthday."

"Not true. You decorated, bought the flowers, the cake, and food. It was amazing and already too much."

He brushed off her complaints. "Not enough."

Stacey felt the heat rising. Gifts made her uncomfortable, like she would upset the giver if she didn't act thankful enough. But this... from him... is so much different. Her heart thundered in her chest. She had no clue what could be in the box, but many things crossed her mind.

At least she knew from the size that it wasn't something serious, like a piece of jewelry. Yet she couldn't tell if her heart was beating because she was embarrassed by what it could be or upset that it wasn't something more intimate—like jewelry.

He sat on the edge of her bed watching as she undid the bow and then the paper. She lifted off the lid, and her breath hitched. On top of the yellow tissue paper sat a small, long, rectangular box. The same wrapping paper and the same bow, just much smaller.

This had to be jewelry. She might have a heart attack if her heart didn't settle. She sat frozen for a long second with the box in her hands.

Her hands started shaking, and Tristan closed his hands over hers. "It's a present, Stacey. It doesn't mean anything long-term. I just saw it and thought of you."

She looked into his eyes, took a breath, and opened the box. A sigh escaped her lips, and her sight became blurry. "Tristan." She pulled out the necklace. It was sterling silver with small yellow beads. The charm was a sterling silver black-eyed Susan flower. It was beautiful. "It's perfect."

Her eyes locked onto his, and her heart skipped a beat. She reached behind her neck, but fumbled with the clasp.

He hooked it for her.

It fell in the middle of her chest, right by her heart. That heart that was flipping and skipping everywhere. She went to her mirror. It was more than perfect. The yellow of the beads reflected the lights, and the flower was amazing. He came behind her, and their eyes locked in their reflection. "Thank you. Thank you so much."

"It's not too much, is it? Too serious?" He asked her as he turned her to face him.

She shook her head and leaned in to thank him properly. Their lips met, and her body warmed. She curled her fingers in his hair, pulling him closer to her.

She needed to feel him, to have him. To devour him.

But she pulled away. She needed to get something off her chest. She was waiting for this night to tell him. "Tristan." She held his gaze and searched it for anything that might cause her to question her feelings for him. There was nothing there but genuine emotion. What she felt was real.

"What?" He smoothed her hair with his hands.

Just do it. He's everything you want. She took a deep breath. "I want us to be more."

She felt him stiffen.

She moved her hand to brush his face. "I know what I said all this time. I know I've battled you about your feelings, but I can't fight any longer. I want, no... I need a relationship with you. I want to know you're mine, and I'm yours."

There it was. The crease in his cheek. Her heart fluttered wildly.

"Really? Are you sure?" His smile became contagious, and she caught the sickness.

She thought her face would break with how wide her smile became. She nodded. "More sure than I've ever been about anything."

His mouth was on hers in an instant, crushing against hers. His hands grasped the back of her head as she gripped his shirt in her fists. Their kiss became intense and wild. Desperate.

But then he pulled away, and she thought she was going to die, and her breath was ragged.

"I have another present. This one...anyway." He walked away from her and brought back the box and placed it in her hands.

"Tristan."

He gestured for her to open it, and she removed the yellow tissue paper. Wow. This was going to be fun. Her eyes became sweltering lava as she held up a see-through black negligee. It was short. It will barely cover her bottom and was cut low in the front. Very low cut.

She shot him a wicked smile. "Get in the bed. I'll be back in a minute."

She slipped into her bathroom and quickly stripped off her clothes. It didn't take long to slip the negligée over her head. She pulled a brush through her dirty blonde hair and admired her reflection.

The negligee highlighted her cleavage and fit all her curves perfectly. The lace was in the perfect spots, with skin showing through. Yeah. This would do. It would do fine.

She opened the door. Tristan was in her bed, leaning back on pillows without the blanket. Naked in all his glory.

Her eyes wandered up and down his muscular chest and his other parts, which were already standing at attention.

She leaned against the doorway. "Well, what do you think?"

A very manly grunt left him, and a lick of his lips was all the response he gave her. His eyes roamed over her body. Causing heat to sizzle throughout her and her pulse to pick up speed.

She sauntered over to the bed, allowing his eyes to stroll all over her a little longer and take her all in. She took her hand and dragged it slowly from his neck, across his chest to his waist.

He caught it before she could touch other parts and shook his head. "It's your birthday. I need to give you a present." He sat up and devoured her mouth with his. Her arms wrapped around his neck and head. He pulled her onto the bed, laying her on her back. His hands traveled over the thin material of the negligee, and they burned a path down her body as they slowly passed over every inch of her, then back up to her neck.

Her breath was hard, and her pulse pounded.

His hand went behind her head, and his lips met hers in a gentle kiss. "You are amazing, Stacey. Thank you for letting me be yours. I..." He hesitated, and his gaze fixed on hers, his eyes a deep smoky gray.

Her breath froze. Her heart swelled. Her emotions were spinning out of control. Just being here with him wasn't enough. She needed more.

"I'm glad you chose us." His hand lifted her face to his. The kiss was intense, like nothing before. There was still something left unsaid.

She loved him. That thought caught her by surprise. She breathed in. She couldn't move. Did she? She's never felt this before. She didn't know.

"Stace? You okay? I'm sorry if I.." He pulled away.

She placed her fingers over his mouth. "Don't. You don't need to be sorry for anything, Tristan. Give me a second."

Her heart was going to explode. She had to tell him. Her hazel eyes searched his and held them tight. She didn't love. She didn't do relationships—in the past—but she does now. She did with him.

"I love you." The words escaped from her mouth almost in a whisper.

His eyes moved and searched hers. A smile grew on his lips. "What? Really?"

Stacey closed her eyes and searched her soul. That was a surprise, but was it true? What did she feel now?

She felt calm. Happy. Relaxed. Secure.

She may have sworn off love and relationships because of her past, but she's never known love like Tristan. Her face glowed. "Yes, Tristan. I love you."

He pressed his mouth to hers and really kissed her. If this was what love felt like as a kiss, she never wanted to feel another kiss again.

Her insides ignited like sparks to a flame. Her heart was jolted back alive, and it beat to a new rhythm.

A rhythm that put her nerve endings on high alert. A rhythm that healed her heart.

A rhythm that was pure Tristan.

"Stacey, I've been trying so hard not to say those words, scared I'd frighten you away. I love you, too."

She lifted her lips to his, and the kiss became intense.

He yanked the black lace over her head and threw it to the side. He kissed every part of her body. And every piece of skin his lips touched continued to ignite. First her neck, then down her chest to her breasts, first the left one, then he moved to the right. He continued kissing down her stomach to the sensitive area between her thighs. There he stayed and sent her to heaven until she had all she could take.

His lips dragged back up slowly, taking his time once again, until he finally found her mouth. Her hands squeezed his tight buttocks, and she guided him inside her.

His eyes held hers, and they made love with their gaze never leaving each other. It was the most amazing sex Stacey could ever remember.

When they finished, they laid together, his arms around her and his hands in her hair, combing the strands from her face. Her body was weak, her legs shaking.

Stacey's ear was against his chest, and she listened to his heart. He was amazing. This was perfect.

He kissed her temple, and she felt him stiffen beneath her, and his breathing changed. She leaned up to get a better view of him. "Is everything okay?" Her hand went up to brush the creases between his eyes.

Tristan combed some hair behind her ear and held her face in his hand. He was silent for a beat.

Her heart gave a hard thump. There's something wrong.

He finally shook his head. "It's nothing. I just can't believe you told me you love me."

That was it. Her heart went back to a regular rhythm. Of course, she loved him. "What is there not to love? I'm just sorry it took me so long to put my junk in the past." She kissed him tenderly.

Their foreheads touched when they pulled away, their connection broken. "I love you, Stacey. Happy birthday, gorgeous." He pressed her mouth to his and held her in a tight embrace.

God, she loved him. She loved being here with him. She was so glad he was hers. She rolled over, and he tucked his arms tightly around her. She could stay here wrapped in him forever.

CHAPTER 22

S tacey stared out the window as she sat pressed up against Tristan in his truck, her head resting on his shoulder. Every nerve ending in her body was at attention and focused on his arm wrapped around her shoulder. They were stuck together all morning. And what an amazing morning it was.

Waking up against his chest with his arm wrapped around her gave her a calm and peaceful feeling that filled every pore, making her body tingle with pleasure. When she remembered she told him she loved him, warmth spread through her, making her adjust herself and wiggle closer to him, which caused him to moan, and parts of him woke up and pressed into her lower back.

The flame that had had a hard time going out last night was reignited. She kissed his chest as she rolled on top of him, sliding his hardness inside her.

His eyes opened and popped wide until his body took over what she had started.

The intensity of his gaze when they made love after she woke him up still made her shiver. She blinked, trying to remember she was in the cab of his truck but stretched and kissed him lightly on his neck.

"Mmm. What's that for?" Tristan glanced down quickly, then squeezed his arm tighter around her shoulder, pulling her closer to his side.

"Just remembering the look you gave me when you woke up this morning."

"Correction. When you woke me up." His smile filled his face. "And yeah. That was an amazing way to wake up." He moved his arm and grabbed her hand that was lying on his thigh, placing it over the hard bulge in his lap.

Wow!

He winked. "It's your touch, gorgeous." His voice was throaty.

Her breath stopped. She swallowed the lump in her throat. Her hand started rubbing over the bulge. Oh, that was a bad idea. There was a tingling between her legs.

Tristan sucked in his bottom lip and suddenly jerked the wheel of the truck, turning off the road onto a dirt path.

Stacey sat up tall. What was he doing?

They made a sharp turn, and all around them was nothing but trees. He slammed the truck into park, undid their seat belts, and had Stacey in his arms before she could even register that they had stopped.

"It's gonna be a long day. And I want you. Now." His hand went behind her neck, and his lips clamped onto hers.

She grabbed his shirt, pulling him even closer. Her breath was ragged.

His was rough.

They kissed and felt and pulled off shirts. Wiggled with difficulty out of jeans.

She couldn't get enough. They were in a truck on the side of a road. Trees all around them. Nothing but privacy. This was crazy. Who cares? Her body was so hot she thought it would combust with desire. She needed him like fire needed oxygen. She wanted him more than anything she had ever wanted before.

"Tristan?" It was a question. Her breath came quickly.

He reached for the glove compartment and fumbled around until he found the condoms they had put in there this morning.

Stacey took it from his hand, tearing it open, panting. "I want to." She peered down at his hardness. Her stomach ignited some more, and her heart fluttered wildly. Damn. With shaking hands, she protected them both, straddled him, then slid him into her.

They moved together. Hard, yet slow. His hands were on her lower back, helping her. Their eyes never left each other.

Finally, she leaned her forehead to his, and they watched each other come to their end.

They both had to catch their breath. Their lips locked.

He brushed the hair from her face as they stared long and hard into each other's eyes.

Tristan cleared his throat. "You are so amazing. God, I love you." He caressed her cheek. "So much."

Stacey's heart slowed, and her body relaxed. She tried to memorize every line, every aspect of his face. "I love you, Tristan. It's such a frightening feeling, but I do."

He kissed her again. "I'll never give you a reason to fear our love. I promise." He glanced away, then he breathed hard. "I'd love to stay here with you, but my aunt and uncle are expecting me soon. We really gotta go."

Stacey agreed, and they sat up and dressed.

"Where is here? Where are we?" She looked around, and all around them were tall oaks and cypress trees. Well, she guesses that's what they were. She's not an arborist by any means. For all she knows, these could just be evergreens. Is that a kind of tree?

"At the very back of my family's land. If you keep going down this road, you'll get to a gate and the back of our cow pasture."

Stacey fell back against the seat and let out a deep breath. That's right. His family's land. His family had lots of money, and she was going to their property to be a part of a yearly fundraiser.

"Hey." Tristan turned her toward him. "Yes, we have lots of property, horses, a heated pool, and a large house. Yes, you'll be seeing lots of things that money bought." He held her face. "I want you to feel comfortable there because I want you to be a part of my life. It's only stuff, but we are real people, and my family is pretty great." He placed a quick kiss on her lips, climbed back behind the wheel, and turned the truck around.

Stacey sat staring out the window, and she wiped her hands on her jeans.

Tristan had known her long enough that he knew she only did that when she was nervous. "Hey? Everything's going to be okay."

She just nodded and stared.

He grabbed her hand and brought it to his lips, wanting to kiss the nerves away. "My Aunt Elie and Uncle Don are going to love you. You'll love them, too. Yes, they have money, but they're so down to earth and real, and..." He stopped.

"Tristan, what's wrong?"

He shook his head and kissed her fingers again. "Nothing gorgeous." His smile almost reached his ears.

He drove a bit further before he pulled off the road again, but this time, it was on asphalt. Well taken care of asphalt.

No way. Her eyes bulged. He stopped in front of a large black metal gate with a large black 'W' on it.

She turned to him as he pushed in numbers on a pad. "My birth-date, in case you ever need to get in." He winked at her.

The gate slowly moved, opening toward them. "W?" His last name was Calhoun. She never asked what Adler's name was.

"Warfield. Remember, I told you my uncle owned Warfield Meats?" He put his foot on the gas, and they drove through.

"Adler Warfield." She made the connection. "That name fits him. It sounds like it would belong on a guy who thinks a lot of himself and is a womanizer."

Tristan let out a deep laugh. "You say it like it's a bad thing."

"Isn't it?"

His face was all fun. "Adler? No, yeah, he thinks a lot of himself. Wait until you see where he grew up. But he's not so tough. One day, a girl will get under that rough exterior and find out he's a teddy bear waiting to be loved."

That made Stacey laugh. Picturing the hard-headed, slightly con-ceited guy she sort of knew compared with a cuddly teddy bear! Not in a million years.

Her laughter dried up quickly as they drove up the immaculate driveway. Trees lined the driveway, with rose bushes between them.

Everything was perfect. Everything in its place.

Then the house came into view, and her jaw dropped.

It was a sprawling mansion with an immense entrance onto the porch. The porch seemed to go on forever, and it wrapped around the side of the house out of view. She placed her hand on his leg.

Her eyes were huge, and her heart thumped wildly. She thought she was going to hyperventilate. "Holy shit! You live here?"

Tristan stopped the car. She felt his hand on her cheek, but her eyes roamed at what was in front of her. This house was immense. This house was amazing.

Behind it, from what she could see, the property just seemed to go on and on to the right. To the left, and following the driveway, there was a brick wall topped with more black iron and what seemed to be a nice brick ranch behind a three, no, four-car garage.

Her lungs deflated.

"It's just a house. A really large over the top house, but just a house with walls, a roof, and furniture." Tristan was watching her.

She turned toward him and knew she looked panicked. Hell, she was panicked.

He shifted the truck into park and placed both his hands on her face. "Look at me, Stacey."

She kept her eyes down, focused on her lap.

"Dammit, Stace. Look at me." His command did nothing to calm her, but it did get her attention.

She closed her eyes and took a deep breath. She kept breathing in until she thought her lungs would explode. Then she let it out. Slowly and with control. She felt better. She felt calm. She lifted her gaze to his.

He bent his head . "You good? I need you to be good."

She searched his face. Her heart calmed, and she nodded.

A horn blared. She jumped.

"Dick!" Tristan rolled down his window and held out his hand with the international symbol of fuck off in plain view.

Stacey turned to see the black Mustang behind them, right on their bumper, with an auburn-haired passenger. Was that Desiree? She looked harder, and the passenger waved.

Yep. "Shit."

Tristan turned to her as he pulled his truck into a garage she hadn't seen before. "What?"

"Adler's with Desiree. They just met last night."

Tristan shrugged. "Well, at least you'll know someone else." He leaned over to kiss her. "Come on. I want to show you around."

They got out of the truck. He wrapped his arms around her, which was good because, one, her nerves were starting up again and his arms kept her from running away, and two, he calmed her. His eyes caught hers. "Promise me something."

She couldn't talk, so she just nodded.

"Don't hold any of what you're getting ready to see against me. Remember, it's not mine. I wasn't even born into it. I was adopted into it, sort of. It's just stuff, and it doesn't matter, okay?"

She didn't move. Just stared at him. At his perfection, his handsomeness.

"Hey…" He bent down. Their lips met.

The other garage door opened. How big was this garage?

He kissed her again.

She found her voice. "Yes, okay." Their eyes held until a car pulled in. It got her attention. She took in her surroundings. They were in a giant two-car garage. Well, just two doors, but it could fit almost four cars. And here came the mustang. She turned back to Tristan. "Did you know he was with Desiree?"

He shook his head. "I was busy last night and didn't think at all about my cousin. I was with a gorgeous woman who loves me."

Stacey's pulse raced, and heart skipped. Another kiss. Heated, sexy. How will she be able to get through this day and keep her hands off him?

"Hey, lovebirds, enough. You're not alone."

Tristan sent his cousin the middle finger again and pulled Stacey into the house.

Stacey stood and took in her surroundings. The seemingly brand-new stainless-steel appliances gave the kitchen a modern feel, while the crisp white cabinets made the kitchen feel open and airy. The counters were black granite with a large sink under a window, and another sink in the island. The kitchen opened onto a large living area. This area had a large, comfortable-looking L-shaped couch and an extremely large flat-screen television, which took up the entire wall. Yep, men lived here. The stand under the TV held what Stacey figured was a gaming station. Typical.

She was drawn to one side of the living area. To the glass wall with extra-wide sliding doors. The doors opened onto the pool patio. Her mouth fell as she stared at the waterfall and faux rocks that surrounded it. "Oh, my gosh. It's beautiful. Do you actually swim in there?"

Tristan laughed and wrapped his arms around her as Adler and Desiree walked in.

"He doesn't swim often. Don't let him tell you he does."

Stacey felt Tristan's head rest on top of hers. She leaned back into his arms and gave him a squeeze before pulling away and walking over to give Desiree a hug. "I never got a chance to thank you for making the cake for my party last night. It was delicious."

Desiree was a beautiful woman, who spent a long time getting her shit together, and now worked in a small bakery on Main Street. She makes the cakes and baked goods for all the parties in town.

"I'd like to take the credit, but that wasn't mine."

Stacey's eyes popped. "What?" She spun toward Tristan.

His hands went out. "Sorry. I didn't know Desiree. I had no clue she worked at the bakery. I just called the one we always use. It won't happen again." He winked.

Adler caught his arm and forced his attention back on him, and they walked off to the kitchen, lost in a deep conversation.

I wonder what they're talking about. Stacey squinched her face but turned back to Desiree. She shrugged. "Sorry about that."

Desiree waved it off. "Not a big deal. Like he said, he didn't know me."

"Yeah, so about that." Stacey lifted her brows and gestured toward the guys.

Desiree shrugged and whispered in her ear. "We exchanged numbers last night and talked for hours after I got home. He asked, if I wanted to come today."

"Well then, at least if I'm left alone, I have a friend."

Desiree draped her arm over Stacey's shoulders. "We may need to help each other not get lost. This place is huge and amazing. Have you been here before?'"

Stacey shook her head. She turned and watched Tristan and Adler.

They were still in a deep conversation, but she walked over to them, anyway. "Hi, Adler."

The conversation stopped, and she wrapped her arms around Tristan. "Hey, can we get a tour before we get left alone and become lost in the never-ending abyss of this property?"

Tristan's eyes bore into Adler.

Adler's held his. "Hi, Stacey."

Tristan turned away from him and placed a kiss on her head. "Of course."

"I'm surprised you two are here already. I figured you would have been late with all the birthday celebrating you were going to do last night. Or did you not get enough exercise?" Adler asked.

"I think we celebrated just enough. We celebrated a bit last night, this morning, and in the truck on the way over here," answered Stacey. She wiggled her eyebrows at Adler.

He froze and just looked at them. Speechless. A first, she was sure.

She glanced at Tristan. "I could go another round or two."

There was that cheek crease. "Or three?" He dipped her low and planted one on her lips.

"God, you two, is this how it's gonna be all day? You know this fundraiser is G-rated. We may be able to get by with PG, but..." he gestured through the air. "This stuff all the time will make its way to X-rated, and I know Dad won't be okay with that."

Desiree laughed.

The guys took them on a tour of the house and the property. To do this, they had to ride in the ATV. That in itself was an experience, as the most exciting thing Stacey ever rode was the rollercoasters at Dollywood theme park in Pigeon Forge, Tennessee.

Desiree, on the other hand, hopped right in and had an in-depth discussion with Adler about her dad's four-wheeler and their dirt bike that she learned to ride when she was seven.

She had Adler drooling over every word. Stacey chuckled when she saw him having to adjust his junk when they got out at the stables.

Desiree was just what Adler needed.

CHAPTER 23

Stacey had never been around horses. She always thought they were large, menacing creatures. Pretty from afar and majestic, but not something she needed to meet up close.

But here she was, standing in a pasture among four of these beasts. The one she was petting was a chestnut mare—according to Tristan—who went by the name of Ginger. Tristan stood with his arm under the horse's head so it rested on his shoulder. He was so relaxed around these beasts, and Stacey swore that Ginger was sending her the message, *This is my man. Stay away.*

"Ginger loves apples." He held out one toward Stacey.

Stacey raised her brow, staring at the piece of round red fruit in his hand. "Are you sure this horse won't bite my hand off?" She held the apple flat in her palm like Tristan demonstrated.

He released a deep, throaty chuckle. Man, that was sexy.

"I promise. Here." He took the apple from her and grabbed her hand, placing it on the side of the horse's head. It was soft and as long as she petted it in the direction of the fur, it felt like silk. The other way, not so much. The horse tossed her head, making Stacey step back, and laugh.

"There. See. She's not gonna eat you. She likes you. Now, take the apple and feed her like I showed you."

Stacey grabbed the apple, and placed it in her flattened hand, and stuck her palm out to the horse with surprised calm. The horse took it from her.

Its head nodded like she actually thanked Stacey for her favorite snack. She watched the horse's mouth as she chewed the apple and came back for more, nudging toward her pocket.

"Hey, that's all I've got for you."

"So, are we getting used to the horses?" Adler came ambling over with one arm over Desiree's shoulder and the other holding the reins to a brown horse with spots on its backside.

This horse was a little taller than Ginger and a lot more devilish. It bit Ginger on the butt, causing a bit of a ruckus. Ginger pranced sideways and reared up slightly, kicking her legs.

Stacey scrambled out of the pasture through the rails, not able to get away quick enough. Her heart thumped wildly in her chest.

Adler roared with laughter. "You might be a girl from a small town, but that doesn't mean you're from the country."

Asshole. Stacey pushed her shoulders back. "I never said I was from the country or ever went to the country. This is my first time on a farm." Adler looked around, his hands in the air. "Well, this isn't a farm, honey. Just a cattle and horse ranch. A farm has goats, pigs, or chickens, also. None of those things are here."

Stacey's insides curdled, and she scrunched her eyes. What a jerk. Who does he think he is? Rich and rude? Tristan coaxed her back between the rails and draped an arm over her shoulder. "Okay, let's get to the main yard. I'm sure everyone's going to be here soon."

"What are we going to do while you two are busy?" Desiree gestured between Stacey and herself.

This is something Stacey wanted to hear. Hopefully, she wasn't going to be expected to actually get on one of these things.

Tristan shrugged and walked the horse back to Jonathan, the ranch hand. "You two can do whatever you feel comfortable doing. You can stand and watch us with the kids, help bring the horses to and from the stable, and help guide the kiddos. Between Jonathan and Carla and us, you'll have lots of help and experience behind you.

Stacey turned to say something to Desiree but stopped when she saw her guiding the huge beast that Adler had earlier. "How do you know anything about horses, Des?"

The pretty brunette shrugged. "I don't, really. I just went riding a few times with a friend of mine. She has horses. They aren't as scary as they look, Stace. Promise."

Stacey rolled her eyes, and Tristan's arm went around her waist.

He leaned into her ear. "Just relax."

She looked up at him, and, dang it, there was that crease. She felt her body relax.

The guys rode in front of the ATV, discussing some things they wanted to do with the kids. Desiree and Stacey rode in the back.

"Hey, you okay?" Desiree asked as Stacey held on for her life, trying not to fall out of the ATV as they bumped and sped over the uneven terrain.

She looked into Desiree's warm brown eyes. "Yeah, I'm glad you're here. I'm a little out of my element. All this and big animals." She waved her arm through the air. "Meeting parents, well, aunt and uncle." She breathed in deep and out hard.

Desiree's arm went over her shoulder. "Well, at least they know you're Tristan's girlfriend. Picture being the flavor of the month."

Stacey's face crinkled. "I love you, and I don't want you to get hurt, but it's more like the flavor of the week."

Desiree flinched. "Ouch."

"Sorry, but if anyone can handle Adler, you can."

Desiree waggled her eyebrows. "Yeah, well, I can handle what I know so far, and damn, he is just plain hot. I can't wait to see what he looks like out of those clothes."

They pulled up on the opposite side of the main house, and Stacey's eyes went wide at what she saw. There were a couple of large white tents set up on the vast lawn. One had tables with chairs and a buffet. There were large grills out the rear of the tent, and the smells from those grills were amazing.

The other tent had a dance floor, chairs, and a band setting up. Wow! Dinner, dancing, and horseback riding. There were also large inflatable jump houses and a slide. A guy was practicing with balloon animals. They had it all. Stacey smiled as she looked around. Yeah, it was a lot, but it might actually be fun.

"Penny for your thoughts." Tristan wrapped an arm around her shoulder and brought her back to the present.

"This is just all so much and amazing." She was in awe and didn't hide it in her voice.

"Yeah, Uncle Don always goes above and beyond." Tristan gave her a quick peck. "There he is. Let's go. He's gonna love you. I do."

Her insides flopped.

Tristan's uncle Don was the spitting image of Adler. Just bigger and more important-looking.

Her insides squeezed into a knot. She thought she was going to throw up.

Adler was introducing Desiree to his father when they caught up with them. Desiree had her hand out and was shaking his. "Yes, sir. I love horses. I don't have anywhere near as much experience as Adler, but I have gone to the stables with a friend and ridden a couple of times. I'm looking forward to spending the day with the horses and kids."

"Well, good to hear. Just make sure this one treats you right and uses manners." His baritone voice carried to Stacey's ears, and the nerves started again.

"Sir, not to worry. I'll keep Adler on his toes." Desiree assured him.

Adler's dad let out a loud belly laugh and slapped his son on the shoulder. "Boy, I like her. She'll hold your hand to the grindstone."

Adler rolled his eyes.

"Hi, Uncle Don," Tristan said.

Don held his stomach and tried to gain control. His face lit up when he looked at Tristan. "Hey there, Trist." He wrapped his nephew in a tight hug. His eyes quickly fell on Stacey. "So, I'm going to guess that this is the girl who has caught your eye and taken all your attention."

Tristan's face glowed with pride. "Yes, sir." He placed his arm around Stacey. "This is Stacey. Stace, my Uncle Don."

Don grabbed Stacey's hand in his two large, beefy palms. Stacey gave him a nervous smile. "Hi, Mr. Warfield. It's nice to meet you."

"Oh, please." The man bellowed. "Call me Don. Mr. Warfield was my dad, and I'm not that old yet. Am I? Do I look old?"

Stacey smiled and felt herself relax. "No, sir, you don't look old at all. You could easily pass as Adler's older brother."

Adler let out a breath. "Oh, Lord. Really?"

Desiree laughed, elbowing him in the side as she grabbed his hand. The big, bellowing laugh came again. "I like her, Trist."

Stacey grabbed Tristan's arm and cuddled close.

"You two are good for each other. I can tell. Have you seen your aunt yet?" Don looked around.

"Not yet. We just got here. She wasn't at the stables," Tristan told him. He fidgeted and put a little space between him and Stacey.

"Well, I know she wanted to talk to you both, give you last-minute instructions, and make sure you were both here and ready to go."

"Translation," Adler added. "She was making sure I was here, and Tristan was prepared to be in charge, thinking I wanted nothing to do with the little brats and might have tried my best to get out of it like I did last year." He turned to his dad. "Well, you can tell my mother that she will be disappointed. I am here and ready to work with the brats. And I'm looking forward to it."

Don took his hand and brushed off Adler's shoulder. "Let's get that chip off your shoulder, son."

Adler jerked away from his dad's hand.

Don continued. "One day, you'll see that the reason Tristan doesn't get picked on is because..."

"He's the responsible one and can always be relied on. Yada, yada, yada. Yeah, I know. I've heard it a million times." He grabbed Desiree's hand and pulled her toward the grills. "We're going to get some lunch, then head to the stables. People are starting to show up."

"Bye, Don. See you later." Desiree said over her shoulder as Adler pulled her away.

Don turned to Tristan and Stacey. "I like her. She actually looks like a normal, well-adjusted girl, and she's actually wearing clothes and can talk in a complete sentence."

They both laughed. And Stacey spoke up for her friend. "Yeah, Desiree is a great person. She's a friend of mine. She doesn't take crap from anyone. I think she'll be good for his ego."

Don feigned looking hurt, placing his large hand over his heart. "What are you saying? My son has a big ego?"

Tristan grabbed Stacey's hand to end the conversation. "Oh, Uncle Don, just a little bit."

Don patted Tristan's shoulders. "Oh, Trist. You two have a good day. It was wonderful meeting you, Stacey. I'll see you later tonight at the dance."

Stacey smiled and realized quickly that her nerves were gone. "It was good meeting you, Don. See you later."

Tristan led her to the grills. She liked Don. He was a jovial man and seemed like a large teddy bear. "I like your uncle. He's funny and seems much gentler than my first impression."

"Yeah, he is really a good guy. A gentle giant. It's my aunt who's a handful at times. But they balance each other well. I'm lucky to have them."

A look of respect, and something else that Stacey couldn't quite figure out, appeared on Tristan's face. Her heart went out to him. His aunt and uncle brought him into their family. They stepped up, accepting him like a son, and he appreciated everything they did for him and gave him. She held on tighter to his hand. He had every reason to be a jerk and mad at the world, but he wasn't. He was a great guy, and Stacey was glad he was hers.

CHAPTER 24

The afternoon wore on. And thankfully, the typical chaotic October weather held off, and it was a perfect day for being at the stables. The temperature was comfortable, the sun was bright, and there was a gentle breeze.

The stables were bustling with activity as kids and teens came to ride or returned to the main house every thirty minutes by a tractor pulling a flatbed loaded with hay.

Jonathan and Carla were leading younger riders on ponies. The ponies appeared absolutely bored as they followed behind, and the youngsters on their backs either squealed with joy or looked scared to death.

Tristan was leading a black-spotted Appaloosa, and his passenger was a spunky girl around eleven years old. Her friend was with Adler. *These girls have mouths on them. One more time around, and they will be able to ride a bit on their own. Thank God.* Tristan needed some space, and he knew Adler really did.

Stacey and Desiree leaned on the fence off to the side, laughing and whispering between themselves as they watched Adler and Tristan interacting with the kids.

"Okay, do you understand how to control her? I think you'll do fine. Just walk with her around the pasture and back to me," Tristan instructed.

"Yes, sir, I'll be sure to come back to you, don't you worry."

Her friend added. "Yeah. We won't be gone long. I hope you won't miss us." She winked at Adler as she walked her horse away.

The guys headed back to the fence. Both rolled their eyes.

"God, I hope they're done soon." Adler sighed.

"No kidding." Tristan leaned against the fence, letting out a long sigh.

Stacey laughed as she leaned over the fence to kiss his cheek. "Has someone had a hard twenty minutes?"

"Those two are going to be a handful when guys wake up and notice them. The things they're saying. I didn't know kids that young knew that stuff." Tristan pulled Stacey's arms. She crawled between the rails to get to him.

"It's the internet. It's ruining them." Adler leaned his back against the rail and his boot on the bottom.

Desiree climbed through. "Damn, you two sound like two old men. You are just thirty, right?" Adler wrapped his arm around her shoulder.

They all stood in silence. Watching the pasture, the horses, and the riders.

Tristan's gaze traveled over Stacey. Her hair blew gently in the afternoon breeze, and her face looked relaxed. He liked her being here. She was the first girl in a very long time he had shared his life with and shown his home to. She was gorgeous, and being here made her seem different. He loved everything about her. He let out a pent-up breath. He needed to tell her about his aunt. If she runs into them before he can talk to Stacey...*Why have you put it off so long? She has trust issues, especially with rich guys, and here you are.*

She looked up at him, a soft smile slowly covering her face. "What?" She mouthed.

He reached out to place her hair behind her ear. *Say something now.* His voice caught in his throat. "Nothing." He shook his head. "Just watching you. You look like you belong here." *Great* job, dumbass. He touched her cheek. Her skin was soft and warmed by the sun. His eyes roamed over her skin, her lips. He leaned down and kissed those lips softly.

He forgot where he was as he became mesmerized by everything Stacey. Their kiss continued, and his heart sped up. She amazed him. His heart loved her. He loved her. Then why couldn't he be honest?

"Hey, you're getting the evil eye thrown at you."

Adler's comment interrupted Tristan's moment. He heard horses approaching and slowly pulled away.

Stacey glanced at the approaching girl on horseback. "Your fan awaits." She smiled and gave a small laugh.

He winked and walked away, for now. He had all day, and the thought of dancing with her in his arms tonight was enough to get him through this nightmare of a middle schooler and the possibility of Stacey being angry with him when he finally got around to letting her know about his aunt. She'll understand. It won't be a big deal.

What an awesome day.

Stacey and Desiree were lounging in the grass under a large tree, waiting for the guys to send the last group of kids back to the main house. Tristan was fun to watch. He seemed so at home and relaxed around the kids and the horses.

Adler was a different story. He was relaxed around the horses, yes. Kids, not so much. He rolled his eyes as the guys walked toward the girls. "Desiree, we always eat around six, then the real fun starts. Let's go get cleaned up and take a break. I need a drink or five."

Desiree grabbed his hand and laughed. "Hard day?"

"You have no idea." He shook his head, and they turned to go.

Tristan stopped Stacey. "Would you be willing to go for a ride?"

"What, on a horse?" Stacey's heart skipped, and the nerves that had been gone all day returned.

"You'll be fine. Ride Dandelion." He gestured to the brown horse Stacey had spent some time with earlier. "She's gentle, and you're used to each other."

Stacey let out a breath. "Fine. You're right. We're friends. Remember that Dandelion."

CHAPTER 25

Tristan and Stacey mounted the horses, and Stacey's followed Tristan's to the back of the pasture, and they exited into the hills beyond. He took it slow, thankfully. She relaxed as she got used to the rhythm of the horse. Dandelion was a gentle horse and knew where she was going and just followed Tristan over hills covered with the flower, her namesake.

They didn't talk as they rode, which was fine with Stacey.

Her eyes roamed the acres of pasture and hills all around her. She was surrounded by the sights, sounds, and smells of nature; sometimes, they weren't that pleasant, and her nose curled, but mostly, it was stunning. Dotted throughout the hills in the distance were quite a lot of cattle grazing in the grass.

Soon, they made a turn, and Stacey's breath caught. In front of her, the rolling hills turned into a grassy meadow with a large oak tree next to a pond. On the other side of the oak, there was what looked like an old log cabin. One that might have been built by early pioneers. Tristan hopped off his horse, which went to drink from the pond and eat the surrounding grass. He helped her down, and her horse did the same.

She looked around in awe. "Tristan, this place is beautiful." She walked over to the dilapidated house, and on closer inspection, she noticed that it had been recently repaired. She peered through the door. There was a picnic table and a couple of rocking chairs inside, and it was surprisingly clean.

She turned in confusion.

"Neat, huh? The cabin's been here at least a hundred years. My uncle keeps it up as a place to get out of the rain and for shelter if you're riding. Adler and I used to spend the night in here as often as we could, doing secret guy stuff."

"Really?" Yeah, she could see it. Little Adler and little Tristan talking about who knows what under the stars. A smile warmed her features. "Who else have you slept with in here?"

Tristan threw his head back, laughing. "Oh, one day, maybe I'll answer that. But I can tell you we had many parties out here." He pulled her into his arms. "I can also tell you I haven't brought a girl out here for…" He looked off into the distance, thinking. "It's got to be at least three years. Maybe more."

What? She wasn't sure she believed him. "No way."

"I didn't say I haven't had sex in over three years. I just haven't brought anyone out here." He closed the space between them and wrapped her in his arms. "I'm thinking that my drought might be coming to an end."

Stacey's heart did that now familiar pounding when he was this close to her and looked at her with that smoky-eyed look. "Oh really? You think I'm gonna end your drought in this dirty and dusty old house?" She pulled out of his grasp and walked farther into the cabin, exploring. "What if I tell you I don't like dark, dirty places?"

She felt his presence close and walked out the back of the cabin. The meadow spread out in front of her. Butterflies and dragonflies fluttered about, landing on the many wildflowers that covered the landscape. She turned toward the pond and leaned against the oak tree. The trunk was double the width of any she had seen before. It was old and tall, and the temperature under it must have been at least five degrees cooler. This place was amazing, and the view was breathtaking. To the side of the tree was a patch of black-eyed Susan flowers. Stacey bent down to pick one, but Tristan beat her to it and leaned on the trunk in front of her, holding the perfect gold and brown flower out to her.

A smile crept across her face, and her hands reached out to take it from him. "It's beautiful." She said as she touched the soft petals.

"Not as beautiful as you." He tucked her hair behind her ears.

She peered at him through her eyelashes and caught his smoldering gaze. Her heart skipped, and the tingling she felt became a surge of electricity flowing through her body. Her lips suddenly longed to touch his. To feel their warmth. "Kiss me." She whispered.

Slowly, he closed the space between them. Gently, their lips touched. The electricity flowed.

The kiss exploded.

His hands held her tightly, making her feel safe, and slowly caressed her back and into her hair.

A soft moan escaped from her as she melted into him.

Even though the kiss deepened, it wasn't rushed. It wasn't desperate. It was calm, sweet, relaxed. Just like her heart when she was with him.

He lowered her onto the grass. It was so soft and thick, it felt like a satin cushion beneath her. He stopped to unbutton his pants as she did hers, and she shimmied out of them and had to kick off her boots to finish the job.

Tristan unbuttoned her shirt, and her skin was bare in the cool air. He leaned over her and caressed her stomach with his lips, then her neck. Goosebumps appeared all over her skin, and she shivered under his touch.

He brushed his hand over her cheek. "I love you." He whispered as his eyes burned their way into her soul.

Her hand came up to his face, and she combed her fingers through his hair. "I love you, too." And she did. She loved him so much she was scared her heart was going to explode.

They held each other's gaze and searched each other's faces and bodies.

Finally, their lips met in a slow, sweet, delicate kiss.

Tristan finally placed his naked body over hers, slipped on a condom, and slid into her. They made love slowly, carefully, and without any rush.

It filled Stacey's heart with happiness. She held him close. Moved with him. The world fell away. Even the birds ceased to exist.

They rode slowly back to the stables.

It was a perfect afternoon.

Stacey was amazed that someone who was brought up with all this was still able to be so loving, so affectionate. Her horse stayed right behind him, and she watched how he moved effortlessly with his horse. His back was strong, confident, and muscular. His hair was blowing softly.

He turned in his saddle and smiled a smile that always stopped her heart. "You good?"

She nodded. "Perfect."

He easily hopped out of his saddle when they got close to the barn. He held her reins as she placed her feet back on the earth. They walked the horses into the barn and got them settled for the night.

They were cleaned up and headed toward the main house in Tristan's truck. It was a good thing because Stacey was starving. "I've had such a good time today. And thank you for being you."

"What do you mean by that?" He pulled next to Adler's jeep, away from the rest of the crowd.

Stacey turned to him. "All this. It's so amazing, and I'll be honest, it's a lot overwhelming. You've grown up with all this, yet you don't let it get to your head, showing off your money and acting spoiled. Like Adler."

"He's not that bad."

She raised an eyebrow.

"He grows on you."

Stacey smiled. Yeah, he does. She nodded. "Yeah, maybe a little. So even though I wish you would have been a little more honest, I can see you don't see this as who you are. It's just where you grew up."

Tristan grabbed her hand, and a serious look crossed his face.

"What's up?" She's felt this from him before. There's something he's not saying.

Just then, someone pounded on the window behind Stacey, and she about jumped out of her skin, and let out a yelp.

Adler opened the door. "Come on, you two. We thought you'd never show up. Dancing's started, and you almost missed eating."

They both climbed out.

Adler placed an arm around Stacey. "Scare you?"

She narrowed her eyes into slits, and she elbowed him hard in the side. "Just a little. Jerk."

His laughter was infectious. "So, how'd you like the meadow?"

Tristan moved some hair from her neck.

She turned toward him. "It was amazing." A buzz went through her skin as she remembered the feeling of the breeze on her bare stomach, the rush of their slow lovemaking.

Tristan winked.

"Yep, I'm sure you had tons of fun just riding. Anyway, you have one more obstacle to make it through." Adler's arm went around Desiree. "My mom is waiting to meet the girl who captured her amazing nephew's heart."

Stacey felt nerves crawl through her. She knew Tristan was close to his aunt. "Come on. I want to get this over with. I'm sure she'll be great." Stacey pulled Tristan's hand to follow Adler and Destiny.

But he held her back.

She turned toward him. She was ready to go. The look on his face froze her in her tracks. Why was he avoiding her eyes? "You're avoiding looking at me, Tristan. What's wrong?" Her heart thumped hard against her chest.

His hands grabbed her arms. "Stacey, I...I should have told you something sooner." His eyes flicked to the movement behind Stacey.

She watched as his body seemed to deflate. "Tristan? What's wrong?" She spun, and her heart stopped. *What the hell?* Her eyes blinked rapidly. Adler, Desiree, and a tall, thin, dark-haired beauty were walking toward them.

"Well, hello. I'm surprised to see you here. Ms. Kempt. Am I right?"

Dr. Bitchy in the flesh. Why was she here? Stacey looked between Dr. Bitchy, or Hensley and Adler. Their hair color was the same, but not much else. But then she smiled. And it was there Adler resembled her.

Stacey turned to Tristan. Her hand rubbed the side of her neck. What was going on? She needed some answers. She watched as a look of dread passed between Tristan and Adler. Adler pinched his lips.

Dr. Hensley broke the silence. "So, what a pleasant surprise. You're the one who caught my nephew's heart."

Elie turned to Tristan. "You didn't tell me your girlfriend was a nurse. It never dawned on you I might know her?"

Stacey finally got her bearings and felt her heart harden. Tristan knew who she was having problems with but never said anything. He and Adler kept this from her. Fury flooded her heart. Stacey closed her eyes and released her breath. When she opened them, they grabbed onto Tristan's. "Dr. Hensley, he knew. He just never said anything."

Fear flashed in Tristan's eyes.

Her heart picked up. He deceived her. *What the hell? He kept this from me. He lied. How stupid could I be to think he was different?*

"Well, maybe we can talk about your interview sometime tonight. Go grab yourselves some food and enjoy the rest of the night." Dr. Hensley smiled before she walked away.

Chapter 26

The four of them stood silently.

Stacey couldn't take her eyes off Tristan. What did she just witness? Her insides were a churning pile of molten mess, but she refused to back down.

He finally looked away.

Adler was the one who broke the silence. "I guess you didn't get around to telling her." Tristan's head shot up, and he glared at his cousin.

Adler lifted his hands in surrender. "Come on, Des. Let's grab some food."

Desiree placed her hand on Stacey's arm. "Stace, are you okay?"

Stacey nodded, but it was a lie. She wasn't okay. Tears welled up in her eyes, and she blinked rapidly to hold them back.

Desiree and Adler walked away.

She leaned against the side of Tristan's truck, hidden from all the guests' wandering eyes. Exhaustion filled her body as she willed the tears not to fall. Why didn't he say anything? Seeing Dr. Hensley threw her off—she was his aunt. Stacey's eyes traveled up his body and met his gaze.

He raked his hands through his hair, and emotion creased his face. Was it concern, guilt, or worry? She wasn't sure.

"Tristan." Her voice was thick, and a tear escaped from her eye.

He reached out and grasped her hands. The shock that ran through her didn't warm her as usual, but made her feel sick.

He lied to her. She can handle a lot, but lying is not okay.

"Stace." His voice cracked, and he cleared his throat. "I meant to say something today, but there wasn't a good time."

So many feelings swam around in her chest. Love. Frustration. Confusion. Hurt. Her heart was mush and falling apart.

Finally, she got her mind straight. "You know, last night when I said her name, that would have been a perfect time to let me know that the woman I was calling Dr. Bitchy was your aunt. Every time today, the fact she wanted to meet me came up, but you still said nothing. There were plenty of good times. You just decided it didn't matter. It wasn't important." Her gaze finally grabbed his and held tight. "It would have just taken a few minutes of your precious time to pull me off to the side and tell me."

Tristan's gaze fell.

Her heart smashed against her chest. "I could tell there was something. There were times things seemed off." She held her ground. "You thought of telling me a few times, didn't you?" Her voice was soft.

She watched as Tristan's stance changed. His shoulders went back. His head came up. "Stacey, it's not a big deal. I didn't tell you that your 'doctor bitchy' is my Aunt Eli. I should have. At first, I was surprised that anyone could see her like that. She's the sweetest lady ever. She loves and cares for everyone. You said yourself that she got you the interview because you were the best nurse there. Maybe you should have listened to those words." Tristan's words became heated, and his features changed. "She must see something in you and wanted to help you get a better job at a better hospital."

Her heart nearly thumped out of her chest. "Fine. Whatever. You still could have told me. Said something. If your aunt is as wonderful as you say she is, I think you would have stood up for her." She froze. The silence hung in the air for a beat before she spoke again. Her voice was eerily calm. "This is probably what you and Adler were talking about in all your secret little intense conversations. Isn't it?"

Tristan released her hands. His gaze became hard. "Yes. It was. I know how you are. I was trying to figure out how to tell you without you getting all bent out of shape about my aunt being one of the rich, bitchy doctors that you hate so much. You made it difficult because of your ridiculous security issues."

He just called what I feel ridiculous. She felt something crack inside her. "You think I'm ridiculous?" She could feel her eyes needed to spill, but she wouldn't cry in front of a guy. "This is stupid. Take me home, Tristan."

His eyes became small. "Take you home? Why? We haven't eaten yet. Come on, Stacey. It's just a misunderstanding. We can work it out." He reached for her hands.

She jerked away from him and stomped to the passenger side and opened the door. Her eyes caught his. "Take me home. Now." She climbed into the front seat, and he followed. He turned toward her, but she ignored him, choosing to stare out the window. He mumbled something under his breath as he turned the key in the ignition. She could make out a few curses and the word stupid. *Whatever.*

Finally, he pulled out, leaving tire marks in the grass.

The music rising from under the canopy slowly died away. So much for romantic dancing under the stars with the man of her dreams. Again, she found herself faced with the immaturity and self-centeredness of a rich man. This one, she hoped, was different. But as usual, he showed his true colors.

When it came down to it, all men were untrustworthy, egotistical, and selfish. Was it only last night she told him she loved him? Was it just this morning they made love here in the cab? That all seemed like a different life.

She grabbed her phone from her pocket and sent a quick text to Kristen, letting her know that her plans had changed. She would be home and was on her way. She placed her phone back in her pocket, ignored it when it vibrated, and laid her head on the back of her seat to watch as the dark world passed by on the interstate.

What the hell happened tonight? How did they go from having an amazing time to that argument? Why didn't he just tell the truth about Dr. Hensley? *How would I have reacted if he had?* She had no idea, and now it didn't matter because she wouldn't have the chance to find out. Her feelings were all knotted up, like a necklace forgotten at the bottom of a jewelry box. Impossible to straighten out.

Finally, they pulled into her driveway, and she reached for the handle, but his hand was on her arm and held her back. "Don't leave, Stacey. Let's talk this out." His voice was soft and filled with emotion.

She froze and breathed in a shaky breath. She closed her eyes. *Get control. Don't let him see how upset you are. Don't give him the upper hand.*

She had control again and turned and looked at him. Her gaze was blank. Her eyebrows were up, waiting for him to talk. Waiting for him to say something worth listening to.

"You look like you're done. You've made a decision." Tristan's voice was irritable. He was upset with her? "Am I not human? I made a mistake. I'm sorry." His voice was harsh.

Stacey nodded. "You sound sorry." Her words oozed with sarcasm.

Tristan let out a loud, frustrated breath, and his eyes were on the ceiling. "Don't walk away from us, Stacey. I disappointed you; I messed up. I'm sorry. It happens in relationships."

"Yeah, and that's why I don't do relationships. People are selfish and disappointing. I knew better than to get into anything more than dates and sex. I knew not to open my heart. This always happens." Her pulse raced, and a lump formed in her stomach.

She swallowed it down and looked into his eyes, which were now wide and pleading. Her voice became quiet. "It's not worth it, Tristan."

He opened his mouth to say something, but she shook her head and turned away. Without looking back, she climbed out of his truck and walked into her house.

Kristen was in the kitchen, leaning against the counter, drinking a bottle of water when Stacey walked in.

"Why are you home so early? What happened?" She asked as she handed a water bottle to Stacey.

Stacey took it, unscrewed the top, and took a drink. Swallowing the water again pushed the lump back down deep where it needed to stay. "Let's just say he didn't disappoint."

Kristen let out a loud sigh. "Stace, come on. Whatever it was, it can't be that bad. You said He was just about perfect."

Stacey banged the water bottle down on the counter. "Yeah, and I also said that there had to be something I was missing. And there was. I let my guard down around a spoiled rich kid, and he turned out to be a manipulating liar." Her voice grew louder, and her pulse raced.

She needed to calm down. This shouldn't surprise her. All guys turn out to be manipulating. That's why she didn't do relationships.

Kristen reached out, but she put her arms up to keep her away. "I can't now, Kristen. Just don't."

She walked to her room and slammed the door.

CHAPTER 27

Tristan sat stunned as Stacey left his truck, walked away, and never looked back. His heart split in two. "What the hell just happened?" He raked his hands through his hair and held it in place. *Did she really just walk away from me? From us?* His thoughts were wild, but he didn't want to believe it. No, he couldn't believe this really all just happened.

He picked up his phone and sent her a text. He wanted her to come back out and talk. Their relationship was too important to just walk away from.

He waited for an answer, but none came.

Anger caused his heart to speed up, and he punched the dash and pounded on his steering wheel. Now, not only his heart hurt but also his hands and fists. "Great job, Tristan."

Was he talking about hurting his hands or not coming clean about Aunt Elie?

He wasn't sure.

A light came on in Stacey's bedroom. It cast a soft glow between the folds of her blinds. He wanted more than anything to go in there and put his arms around her and hold her until she realized her mistake.

He opened his truck door and stepped out. He leaned against it and stared at her window. All he had to do was walk to the door and knock. Someone would let him in, and he would get her to listen to him until she forgave him.

Forgave him for what? It's not like he intentionally kept something from her or lied about who he was. She was so damned negative about everything when it came to guys and relationships. But she finally opened up and gave her heart to him. He could have at least told her about his aunt.

Hindsight and all that bullshit. DAMN!!! He hopped back in his truck and slammed the door. The tug of war inside his heart was driving him crazy. He let out a yell, put the truck in gear, and pulled out of her driveway.

Tristan made it home and was pulling through the gates in record time.

It was a good thing he didn't pass any cops. He was sure he was going over one hundred. That would have been just what he needed to end this perfectly shitty night—a trip to jail for reckless driving.

The dancing was in full swing when he drove up the driveway. He forgot about the fundraiser. He could just say, fuck it, turn toward the party, find someone to dance with, and forget about this nightmare. He was sure that there would be some willing participants who would gladly spend quality time with him, both in his arms and in his bed. That's what he would have done in the past. That's what he would have done before Stacey.

He sighed and kept following the driveway. He was no longer in the mood for partying. If he couldn't dance with her, he wouldn't dance at all.

Once he parked in the garage, he headed toward the bar and made himself a drink—Jack and Coke—he wanted something strong. Stronger than beer. Before he walked away, he poured himself a shot and downed the dark whiskey, enjoying the burn as it coated his throat.

Once he filled the ice bucket, he grabbed the bottle of Jack, the open can of Coke, and one other, and went out to the patio, turned on the gas fireplace, and sat by the pool near the fake cheer of the fireplace, ready to finish his night.

Just himself and ole Jack.

Shit. He dumped the rest of the second Coke can into his glass and filled it with ice. This would be his last drink. Make it count. He poured Jack until the glass was filled. When he sipped, he grimaced. Good and strong. Perfect.

He checked his phone, and the last text he sent was still not answered. Rage filtered through his veins. She was ignoring him. "What the hell?" He spoke to the air and let his phone fly. It crashed into the brick wall, and he heard what sounded like a few pieces hit the ground. It didn't matter. If she wasn't going to text him back, he didn't need it.

"Bro, what's wrong?"

Adler. "What are you doing here?" Tristan's words slurred when he spoke, and his legs wobbled when he pushed himself out of the chair. He watched as Adler came to his rescue before he tumbled into the gas fireplace, and Desiree went to pick up his phone or the pieces. He didn't know at this point.

"I, my dear cousin, was bringing my beautiful date back to our place and was hopefully going to have my way with her."

Desiree smacked his arm.

"Ouch." He laughed. "But it looks like we're going to be babysitting you instead. What an awesome trade-off."

Desiree intercepted the conversation. "I guess Stacey didn't appreciate that you didn't tell her you knew the doctor bitchy she was complaining about?"

Tristan shot her a look.

"He filled me in." She pointed at Adler. "It then made sense. I was there when she was talking about it."

"Was that just last night?" How could things have become so messed up in such a short amount of time? His head was swimming. "I think I'll lie here and sleep." He slurred.

Desiree raised her eyes.

Tristan breathed hard, and Adler led him to the couch. "Des, grab the comforter from the spare room. "

"Are you crazy? It's going to be cold tonight."

He brushed her concerns away. "Trust me. He'll be fine. It's not the first time one of us has passed out on this couch."

⁕⁕⁕

Stacey lay in her bed. She had cried all the tears she had, which, surprisingly, was more than she had ever cried before. It could be because she was never truly in love with anyone before, but she refused to go there.

Was it just last night that she opened her heart to him and told him she loved him? Did she honestly think that what they did today was more than sex? That they actually made...she hated to think it... love?

There was a pain so deep in her chest she needed it out. Why did he turn out like all the others? *I thought he was different. I thought I could trust him.* She knew better. A sigh left her throat. When she thought of the time they spent talking, dancing, being together, making love…She knew things were different with Tristan. She couldn't have been wrong about him.

Finally, she grabbed her phone and noticed his text. He wanted to talk.

She answered him.

> **It's late. But let's talk to-**
> **morrow.**
> **Come over around ten. I**
> **miss you already.**

She waited and waited. No response.

She went and brushed her teeth and washed her face, getting ready for bed.

Still no answer.

She grabbed a book and tried to read, but no luck. She couldn't focus, so she checked her phone one last time. He still hadn't answered.

She fell asleep wondering why he was ignoring her, and her anger crept back in.

CHAPTER 28

S tacey rolled over as rays of sunlight filled her room.

Her eyes fluttered open just a sliver. At first, she forgot what day it was. She grabbed her phone. It was nine, and it was Sunday.

Memories of last night came flooding back to her, and she checked to see if she had a text from Tristan. Her heart fell when there was still nothing there.

Maybe he read it and answered and forgot to press send. Just in case, she hopped out of bed and into the shower. The hot water felt good as it washed away the tears and heartache. Being Sunday, she headed downstairs to grab a cup of coffee and a banana. She'd wait to eat when she met everyone at The Pizza Place after they got out of church, or maybe she'd end up with Tristan talking, or even better yet, making up.

She stood in the kitchen by the window, watching squirrels in the yard. Her heart fluttered as she thought of him. She could feel his hands on hers as he pulled her to him, their lips connecting and leading to... other things. Her body tingled just thinking about it. *This mess is just a big misunderstanding. He didn't lie intentionally.* Her heart fell, and a weight filled her. *But there were plenty of times that he could have said something. It wouldn't have been hard.*

Yes, it would have been very simple. Her insides boiled as she thought more about it. He deceived her knowingly and purposely. *If he shows up, we'll talk, but his explanation better be good.*

As ten o'clock came and went, and ten-thirty turned to eleven, the lump in her chest that she was trying to ignore took over and exploded. She thought her heart was going to break as the tears rushed out. She was hoping things would have been easy to mend, but with him not returning her messages, it wasn't feeling like he really cared.

Fine.

Anger fueled her, and she picked up the phone to dial his number. It went straight to voice mail. Either he had his phone turned off or had blocked her. That jack ass!

Her day switched gears. Since she hadn't heard from Tristan, she needed to be by herself. She skipped eating with her friends and got back into comfy clothes, knowing that Kristen would be getting back to her as soon as she could.

She wasn't disappointed.

She was cuddled under a blanket on the couch, bingeing Netflix, when the smell of pizza filled her nostrils and her best friend's voice filled her ears. It wasn't just Kristen, though. Elizabeth was with her. She sat up and forced a smile. Maybe they could help her get out of this funk.

Kristen placed a Diet Coke on the coffee table along with some leftover pepperoni pizza as Elizabeth plopped in the chair. Stacey grabbed a piece and let the delicious flavors fill her mouth.

Kristen's eyes blazed into hers. *They want me to talk.* She felt tears rising to the surface. *I can't cry anymore.* She kept eating. Maybe she could eat until the tears passed.

"Girl, come on." Kristen huffed. "What exactly happened last night? It seemed like things were going amazingly well at your party."

Was her party just two days ago? Did she really tell him she loved him? She buried her face in her hands. Why did she do that? Ugg!

"Okay, what's going on inside that head of yours?" Elizabeth asked.

"Yeah, there's something big. I can smell it." Kristen leaned forward and laid her hand on Stacey's knee.

Dammit, Kristen! Stacey caved and found herself spilling everything. The feelings she had for Tristan, the feelings he said to have for her. Their amazing night, and the meeting of Doctor Bitchy, who was really his amazing Aunt Elie.

"What?" Kristen's mouth almost hit the floor.

Stacey's eyes were wide. "I know. Picture how shocked I was when I saw her there and realized he had kept that from me. I was so mad, I asked him to bring me home." She searched her friends' faces. They were exchanging glances.

Kristen spoke up. "Stace, we don't hear that he said anything wrong."

Stacey's heart fell. "He lied." Tears streamed down her face. "I trusted him, gave him my heart, and he threw it back at me. I thought he was different." She shook her head, and her voice came out in a whisper. "I was wrong."

"Oh, Stace." Kristen's voice was filled with concern. "We know he lied. Or, you see it as a lie. But was it really? Could it have been he just didn't know how to tell you?"

"Yeah," Elizabeth added. "From what we saw Friday night, you two are great together. He made you shine in a way I've never seen before."

"Really, Liz? I figured you'd understand. You, of all people, know the importance of trust and how much it hurts when that trust gets broken."

Elizabeth's face creased. "What do you mean? Me, of all people?"

"Last year, you were ready to raise Grant on your own, without Brady. You left him because of his stupidity. He broke your trust."

Elizabeth shook her head. "That's far from the truth, Stacey. Yeah, I was ready to leave him and willing to walk away from what we had, but the circumstances were a bit different. His lies affected our family. We had to start over and figure things out. It's not quite the same."

God, she was hurting. He didn't cheat. He lied. She couldn't hold the tears back anymore, and the dam broke. Kristen and Elizabeth wrapped her in a hug and let her cry. Finally, with her face wet and snotty, she unwrapped herself from their cocoon and accepted the napkin from Elizabeth. Her eyes met Kristen's. "I trusted him. I..." She couldn't finish.

Kristen held her again. "I know, but Stacey, he made a mistake. He's human. It's going to happen. Don't compare him to all the jerks you've dated in the past. He's nothing like them. And he's nowhere near the shit rating of Carl." Kristen held Stacey at arm's length and held her gaze. "I think you both need to talk things out."

Stacey nodded. "I know, and I agree. After I got home and had time to think, I realized I had overreacted a little and tried to call him, but he's been ignoring me. He hasn't called back or sent me a message." She let out a big breath. "That proves he knows he screwed up and refuses to do anything about it." She looked at her friends. She was hurt, but it was much more than just that. She was also upset, pissed, and irritated.

"Maybe he just needs time also, Stace," said Elizabeth. "There's probably a perfectly good reason he hasn't gotten back to you."

Stacey's breathing calmed, and she nodded. When she spoke, her voice came out in a whisper. "I know. You're right." She was so glad they were here. "Thanks, y'all."

Chapter 29

S tacey jumped out of bed Monday morning before her alarm went off, eager to get to work. A change of scenery and the reliability of chaos and action of work seemed like a great way to get her mind on something else. She never heard from Tristan yesterday, but Kristen and Elizabeth helped her try and keep her mind off things. They watched a couple of *Harry Potter* movies until it was late, and she had to get to bed.

"Hi, Stacey." Nancy said. "Do you have a minute? I need to talk to you before you start your day."

"Sure. What's up?" Stacey took her coffee and joined Nancy at the table.

Nancy's face was lit up. "Well, it seems like you left a great impression at your interview on Friday."

Stacey's heart jumped. With all the drama of her weekend, she almost forgot she'd had the interview. Thinking back now, she thought about the feeling she got on the floor and the good vibe that filled her entire being. "I really loved it, surprisingly."

"Well, they really loved you and wanted to know if we'd be willing to let you go early. They want you to start on Friday and work the weekend."

Stacey's eyes popped, and her mouth fell open. "Really? Friday?" She dug through her feelings. Did she want that this soon? Surprisingly, yes. Yes, she did. Her heart beat faster. A bigger hospital. There was so much more action and people. It would push her as a nurse. She was so ready for this. She raised her eyebrow. *Wasn't that Dr. Hensley's reasoning for putting my name in for the job?* One corner of her mouth ticked up. *Thank you, Dr. Hensley.* "Yes, I'd love to work there. And starting Friday? Absolutely." Stacey stood.

Nancy gave her a squeeze. "I'm so proud of you. You'll be using your amazing gifts at a hospital that will help you grow. That is such a great opportunity."

Stacey was on cloud nine.

Wednesday night, when work was finished, there was a cake celebrating those who were moving on to something bigger.

Stacey entered the break room with Karolyn, who had accepted a job on a different floor of County. Many of the staff were standing around, enjoying the celebration. Stacey, still flying high after a very busy week, picked up a slice of chocolate cake and talked with some co-workers.

"Excuse me, Nurse Kempt. Can we talk?"

Stacey's heart picked up speed. Dr. Hensley. What's she doing here? "Sure." Stacey placed her plate in the trash and followed the doctor out of the room, wiping her hands on the butt of her scrubs. She took a deep breath. Calm down.

Doctor Hensley stopped in the next empty room. "I'm glad to hear you accepted the job."

"Thank you. I start on Friday. I'm really looking forward to it. I enjoyed my experience last week when I visited for my interview." Stacy couldn't keep the excitement out of her voice. Her eyes met the doctor's. "I need to tell you thank you for putting my name out there. I really appreciate it." Stacey meant it.

Doctor Hensley put her hand up. "Don't thank me. You deserved it. Your record is impressive. The larger hospitals need your kind of talent to better serve their patients."

This woman thought she could add something real to a larger hospital. Stacey's chin jutted up, and her face beamed. Someone noticed her work.

"There's something else we need to discuss, and it isn't hospital related."

The lump that Stacey was trying hard to ignore started rising again.

Dr. Hensley's expression changed. It softened. "I want to talk to you personally about Tristan. Will you give me a minute?"

This was a bit weird, a personal conversation with a higher-up at work, but Stacey nodded.

Dr. Hensley gave her a small smile. "When my sister passed, there was no doubt Don and I were going to keep Tristan and raise him as our own. He's a great young man." The doctor's eyes rose to meet Stacey's. "He has never given his heart away lightly. I know that because we haven't met many girls he's dated. Unlike Adler, Tristan doesn't date often. His heart is much more guarded. I don't know what happened, but I know that since the family picnic, he's been by himself and quieter than he has been in months. If he contacts you again, please give him a chance to explain himself. He's worth it." Doctor Hensley reached out and touched Stacey's arm. "Good luck Friday. The hospital is lucky to have you."

"Thank you, and I will." Wow. She is really nice. Stacey watched as she walked away. Did Tristan talk to his aunt? Why hadn't he contacted her yet? Stacey pulled her phone from her pocket and scrolled until she found her text with Tristan. Her last one was still not answered.

Can we talk? She typed in.

She stopped and looked at the words. If he wanted to talk, wouldn't he have texted her?

She let out a sigh and deleted it.

Jacob and Kristen's cars weren't the only ones in her driveway when she pulled in.

What the hell?

She walked in, and the kitchen was filled with her friends. Elizabeth, Jessica, Kristen, and Desiree.

Her eyes froze on Desiree. She only came by for birthdays or large get-togethers. She was never part of their small friend circle. Everyone else she could understand. They are always in each other's business, like friends usually are.

Ignoring their presence, she walked to the refrigerator to get out a Diet Coke, popped the top, and leaned against the counter taking a deep drink. Finally, she looked at them and crossed her arms over her chest.

"Surprise!" they yelled. They stepped away from the table. There was a cake sitting there.

What is this? She was so focused on them getting into her business that she didn't think they would be planning anything. "A cake?" Printed on the cake was, "Here's to bigger and better things. Congratulations!"

"Oh, my God. This is awesome. Thank you." Stacey's face was all smiles. "I didn't get to finish my cake at work, so let's dig in. Someone make coffee."

"Already done." Kristen brought over the carafe, and half and half.

Elizabeth cut the cake while Jessica passed them around the table. The girls sat and ate very large pieces of cake.

"Liz, these pieces are huge." Jessica's eyes were as large as the cake.

"Yeah, well, eat as much as you want. I'm looking forward to eating all of mine. I need to eat something. I'm working hard to get into my dress and am tired of salad and chicken."

"So, how are your wedding plans going?" Stacey asked.

They spent the next few minutes talking about Elizabeth and Brady's wedding. Jessica, the maid of honor, was filling them in on what the bridesmaids were going to wear. Desiree discussed the cake and food.

"I asked Adler to go with me," Desiree said.

"Damn, Des," said Kristen. "You've been seeing Adler?"

"Since Friday night. Spent all weekend with him." Desiree's look was pure mischief.

"You've got good taste," Jessica informed her.

Stacey's body felt numb. She looked up. "You're not going to last that long. He doesn't stay with one girl." *Where did that come from, Stacey?*

Desiree stood up. "Look, just because you're making the worst choice of your life and ditching Tristan for no reason…"

What! Desiree knew nothing about what was going on between her and Tristan. "No reason? What do you know about what happened?" Her eyes welled up with tears, and when she spoke, her voice was thick with emotion. "He lied to me." The words tore from her chest. "I loved him, and he lied." Tears spilled down her cheeks.

"Stace." Kristen's arms wrapped her in a cocoon of warmth. "What he did was shitty. I agree. He should have told you about his aunt. I know you love him. That's why you're hurting so much."

Stacey cried on Kristen's shoulder. This was the first time since college she had cried like this over a guy. But this seemed so much different.

"It's okay to love, Stacey. And sometimes love hurts. It hurts badly." Elizabeth wrapped them both in her arms.

Stacey pulled away and started wiping at her tears.

Desiree's voice was softer. "I know for a fact he really wants to talk. He just got a phone yesterday."

"What are you talking about?" Stacey gave Desiree a blank look.

"Well, to make a long story short, when he came back Saturday night, he threw his phone against the wall, and it shattered."

Stacey blinked rapidly. *He broke his phone.* Her jaw dropped.

Desiree snickered. "Yeah. You did that. See how upset he is?"

Jessica laughed. "He's either upset or has major anger issues."

"Well, either way, he's wanting to talk." Desiree focused on Stacey, her brows up.

Stacey's pulse picked up speed. "How do you know?" She needed to make sure her heart wasn't racing for no reason.

"Adler and I were sitting by the pool last night talking to him. He's not sure exactly what happened, and he's miserable." Desiree's phone pinged. She glanced at it. "It's Adler. He wants to know whether I've talked to you yet. So? Do you want to talk to him?" Desiree's eyes questioned Stacey's.

Yes. More than anything. Everyone's faces held encouragement. She nodded. "Yes," she whispered.

Desiree texted something back.

Almost immediately, Stacey's phone pinged. Her heart leaped in her chest.

Holy shit! It was Tristan. She looked at her friends. Her eyes were wide. "He wants to come over now." Her pulse started racing.

Elizabeth jumped up. "It's late. I gotta go and make sure Mom could get Grant to bed. Good night, everyone." She gave hugs around the circle.

"Yep, I gotta run also. It's getting late." Jessica followed Elizabeth's example.

"My honey's in bed waiting for me." Kristen hugged her and gave her a kiss on the cheek. "You've got this, Stace. Follow your heart for once."

Stacey and Desiree were the only ones left. They worked silently as they cleaned the table and put away the cake. Stacey finally broke the silence. "What do you think about everything?"

"Look, I'm not really sure what happened, but I know he doesn't think he lied. I think it's just a big misunderstanding, and you both need to talk things out." And Desiree was gone.

Stacey sat on the deck, waiting for the lights of Tristan's car to enter her driveway. Her thoughts kept flip-flopping back and forth. First, she admitted to herself that she had blown things out of proportion. She knew she could do that. But she had a problem with the fact that he hadn't told her about his aunt. All he had to do was say something. It wouldn't have been hard, but he chose to ignore it. That was what she couldn't forget. That was what bothered her the most.

Well, she would hear it directly from the horse's mouth. He pulled into the driveway.

As he parked, she stood up and leaned on the railing. Her breath caught as he got out of his car and walked closer to her. Even on this chilly March night, he was dressed only in a t-shirt and jeans. A pair of cowboy boots on his feet.

Her eyes met his as he got closer, and they wouldn't leave the confines of each other. His smoky grays pulled her in like a tornado in a storm. Her insides clutched, and her pulse raced.

He climbed the steps, then was there in front of her with his hands shoved in his back pockets and a small smile on his face. Man, did he look adorable.

Heat grew in her gut as she returned his smile. This was the right thing. They could make this work. "Hi. I'm glad you're here." Her voice was small, and her eyes still didn't want to leave the confines of his.

"Hey, me too."

They walked toward each other. Automatically, their hands met as if they were pulled together by a magnetic force. When their fingers intertwined, electricity shot through her, and she felt their connection.

"I'm sorry I overreacted." She blurted the words out before knowing she would.

Tristan shook his head. "I should have told you. I'm so sorry."

Stacey opened her mouth, but he held up a hand to stop her. "Let me finish." That hand tucked some hair behind her ears. "I knew you had trust issues from the beginning, and lying was a definite no. And I agree. It is with me also. You can't have a relationship if you can't trust each other." He looked away before he continued.

She gave him time. They needed to get this all out.

"I wish I could verbalize why I didn't say anything. There were plenty of times, perfect times, to tell you about my aunt. I just..." He shrugged and turned his gaze back to her.

The smile grew on Stacey's face. It wasn't all him, though. "I didn't make it easy for you. Spouting all my insecurities about rich people and how much I couldn't stand the doctors at the hospital. I was rude and very insecure. That insecurity almost cost me you."

Their gaze held.

Her heart skipped.

Slowly, they closed the space between them until their lips met.

She melted into him. His kiss, his taste. She missed this. It had only been four days, but it felt like a lifetime.

When the kiss ended, he held her face close to his. His eyes roamed over her, and then slowly his lips came to hers again. This kiss became deeper, more intense. It made up for the time they lost in those four days.

Stacey held her eyes closed tight, willing his smell and taste to her memory.

Tristan spoke, his voice deep. "I need you to know that you can trust me. I'm not like those other rich assholes you've dated." His hands brushed the sides of her face and held her head tight. "I love you, and I screwed up. I was scared you'd leave if you knew who my aunt was, and I lost you anyway because I said nothing. I would take it all back if I could, but I can't, and I'm sorry for all of it."

Her heart swelled. "I'm sorry, too. I didn't need to automatically put you in the same category. You never gave me a reason to." She pulled him to her in a desperate embrace. Her insecurities made her almost lose this amazing person in front of her.

Their embrace led to another kiss, which led to them ending up in her room. The night was amazing, filled with each of them apologizing to the other over and over. Reminding each other of their feelings.

Chapter 30

Stacey took advantage of an empty house and a happy heart to give her enough energy to get through the day. When Jacob and Kristen came home, the oven was filled with food, there was a cake on the counter, and the house was sparkling.

Jacob opened the oven and closed it with wide-eyed surprise. "Okay, sis, what's going on? That's lasagna and garlic bread in the oven. You never make lasagna."

Stacey grabbed plates out of the cabinet and forks and knives. "Here. Instead of asking questions, you two can help set the table."

Kristen grabbed the plates with a smirk. "Does this have anything to do with the extra car in the driveway this morning?"

Stacey's body warmed, and she checked her text. He was on his way and should be here soon. "Not gonna lie, but yes. It does. And he'll be here soon." She got out the salad and dressing.

"So, all went well last night?" Jacob asked.

"Yep."

There was a knock on the door, and her heart jumped. "Now finish setting these out and get the food out of the oven." She threw her oven mitts at Jacob and hurried to the door.

There he stood.

Gray shirt, black pants. Dress shoes. Perfect.

Stacey grabbed Tristan's shirt and pulled him to her so their lips could greet each other, and what a greeting it was. Her body was on fire. Her heart was full. Maybe they could skip dinner. She shut the door, and Jacob stood in their way.

They would have to eat.

Dinner was amazing. The company was better. Stacey thought her face would break from the smile that wouldn't go away. She loved Tristan here, around her table with her brother and best friend.

It felt right. She felt good and complete.

Once dinner was over, Kristen and Jacob promised to clean up since Stacey cooked, so she and Tristan went outside.

They leaned on the deck railing and talked about everything. *I can't believe I doubted him. I doubted this.* She held his hand tighter and looked at him. "I love you." His smile made her insides go squishy.

He put his arms around her waist and placed a kiss on her hair. "I love hearing those words from you. There was a time I thought I was crazy. Continuing to fight for your attention. I've never worked so hard for a first date in my life."

"I'm glad you didn't give up."

"I'll never give up on us." His eyes smoldered deep into hers.

She sucked in a breath. She knew what he said was true.

His hand curled around her neck. "I know you've had bad luck with guys, but we aren't all bad. Some of us don't give our hearts away easily. I haven't been in a relationship for..." He stopped to think. "It's been a long time."

His lips closed in on hers in a kiss that ignited her insides. He kissed her with so much passion that her lips were on fire. Her heart was beating out of control. His mouth left hers and traveled down her neck. Wherever his lips touched skin, shock waves of desire flooded throughout her body. He pulled away, and his breath was rapid.

Her heart was thundering.

He tucked her hair behind her ear. "Maybe we should take this somewhere else."

She liked the sound of that.

CHAPTER 31

Working at Summit Woman's Center was so different, yet Stacey found herself loving every second of it. She was always busy, and the chaos kept her focused. March flew by as Stacey's days were spent at the hospital, and her nights were with Tristan as often as possible.

She was finally into work enough that she'd gotten to know some of the nurses, sand he was taking a much-needed lunch break with her coworkers, Carla and Gina.

Gina was a handful of a girl. Pink hair, multiple piercings in her ears, arms covered with tattoos, and a mouth that went with it. It always impressed Stacey how quickly she could turn off the attitude when she walked into a patient's room and turn it right back on as soon as she left. Everyone always told her she was going to forget where she was one day, and that attitude would get her in trouble.

Carla, on the other hand, was as sweet as she was pretty. She came from a wealthy family and had the best of everything growing up. She lived with some nursing friends in a high-rise condo right in downtown Nashville. Stacey wasn't sure what the rent was, but knew she couldn't afford it and wouldn't want to even if she split it four ways.

They were talking about some of the new moms on the floor and eating a quick lunch when the door opened and quiet fell over the room. Doctors and board members walked in. They do rounds and check in on the different floors from time to time.

Stacey's heart fell. Dr. Hensley was with them. They had talked a couple of times at the house, and they got along well, but Stacey was really hoping to keep her private and work relationships separate.

No such luck.

Dr. Hensley smiled at the girls and greeted Stacey by name.

Stacey nodded. "Hi, Dr. Hensley."

"Are you enjoying your new job? I'm hearing great things about you."

Stacey glanced at the girls sitting with her, then back to the doctor. "I am, thank you. It was a good move, and I'm enjoying it."

"Good to hear. Enjoy your day."

Stacey focused on finishing her lunch. She felt two pairs of eyes watching her every bite. "What?" She tried to look like it wasn't a big deal.

Gina's hands were gesturing back and forth between Stacey and the door that had just closed. "So, what was that about?"

Stacey shook her head.

"Dr. Hensley doesn't usually talk to us lowlifes. What's so special about you?" Carla asked. Gina just shrugged.

Stacey couldn't deny knowing her. She made it obvious that they knew each other. "She helped assign all the nurses of the L and D at County. That's how we met." Not a lie. That is how they met.

"I don't think I've ever talked to her. Just about her." Gina stated as she got back to her lunch.

"You would have if you would've gone to that party with me last summer," said Carla.

Gina looked confused.

"You know the hospital had that fundraiser last August. We had to pay like five dollars. Everyone else had to pay a lot. We got a meal at their ranch, and there was dancing"

Recognition dawned on Gina's face. "That was her house?"

"Yep. You missed out. After the official fundraiser, her sons invited a group of us to stay later. We partied at their 'guest house.'" She put air quotes around guest house. "I come from money, but their guest house was amazing. And their pool...anyway, you missed out on a really good time." Carla's face lit up as she finished her lunch. "She has an amazing son. He's so hot, has a body to die for, and can do amazing things with his mouth."

Gina slapped her friend. "Get out. You got some with the rich bitch's son?"

Carla waggled her brows.

Stacey was shocked. "Adler? You got it on with Adler?"

Gina's eyes went wide. "What, you know her son, too?"

Carla waved her hands to erase the comments. "Not Adler. Her other son. Tristan."

Stacey's stomach fell, and her heart stopped. She didn't comment. Just listened as Carla described Tristan. His smoky eyes. His soft brown hair. How his body felt when she touched him. Stacey's heart was beating hard. Her stomach churned. He told her he hadn't been with anyone in over a year. This was just last summer—maybe eight months ago. She heard enough. She had to get back to work.

Her heart and head were not focused for the rest of her shift. She turned on autopilot mode and finished her night that way. As soon as she was in her car, she thought over what she had heard.

Carla knew Tristan. They met just last summer. She counted on her fingers. August to March is seven months. Tristan told her he hadn't been with anyone in over a year. Again, Tristan didn't tell the entire truth. Her pulse drummed at her temples. She felt a headache coming on. What the hell was his problem?

She sent him a quick text telling him she was tired and he shouldn't come over. She wanted to go right to bed.

But, not surprisingly, when she pulled up to her house, his truck was sitting there, and his amazing body was sitting on the deck waiting for her.

Luckily, Kristen and Jacob weren't home.

She got out and stood strong. The sick feeling that had been entering her stomach lately whenever things didn't feel right with Tristan showed its ugly face, and her head throbbed. She rubbed her temples.

"Hey, gorgeous." His smile lit his features. The crease presented itself. Are you okay?

She needed to ignore all those pieces of him that had their way of getting to her. His concern and the way he called her gorgeous. That damn crease. She returned his hug but knew he could tell something was off. She shook her head and walked away as her sight turned blurry, but she quickly stopped and took a breath.

Face him now and get this out in the open. She turned on him and wiped harshly at her face as the tears fell. "I don't understand you. Why can't you just tell the truth?" She pulled in a shaky breath.

His jaw hung low.

Of course, he was going to feign confusion. What did she expect? "I can't do this. I told you not to come over. You need to go. We're done."

Tristan grabbed her and pulled her around. "What are you talking about, Stacey? Why are we done? What happened now?"

Stacey's insides tore to pieces. Anger rose from her chest. "Does the name Carla sound familiar to you, or are you as shallow as your dipshit cousin, and girls don't mean enough to remember?"

Tristan shook his head. "Carla? I don't..."

She could tell he was digging through his memory.

What. A. Dick. She didn't think him capable of being a typical guy. She should have known better than to put him on a higher pedestal. He belonged on the dick level with the rest of them.

His eyes became enormous, and he pulled away just a little.

He figured it out. "See, you know her. Imagine my surprise when I was talking with some of the nurses at lunch and found out one got to know you last summer. Imagine how confused I was. You told me you haven't been with another woman for over a year. August to now is just seven months." Stacey had never felt this much rage and anger before.

"What are you talking about?" His eyes got wider, and his hands went into his hair. "What? You think I slept with her? I told you I haven't been with anyone in over a year."

She shook her head and walked away. "That's not what she told the entire break room."

"God, she's lying." His voice thundered. "She came to the house for a fundraiser. Adler invited some of the nurses to stay and party. We had too much to drink. She and I made out, but nothing else happened."

She didn't need a man. She didn't need him. What if I'm as easy for him to forget about and throw away? "I can't do this again. I'm done. Please go."

Tristan breathed in deeply. "God, you're being unreasonable. Again!"

Stacey held her own.

His nostrils flared. "Whatever. Call me when you want to talk reason." He stomped to his car and peeled out of the driveway.

Kristen and Jacob pulled in close behind him, and Kristen jumped out of the car quickly. "Stace. What just happened?"

Stacey's insides felt like they were going to split apart. Her heart ached something awful. Her throat was tight, and the throbbing in her head turned into a full-out banging. She waved her hands in the air, not able to get out words.

Jacob touched her arms.

Couldn't these two just leave her alone? She finally got her composure. She put up a hand to calm herself. "Nothing that I didn't expect. It's over. Leave me alone." She barely looked at them as she walked away.

CHAPTER 32

Kristen tried to follow Stacey, but Jacob pulled her arm.

He shook his head. "Leave her alone. She needs time."

She felt anger rise from deep in her belly. Stacey was always there for her. She needed to be there for her friend. "Jacob, she's hurting, and I don't know why."

"I'm sure I do." Jacob interrupted, and his gaze held hers, not letting her look away. "Her trust issues are screwing with her. She has to find a way to put her past relationship issues in the past. Until then, she will always look for something negative about her and Tristan's relationship. She can't find anything, so I know my sister. I'm sure she just made a huge deal out of nothing for the second time."

Kristen stomped toward him. *God, he's infuriating when he's in his I-know-better-than-everyone attitude.* "Exactly, and someone has to talk to her."

"I disagree. She has to grow up and see that not everyone's going to hurt her. Not everyone's going to always leave." He grabbed Kristen's hands.

His face softened. "Kris, I love my sister. If it weren't for her, I wouldn't be here with you. She saved me when I was at my lowest and never gave up on me. Now, she needs to save herself. We can't do it for her. She can't fix everyone and always nurse the world back to health. She needs to start nursing herself."

Kristen dropped her gaze and looked at her toes. He was right. Stacey needed to take care of herself. Put herself first. "How do we get her to see that?"

"Well, for starters, she and I need to separate." Kristen's face scrunched up. *What does that mean?* "What?"

"I need to move out. I need to move in with you."

Kristen's heart leaped. Jacob won't move in with her. She had already asked him. Many times. "I asked you to move in with me. You won't live with a girl full-time until you're married."

Jacob nodded.

Kristen stared at him. *Why is he nodding?* Her heart stopped, and her breath caught.

"You're right. I won't live with you full-time until we're married, and you don't want a big wedding. So, let's get married at the county courthouse, and with all the money we don't spend, we'll go on an amazing honeymoon and finish up your house."

Her jaw dropped. She stopped breathing. Shock. She's in shock.

Jacob's hand pushed on her chin. Her mouth closed.

Did he just say that? The smirk on his face says yes.

"So, what do you think? Will you marry me?"

"Is that a real proposal?" Her voice came out quietly. Almost a whisper.

Jacob lowered his head so their eyes met. Again, he nodded. "Yes. I love you. I've always loved you. I want to marry you and have your babies."

Her eyes went wide. "Babies?"

His laughter came from deep within his chest. "Yes, babies. Our babies will be adorable." He brushed her hair out of her face. "We'll go to the courthouse. A justice of the peace. Stacey will stand for you, Chad for me. We'll have a small celebration with friends here in the yard. A small, simple, no-nonsense wedding. Just like you always wanted."

She couldn't believe what she was hearing. That's not his dream wedding. It's hers. "But you always wanted the big church wedding."

He held her head in his hands. "I want to be married to you. I love you, and you love me. Everything else doesn't matter. I won't move in with you officially until we're married, so say yes."

She looked away, but he held on to her head, and her gaze couldn't look far.

"What do you say?"

Her heart had always beat for him. She had dreamed of marrying this man for so long. Her eyes filled, and she blinked quickly to hold back the tears. "Of course, I'll marry you. You're the only one I've ever loved."

His smile reached his eyes as he crushed his lips on hers and wrapped her in his arms.

She was getting married to Jacob. They are going to be together forever. Her insides swam with emotion. Her heart swelled. She will have little Jacobs. Even that thought didn't scare her.

He was right. Their babies will be perfect. Wow, Mrs. Kristen Kempt. Her smile met her eyes.

Fairy tales do come true.

"She's avoiding us." Jacob placed a cup of fresh coffee in front of Kristin. He joined her outside on the deck as she was enjoying the pleasant spring morning, worrying about Stacey.

It was Saturday, and it's been two days since Stacey's abrupt entrance into the house. She hasn't answered Kristen's text, left for work at the crack of dawn yesterday and stayed out late. They don't know if she's even been home, as her car was gone when they both got up. A random glass sitting in the sink was the only evidence that someone else had been in the house outside of the two of them.

Kristen looked up at him, concern in her eyes and creasing her face. "I know. I just sent her a text. I told her that I was worried and needed to talk to her. I really want to tell her about us. I want her to be the first to know." She sighed. She wasn't used to feeling bad for others, but this is Stacey. Stacey has always taken care of her and been there for her. *I'm the worst friend. What should I do? What if I don't say the right things?*

"She's fine. Maybe she took an extra shift at the hospital and didn't tell us." Jacob started to rub her back.

Kristen didn't think so but couldn't prove him wrong, so she returned to the second thing on her mind. "So, with her not around, when are we going to tell people our news?" She still couldn't believe this was happening. They were going to look at rings today. Suddenly, her finger felt empty and naked.

Hmm, naked. The corners of her mouth ticked up. Last night. Her heart sped up. It was a good night celebrating.

Jacob placed a kiss on her lips, which brought her back to the present. "What has you all in thought world? I hope still not my sister."

Kristen shook her head. "No, I was just remembering our celebration last night and the night before." She got up and sat on his lap. "Sex has always been fun, but engagement sex has been…Wow! If I had known being engaged would be this amazing, I would have encouraged you to propose sooner."

"Really?"

She nodded and placed a kiss on his lips. Mmm. "You are amazing," she whispered. "I love you."

"Well, if you're that excited about the engagement and that much in love with me, I hope you'll be ready to marry me in two weeks."

She froze and swore her heart stopped.

"Surprise! I stopped by the courthouse yesterday and reserved a date. Two Fridays from now, we will be getting married."

Kristen put her hand on her chest over her heart. "I think my heart stopped. I really think you're trying to kill me." Her eyes got wide, and she grabbed his hand, placing it in the same place. "Seriously, feel. Do you feel anything? I don't."

Jacob laughed. And wrapped his arms tight around her. "Your heart is fine. You're breathing. Your heart's beating. You're just nervous. Now, when we tell Chad and Stacey tonight, we'll have a date to tell them. They'll need to get time off work, and we need to have some time to plan the party here. So, we have two weeks to get furniture in that house of yours and get those walls painted and floors finished."

Kristen wasn't dying; she wasn't dreaming. This was real. "You've thought of everything."

"There's not much to think about. We'll have Des do the cake, get some sandwiches and platters from Main Street Deli, and maybe get a tent so we can have somewhere to sit and mingle. A dance floor. We'll be at the courthouse, and when we come back here, our friends will be here to celebrate with us. Small and simple with the perfect ending. You becoming Mrs. Kristen Kempt."

Kristen's heart let her know it was working as the beat it was keeping suddenly sped up. "I like the sound of that."

Jacob smacked her bottom. "Good, now get up, and let's go ring shopping. We have a lot to do and just two weeks to get it all done."

"First, let's make sure Stacey and Chad know they have to come for dinner, and no is not an option." Kristen sent the text to Stacey, and Jacob sent one to Chad.

⁂

Stacey left home early and found herself exactly where she wanted to be.

She needed time to herself without anyone telling her what she needed to do. All she needed was fresh air and nature. This state park was a perfect place. They used to come here with their parents. A nice long hike ending at a waterfall would do her good. Get her to focus and think things through.

She pulled over right before she got to the park to get gas. She leaned against the car as the gas pumped and glanced at her phone. A sigh escaped her. Five messages from Kristen, two from Tristan, and one from Jacob. "I guess I should answer Kristen and Jacob. Let them know I'm alive." She spoke under her breath.

She answered them both and promised that she would be home tonight for their important family meeting that she absolutely couldn't miss. Whatever that could be.

She made Kristen promise it had nothing to do with her and that Chad and Jessica would be the only other two there. She didn't want any surprise guests, aka Tristan.

She read Tristan's two texts. One apologized and said he realized he should have mentioned her, but they only kissed and messed around. He didn't think it mattered. She let out a hard sigh. "That's still more than no relationship in over a year. You lied—again. Why couldn't you just be honest?" The second one just wanted her to text him. She couldn't right now.

She finished the short drive to the park, parked her car, silenced her phone, and started her hike. It was a perfect spring day. This is the season she loved best. Everything was coming alive; the birds were active, and the weather was amazing. She found a good pace and got lost in nature. Before she knew it, she was at the end of the two-mile hike.

The waterfall was magnificent. Stacey wandered around the area, snapping pictures with her camera. She then sat to have a snack and enjoy the scenery and view.

A memory of being here with her brother and parents shot into her mind. Jacob and her dad were off doing who knows what, and her mom was sitting with her on the rock she sat on now. They were talking about senior prom.

Stacey was going with her boyfriend, and Kristen was going with his best friend. Stacey's mom told Stacey something then. *Remember, Stace. Always stay true to who you are. Don't let a guy pressure you into doing anything you don't want to do or becoming something you don't want to be. Stay your* strong, *independent self, but don't scare off the guys either. One day, someone will see how amazing you are. That's a gift. Don't let it get away.*

At the time, Stacey wasn't sure what her mom really meant. But those words meant everything now. Her strong independence was pushing Tristan away.

She pulled her phone out again and read his text. He swears he and Carla never had sex. Yes, they messed around, but can she really hold that against him, or is she just trying to find an excuse to mess things up like Jacob says she's doing?

She breathed out. *Oh, Stacey. Figure your shit out.*

She pushed herself off the rock and started the hike back.

She walked slower. Really enjoying the scenery, she made it back to the car quicker than it had taken her to get there. Probably because the walk back was downhill.

She got into her car, turned on the radio, and drove the two hours home.

CHAPTER 33

Jacob, Kristen, and Chad's cars were the only ones in the driveway when she got there.

She couldn't ignore the small feeling of disappointment that entered her heart. A part of her hoped that Kristen would have ignored her and invited Tristan over, anyway. But then, thinking about it, she knew no one had his number.

Oh well. Let's see what is so dire that she absolutely had to be home for dinner. She walked into the house, and everyone was sitting around the table snacking on a charcuterie board. "Why the fancy food, and where's the beer?"

Jacob jumped up from the table. "Great. You're here." He pulled out a chair. "Here. Sit down."

Stacey sat. What got into him? He's never pulled out her chair.

Jacob went and got the chicken from the oven and veggies and mashed potatoes from the stove. This was a lot of fuss. There must be something big going on.

"Chad, do you have any clue?" Stacey gestured around the table and kitchen.

He shook his head and looked as confused as she was.

"Where's Jessica?" she asked.

"Jacob invited me. Said it was just going to be us four, so she went to see Grams."

They filled their plates and started eating.

Jacob and Kristen kept glancing at each other, and Kristen couldn't sit still.

This behavior was crazy and so out of character. Stacey has known Kristen forever and has never seen her nervous at all. Not even when they had to do impromptu speeches in English class. Kristen just grabbed her topic, glanced at it briefly, and sauntered to the front of the class. She took up her two minutes, like speaking about the evolution of future man was something she studied every day.

Stacey racked her brain for what could be causing her friend's nerves to be on edge. She looked around the table. Everyone was sipping wine except for Kristen. She had sweet tea. She prefers wine. Why isn't she drinking wine?

Then it hit her like a ton of bricks. Stacey's fork clattered to the table, and her eyes went wide. "HOLY SHIT!!" she hollered.

Chad spilled his glass of wine. "Fuck!" He reached for napkins as the wine spread like blood over the table. "What was that for, Stace? You scared me to death."

She reached over to help him mop up the mess that she had caused. "I know what's going on." She whisper-yelled at him.

Jacob and Kristen froze.

Stacey jumped up from the table. "Kristen hasn't sat still since we started eating. She isn't drinking wine like the rest of us. The only thing that could ever make her that nervous and not drink is simple."

She turned to Chad. "I'm gonna be an aunt."

Chad's eyes got wide. Finally, what she said registered, and he jumped up, almost spilling his wine again. "Shit. You're right." He grabbed Jacob and wrapped him in a hug, slapping him on the back. "Dude. You're gonna be a dad. Congratulations."

Stacey was up clapping and trying to get to Kristen.

Kristen's eyes were as wide as saucers, and Jacob was pushing Chad off him.

"HEY!" Kristen yelled at the top of her voice.

They all froze.

"I'm not pregnant!"

Jacob finally successfully pulled away from Chad, straightened his shirt, wrapped his arms around Kristen, and held her close.

Stacey started. "Are you sure? I mean, I've never seen you..."

"Yes, she's sure." Jacob looked at Kristen.

Both of them were so in love. It was great watching them together. She had watched it start so many years ago. But then what...Suddenly, her breath caught. She just connected all the dots.

"We're getting married." Jacob blurted it out.

Her heart swelled with happiness for her two favorite people. Her eyes swam with tears as she pulled them both into a hug, with Chad wrapping all three of them together like a burrito.

Stacey grabbed a napkin and handed one to Kristen. The girls wiped their noses and dried their eyes. "When?" She asked.

Jacob nodded to Kristen.

Kristen put up two fingers. "Well, two weeks. At the courthouse, and we want you two there to stand up for us."

Stacey was stunned. "Two weeks? Holy shit. That's so soon!"

Kristen nodded. "It's going to be a very simple ceremony with a party here for all our friends after. We wanted it quick not to interfere with Brady and Elizabeth, and small because well..."

"That's what you always wanted." Stacey finished for her friend. "It'll be perfect. We have tons to do."

"Hold on." Jacob took the engagement ring they had purchased earlier that day from his pocket. "Now, to do this correctly. And with just us here, it couldn't be any more perfect."

He turned the ring over and over with his fingers and turned to Stacey and Chad. "You two have been our best friends forever. All four of us grew up together. Of course, me and Chad were usually bothering you girls and getting in your way."

The girls nodded.

"Then high school hit, and I fell in love with the only girl who truly ever had my heart." Jacob turned toward Kristen and took her hand in his.

Stacey's throat closed with emotion, and she wrapped her arm around Chad and laid her head on his chest.

He gave her a squeeze.

"Kristen, our history has been rocky most of the time." Jacob smiled.

"All the time." Chad chimed in, making them all laugh.

Jacob shrugged. "Maybe, but we finally figured things out, and I love you more today than I ever thought possible." He reached over and wiped the tears from her cheek with his thumb.

"Please get on with this. I don't do tears." Kristen sniffed.

Jacob winked and dropped to his knee. "Kristen, I love you. I've always loved you. Will you marry me?"

Kristen rolled her eyes and wiped her face with her free hand. "Of course, now stand up and put that ring on my finger already."

Jacob did just what she said. Then he kissed her, lifting her off the ground.

Stacey watched as her brother and her best friend celebrated their love and their promise to one another. Only one thing could make this better, but right now, it wasn't about her. The rest of the night, Stacey made lists of everything they needed to do in the thirteen days they had left and argued with Kristen about the small details. She ignored the texts coming in. Kristen and her brother were more important, and with her job, she had to take advantage of any spare time she had.

The next morning, Stacey and Kristen were up and out early.

The guys were going to wear their suits but were finally talked into buying new shirts and ties.

The girls were heading to the store. Kristen wasn't going to wear a traditional wedding dress, but she did want a new white dress, with Stacey wearing the same style but in a different color. They needed to get the dresses and shoes picked out; they had an appointment at the bakery to choose the cake, and they had to find some simple invitations with a quick turnaround.

With two dresses and two pairs of shoes purchased, the girls headed to the bakery to meet the guys for the appointment with Desiree. They parked on the square and walked a few doors down to the bakery. The smell of freshly baked goods greeted them as soon as they opened the door. Desiree was expecting them and had some cake samples and the wedding cake book set out in the tasting room for them to enjoy.

"Hey. Is Jacob joining us?" Desiree hugged each girl as they entered the store and led them to the back.

"Yeah. He should be here any minute." Kristen fell into the chair and stretched out. "I'm exhausted."

Desiree brought them each a bottle of water. "How was dress shopping?"

"Exhausting." Stacey took a big swig of the water. "It never ceases to amaze me how difficult this woman can be."

"Hey, that's my fiancé you're talking about." Jacob entered the tasting room.

Kristen jumped up at the sound of his voice. "I like the sound of that." She smiled at him.

He greeted her with a kiss. "Me too. Did you find a dress?"

Kristen nodded.

"Is it sexy?"

"Yes, she told you she did, and that's all you get to know." Stacey quickly cut in. "This may not be traditional, but you won't see the dress or her in it until we're at the courthouse."

Jacob put up his hands, surrendering to his sister. "Fine. Let's eat cake. I'm starving."

They all took their seats, and Desiree introduced them to her lineup of cake choices.

After an hour of tasting cake after cake and arguing over what they liked, they finally decided on a two-layer cake. One layer of lemon blueberry and the other strawberry, both with Desiree's signature icing.

Cake, check.

Kristen again relaxed back in her seat. "Now we just have to decide on food, and then that should be everything but the flowers, and they are going to be simple cut flowers." Kristen let out a sigh. "Who knew weddings were so much trouble? This is small, and I'm already finished with all of it. I don't know how Elizabeth's planning such a big wedding. This already has me bored and irritated."

Stacey squeezed her hand. "That's why you have me. I'll do everything and take all the stress off you."

Kristen smiled.

Jacob placed two detailed receipts on the counter. "Well, check the food off your list." He pointed to one receipt. "That's taken care of. Sandwiches and salads from Main Street Deli will be delivered by five forty-five, and The Pizza Place is delivering three kegs of beer, bottles of water, and some wine. Also, by five forty-five."

Kristen read over the receipts. "Food, drinks, cake. Now we're done." She kissed Jacob. "I'll see if Elizabeth and Jessica can be at the house when everything is delivered."

"And we'll have all the tables and chairs set up Thursday night. Done." Stacey swiped her hands against each other. "Maybe I'll keep things this simple when I get married. A wedding planned in one day."

Desiree stood up and started cleaning. "Marriage, Stacey? Does that mean you and Tristan are talking again?"

Stacey glared at her. "Getting into my business, Des? Does that mean you and Casanova are still talking?"

"Talking and other things as often as possible." She wiggled her eyebrows. "Tristan is still moping around, upset because you aren't answering his texts. I told him you'd be here today."

Stacey's jaw dropped. "What? Why?"

"He asked if I'd seen you around. I told him I would be."

Desiree looked behind her friends and could see the front of the shop through the glass in the door. Her face lit up. "Well, we're done here, and everything is written up. Are you going to pay now or at delivery?"

Jacob pulled out his wallet. "Paying now. Getting it all taken care of."

"Awesome. Let's go to the front and take care of this. I think I have more customers to tend to."

Stacey felt like they accomplished so much today. Seeing the smiles on Jacob and Kristen's faces made her beam. She was so happy for them and ecstatic that she and Kristen would finally be sisters. They talked about this very possibility just jokingly many years ago. Knowing Jacob had a crush on Kristen made it so much fun to talk about, and now it's becoming a reality.

Jacob held the door for the women as they left the back of the store.

"After you, sis. Here, let me fix your hair." He stopped her long enough to brush her hair with his hands and tuck some stray strands behind her ear. What is he doing?

She brushed his hands away. "Jacob, enough."

He held his hands up. "Sorry, after you."

Whatever. Weird. She stepped through the door and froze.

CHAPTER 34

D esiree didn't have customers. She had Adler and Tristan, and they were in the front eating donuts and looking fine.

Stacey swallowed hard. And had to fight to keep her pulse under control. Shit. Shit. Shit. She wasn't ready to face him yet.

"Stacey," Kristen whispered loudly to her and pushed her toward Tristan.

Stacey shot daggers at her friend.

Kristen winked.

"Hey." Tristan's voice was quiet and unsure.

She turned toward him in all his amazing glory. His smile was small. His hair was perfectly messed up. His hands were wiping donut crumbs on a napkin.

A thought crossed her mind of those fingers in her mouth and her licking them clean, which caused the butterflies in her stomach to work overtime. She wished they'd go on a break already.

Tristan gestured toward the door. "Can we talk?"

"I'm sure we have more to do here." She turned toward Kristen.

"Nope, we're fine. We've taken enough of your day. Off you go." She all but pushed Tristan and Stacey out the door.

They stumbled onto the sidewalk. They stood on the street with the bakery door closed behind them, looking at each other. Stacey's insides were churning. Getting sick was a possibility, or maybe passing out.

"I'm not from here. Is there anywhere to talk?" Tristan asked.

Stacey breathed in deeply, then let it out. "There's a greenway park area this way." She gestured with her head and started walking. Her hands felt strange hanging by her side as they walked quietly down the street. She wanted to reach out and take his hand but thought better of it, so she put them in her front pockets.

The boutiques and shops were doing bustling Saturday afternoon business. Lots of people were enjoying the sunny afternoon, and Stacey said hi to some that she knew as they passed. The park loomed ahead, and luckily, it seemed pretty empty. They should have privacy.

"Do you want to sit or walk the path?" She pointed to the bridge that crossed the river. "It doesn't go very far. Just around the river to the bridge. Then back."

"Let's walk." Tristan placed his hand lightly on her back and led her toward the path. "Stacey. I want you to understand that I didn't intentionally forget about Carla."

Nothing like getting right to the point. The churning in her stomach picked up. "I know. I just..." Just what? Stacey racked her brain. *Why do you keep finding fault with him?* "I don't know. See, this is why I don't do relationships."

Tristan stopped walking. "What?" His face was red. His breathing was deep.

"I..." she started, but the look on his face stopped her. He was angry. What did she do? "Tristan. You lied to me again. I don't think I believe you forgot about something that happened just seven months ago."

He faced her, and she saw lots of emotion, but not of the good kind. "It wasn't a big deal, Stacey. It meant absolutely nothing, and it never crossed my mind again." He closed his eyes.

"That makes you shallow and no different from any other man. I thought you were different." As soon as she said it, she wanted to take it back.

His eyes filled with rage.

"Tristan, I..."

"Enough." He snapped. "I've tried to understand your reluctance to be in relationships. I know you've been hurt and cheated on. But I'm tired of trying to get you to realize that's not who I am, but you think it is, anyway. I've given you my time, my attention." He gazed off into the distance before catching her eyes again. "I've given you my heart." His voice cracked. He swallowed.

Stacey froze and held her breath. Her heart felt empty.

"You've taken my love for you and keep acting like it doesn't mean anything." He grabbed her hands. "I've never told anyone I've loved them before, Stacey." He shook his head. And closed his mouth. His eyes glistened.

Say something. Her pulse raced. *Say* something, dammit!! Her mouth opened and closed. Nothing came out. It was like she was a fish out of water, gasping for breath.

His eyes begged her to say something. He waited, and then an enormous sigh escaped him. "I can't do this." He put his arms out wide and bit his bottom lip as he walked backward. "I'm sorry." A tear silently fell.

"Tristan, please."

"What? What do you want?" His voice came out quiet and tired. He swiped his hands down his face.

Her heart pleaded with her to say something to stop this from happening, but her mouth wouldn't open.

He sighed again, muttered a swear under his breath, and turned and walked away.

"Don't go," she whispered to his back, so low he couldn't hear her.

He picked up his pace, and the separation between them grew quickly.

"I love you," Stacey said louder, but he was out of reach.

She watched his back retreat, and finally he turned toward the bakery and was out of her sight. *Go after him. What are you doing?*

But she couldn't move. She was frozen in place. Her feet felt like lead, and were unable to listen to her brain. Tears streamed down her face. She reached into her pocket and called an Uber.

Tristan blinked to try to keep the tears from falling, but it was useless. *I can't believe I put myself in this situation again.* His heart was breaking. The reality of the situation hit him like a Mack truck. He was wasting his time. Fuck this. A sigh escaped him. He willed his legs to go faster because he needed to put as much space between Stacey and him as possible. He was going to lose it, and he refused to give her the pleasure of seeing him that upset.

He could see the group hanging out outside the bakery. *Great. Just what I need. An audience.*

Adler spotted him first and walked toward him. Searched his face. "Bro, what happened?" He grabbed his arm, pulling him to a stop.

"I don't need your sympathy right now. Please get out of my way." Tristan pushed him off hard. "This was a waste of my time." Anger fueled him and propelled him forward.

He focused his words on Jacob, his voice loud and harsh. "I did nothing but love your sister. She's messed up." He tapped his temple. "Up here. She's thrown us away, and I'm done." He was in Jacob's face. He needed to take his feelings out on someone, and her brother seemed perfect.

Jacob's hands flew in the air. "Step back and calm down." Jacob's eyes flew to Adler. "Get him out of my face."

Adler nodded and wrapped his arms around Tristan's waist. "Don't do this," he whispered through clenched teeth.

Tristan elbowed him hard, catching Adler in the chin.

Adler stumbled back and touched his fingers to his lip. Blood. "Fuck." He stepped in front of Tristan. "You're pissed, and that's understandable. You want to hit something." He pounded his own chest. "Hit me. Stacey's issues aren't Jacob's problem."

Tristan froze. He wasn't going to hit Adler. Not this time anyway, and he sure didn't want to hit Jacob. *What are you doing?* His shoulders curled over his chest.

Adler pounded him on the chest in the way they did when one of them made a good choice.

Tristan took deep breaths to calm his pulse.

"There you go. Breathe," said Adler. "Calm your stubborn ass down."

Tristan's heart rate slowed, and he felt a little better. He met Adler's eyes. Adler smiled his mischievous grin and patted Tristan's cheek. "There you go. You're calm. Good boy."

God, he hated it when he used that condescending tone. "Back off before I rethink my decision and punch you."

Adler pounded him hard on the shoulders and turned to Jacob, a big smile plastered on his face. "He's good now."

"Look, I'm sorry for how Stacey's acting." Jacob approached Tristan. "Honestly, she's been avoiding us the past couple of days. We have no clue what happened or what's going through her head."

Tristan glanced between Jacob and Kristen. He was tired. "Well, you can both tell her that I'm done trying. I have to be. I've never tried this hard, and it's exhausting. If she figures her shit out, and this is what she wants, she'll have to work for it."

Jacob nodded. "I totally get it. I wish I could explain what's going through her head." He shrugged. "I've got nothing."

His eyes held Jacob's. "I love your sister. But I don't know how much longer I can wait for her."

"I'll talk to her," said Kristen.

He nodded, then turned to Adler and held out his hand. "Keys, please. Desiree can get you home." He had nothing more to do here.

Desiree nodded.

Adler handed over the keys. "Careful."

"Unfortunately, I'm always careful." He walked to the car and headed back. This wasn't the ending he was hoping for.

When he got back to the house, he saddled up his favorite mare and went for a long, fast ride. That always cleared his head.

Jacob and Kristen pulled into the driveway, and Kristen sent Stacey a text. "She's here."

"I don't think she needs me here," Jacob said. "You talk to her. I'm going to Chad's for a bit."

Kristen rushed into the house and stopped in her tracks. Stacey sat at the kitchen table with a glass of wine in front of her.

Kristen poured herself some and sat at the table. "We need to talk about this."

"Where's Jacob?" Stacey's eyes stayed on her wine.

"He went to Chad's. It's just us. How'd you get home?"

Stacey lifted red-rimmed eyes. "Uber."

The silence went on.

Kristen reached across the table and grabbed her friend's hand. "Hey." She shook her arm until Stacey looked up. "You need to talk about this. What's going on? Why are you making this so difficult?"

"Me? Why do you think I'm making this difficult?" Stacey's voice was loud, and fury sparked in her eyes.

A smile grew on Kristen's face. "Good job. We have some feelings."

She always had a way of making Stacey talk. How annoying. "First, he lied about his money."

"It's not his."

Stacey huffed. "Semantics. Then, when he realized that the doctor I was having problems with was his aunt, he didn't say anything." She held up a hand to stop Kristen's comment. "It was deceptive and embarrassing. I was totally caught off guard and shouldn't have been."

Kristen looked up. "Okay. You've got one. He should have said something, but he apologized."

Stacey's eyes rolled. "Then he told me he hadn't had a relationship in over a year."

Kristen rolled her eyes right back. "He wasn't in a relationship. He kissed a girl."

Stacey threw her hands up and widened her eyes as if saying, "Hello, same thing."

Kristen continued. "He wasn't in a relationship. He didn't have sex. Not a lie."

"They kissed and messed around." Stacey's voice was more agitated.

"Still, no sex, no relationship."

Stacey jumped up from the table. "Again, semantics." *Why is she not seeing things my way?*

"Not lies." Kristen leaned on her hands and met Stacey's gaze straight on. "What's the real problem, Stace? I don't see any so far." She raised her voice. This was ridiculous.

Stacey grew quiet.

Kristen waited.

Stacey's eyes were starting to glisten, and finally, a tear fell.

Kristen's heart broke. But she didn't move. She stood strong.

Stacey stood up tall and wiped it away. "This is why I don't do relationships."

Kristen's voice came out soft. "Why? Because they're hard?"

Stacey's head shook. "No. They hurt." More tears fell, but they were still silent. She grabbed a napkin and wiped her face.

Kristen joined her and leaned against the counter. "They don't always hurt."

Stacey laughed. "Really? You and Jacob hurt each other more over the years than anyone I've ever seen. I've watched you both. I've picked up the pieces. Over and over." Her voice was getting louder. "Look at all the hurt Elizabeth has been through with her relationship."

Kristen nodded. "So far, both these couples figured things out and are happy and in love."

"Elizabeth's mom is alone because of Mr. Park's death. Your mom is alone because your dad divorced her. I..." Stacey gasped for air as her sobs overwhelmed her.

Kristen's heart broke, and she placed her hands on Stacey's arms. Her voice was soft. "What. You're what, Stace?"

"I'm scared." Her voice cracked. "Relationships and me, they don't work out."

Kristen wrapped her in a hard hug. "That was in college. That was one time you opened yourself up, and he shit all over it. Carl was an asshole. He cheated and tore your heart out and stomped all over it. After that, you put up a wall around your heart and swore you wouldn't put yourself back in the situation again. Then along came Steven, and the same thing happened." Kristen pulled back. "I'm sorry you were hurt." She caught her eye. "You need to see what came out of that. You became a strong woman. You don't need a man, Stace. But having one who is your partner and beside you through everything is amazing."

Stacey wiped her face again. "God, I hate tears."

"I know. Me too."

Both girls sniffed and then laughed.

Kristen wiped the few tears that fell down her face. "Can I say something else?"

Stacey nodded.

"Your mom and dad would want you to be happy."

Stacey agreed. "I know."

"They also would have loved Tristan. Even though he seems perfect, he isn't. Those little flaws you're finding so much fault in are just that—flaws. We all have them."

Stacey wiped her face as she walked into the living room and fell onto the couch. "I've messed this up so badly. What do I do now?" She buried her face in her hands.

Kristen plopped down next to her. "I suggest you think long and hard before calling him. You need to make sure that a relationship with him is really what you want. If it is, you apologize. He said he's done fighting for you. It's all in your corner now, Stace."

"My inability to trust has made a mess of something amazing."

Kristen nodded. "Yeah, it has."

"Thank you for always speaking the truth, even when the truth hurts," Stacey said. "I love you."

"I love you, too." Kristen answered.

CHAPTER 35

The next week flew by. Between work and wedding plans, Stacey thankfully didn't have much time to focus on her issues with Tristan. She wanted to text him, but needed to make sure she had her feelings straight before she contacted him. There was only one chance left to get things right, and she didn't want to mess anything up. So, instead of texting him, she made lists and helped Kristen get all the little details together for this wedding just over a week away.

It was Thursday, and it had been another busy shift on the floor. Stacey was tired and starving. She walked into the breakroom, ready to grab a bite and get off her feet for a little bit.

She had worked five straight shifts this week but was looking forward to a nice long weekend. She pulled her dinner out of the refrigerator and heated it in the microwave.

Carla was sitting at a table by herself. Stacey felt her insides flop. She didn't want to talk to her and had done a good job of avoiding her all week, but she also couldn't be rude and ignore her. She grabbed her food and a water and took a deep breath.

Carla looked up from the book she was reading. "Oh, hi, Stacey."

"Hey. What are you reading?" Pleasant enough conversation. Tristan doesn't have to come up.

Carla gave her a brief synopsis. "So, basically, a no-thought-necessary romance. Great for the nights here."

"Maybe I could learn a thing or two from someone in that book. My romantic life basically sucks right now." Stacey felt a sick pit in her stomach start to form.

Carla agreed. "Yeah, mine's not much better. I haven't been able to get a decent date in forever. Guys are either creepy or strange." She leaned closer to Stacey and whispered. "One guy I went out with kept leaning over and taking big whiffs of me."

Stacey's eyes went wide.

"Yeah, and he kept saying weird things like 'You smell sweet like sugar.' 'You smell as fresh as fresh-cut grass.'"

"What?" Stacey's mouth was open. That was creepy.

"Yeah. I excused myself for the bathroom and kept walking. Left him at the restaurant. Haven't been out since."

A chill went through Stacey. "My life lately hasn't been that bad, but my past relationships have given me trust issues that have caused me to mess up a pretty amazing relationship I could be having." Why did she just say that to Carla? She hardly knows her.

"Let me guess. He's a great guy, but you've been shit on so much that you're waiting for the real guy to emerge. Am I right?" Carla put her book down and took a cookie from her lunch bag next to her. She offered one to Stacey.

Stacey's eyes went up in question.

"Chocolate chip. Made them myself."

Stacey took a bite. A soft crunch on the outside and soft and chewy on the inside. The perfect cookie. "Mm. This is amazing."

"Secret recipe." Carla winked.

Stacey smiled. "But, yeah, about the guy. You're pretty spot-on." Just tell her it's Tristan. "Can I ask you something? It's pretty personal, so if you don't want to answer, I understand."

Carla shrugged. "Sure. Ask me anything."

Stacey took a deep breath. "It's about Tristan." She waited. The only reaction was a questioning look. "You said you messed around with him." Stacey paused, not knowing how to continue.

"Wait a minute." Carla sat back and crossed her arms. "Is Tristan the guy you're talking about?"

Stacey gave a small nod.

Carla's gaze fell to the table.

Stacey's shoulders met her ears and stayed there. "Doesn't matter. I screwed things up badly. So, I need to know. Did you really have sex with him?" There's nothing like getting to the point.

Carla deflated and shook her head. "No. I implied that for Gina's sake. We just messed around. And that wasn't even much more than kissing. He isn't into one-night stands, and he never called me."

Stacey's stomach churned. He was telling the truth. She took something all out of context. She closed her eyes and took a deep breath, trying to calm her stomach. "Thank you for letting me know." She gave Carla a smile.

"It looks like he means a lot to you. I'm sorry if my implications caused trouble. He's a great guy, and if he cares for you, you're one lucky woman."

Stacey smiled. "He does. Or at least he did. Thank you."

She needed to get back and finish her shift. First though, she sent Tristan a quick text.

**I'm so sorry for every-
thing. I really want to
talk. Can we? Sometime
tomorrow? I have off. Let
me know.**

Tristan was brushing off the mare he had just finished riding. It was a good ride and did what he hoped. It gave him something else to think about. He hadn't heard from Stacey all week, and it was driving him crazy.

"I loved her. Who am I kidding? I still do. I'm crazy about her." He was talking to the horse, and he had her undivided attention. "I've tried hard not to be like other guys, and here I am, still being thrown into the same pot as them." He sighed. "Hopefully, she figures her shit out." *I'm not gonna call her. Our relationship is in her hands, but I'm not gonna wait forever.*

He patted the horse on the side of its face. "Ginger. You are the one girl I've always been able to count on. Thank you." She just stared at him with her large brown eyes and breathed on him, shaking her head.

"Still talking with that horse, huh? What's going on?"

Tristan looked up.

His aunt was dressed in her riding pants, a T-shirt, and the riding boots she loved.

He smiled at her. They looked a lot alike because she favored his mother. He was glad he could look at her and remember his mom. He didn't feel so alone at times like this. When he needed to talk, Adler wouldn't do.

"How do you always know when I need to talk?"

She shrugged and patted. Ginger. "I don't know. Just intuition, I guess. I haven't seen you at dinner all week. You usually come at least once. Adler said last night you weren't in the mood to be around people. I figured you'd be here since you weren't at the house."

"Needed to ride off some steam and keep myself from doing something stupid."

Her eyes raised.

"Nothing that stupid. Just needed to keep myself from texting Stacey."

Aunt Eli looked thoughtful. "Why would that be stupid? I thought you two had worked things out."

Tristan shook his head, led Ginger into her stall, and gave her hay and feed before answering. "We did, but then new things came up." He let out a sigh. "She needs to figure out where she is. I was going to wait for her to contact me, but it's been five days. I don't know how much longer I'm willing to wait."

His aunt laid her hand on his arm. "I'm sure things will work out for the best. Please let me know if you need anything."

He smiled. "Don't worry. I'm good."

"Good to know. And your uncle also told me you're going out to Texas for some training at the ranch. Do you need anything for your trip?"

He shook his head. "Nope. I have everything. I'm gonna pack in the morning. I'll be leaving here around noon for the airport. I'll be back next week."

His phone pinged. He glanced at the text, and a smile ticked up. "She wants to talk." His heart skipped.

"See, she is a smart girl." She wrapped him in a warm hug. "I love you so much, Tristan. You're an amazing man who has a lot to give to a relationship. Take your time and find someone who will make you happy. "

He nodded and gave her a small smile.

She rubbed his cheek. "Have a safe trip."

"Thank you. I will. I love you, too." He watched as his aunt walked away and read the text again. He answered her immediately.

**Tristan: I'm leaving for a
business trip at noon.**

A little while later, he got his answer.

**Stacey: Can I come by to-
morrow morning around
9?**

**Tristan: Sure. See you
then.**

He placed his phone in his pocket and headed back to the house.

Adler and his dad were talking in the kitchen when Tristan walked in. "

"Thank God you're here."

Uncle Don looked flustered. That's an unusual look for him. One Tristan sure wasn't used to seeing. "What's going on?"

"I was looking for you." Don continued. "You need to pack. There will be a car here to get you within the hour. You're heading to the airport now."

Tristan was shocked. Now? "Why?" The training didn't start until Monday. He was going to spend the weekend checking out the cattle and the ranch. He had plenty of time.

"We need you out there ASAP. The training's been moved up. It starts tomorrow. You can't miss it. You need your certification."

Tristan's heart fell. Talking with Stacey would have to wait. "Okay. I'll be ready." He went to pack and just about finished when there was a honk outside.

His car was there. Time to go. He sent Stacey a quick text.

**My schedule changed. I'm
on my way to the airport
now. I'll be home late** on
Wednesday.

Once he got in the car, his phone kept pinging with staff from the Texas office. He was busy talking with them until he got on the plane.

Stacey was in the kitchen early the next morning when Kristen came in.

"Hey, what are you doing?" asked Kristen as she fixed herself a cup of coffee.

"What? This is my house." Stacey gestured around the room. "My kitchen."

Kristen shook her head. "I know, but it's seven a.m., and you're awake. I thought you'd be sleeping." She took her travel cup to the counter and sat next to Stacey.

"I usually would be, but I was planning on going to see Tristan this morning."

Kristen's eyebrow shot up.

"But." Stacey held up her hand. "His trip to Texas was moved up, and he's already there. He left late last night. We'll have to wait till he gets back Wednesday to talk."

"That sucks. But I'm glad you decided to talk with him. I hope everything turns out." She grabbed a banana and put the lid on her coffee mug. "Sorry to change the subject, but are you still able to meet me at my house later? Jacob's gonna pick up sandwiches. We'll finish painting, and then we just need to start moving in furniture."

Stacey nodded. "Yep. I'll see you there around five."

"Great. Later gator." Kristen blew her a kiss and left.

Stacey cleaned the kitchen, did her laundry, and became bored very quickly. Grabbing a book, she headed outside to read and checked her phone. Maybe Tristan messaged her.

Nope. Damn. Call him. If he can't talk, he won't answer.

She dialed and waited as it rang. Her heart thumped hard in her chest. *I really need to fix things. I acted so* stupidly.

There was a click. "Stacey?"

Her heart stopped. It took her a second to find her voice. "Tristan. Umm. Hi."

"I'm sorry." He didn't sound as if he were in Texas. That's the cool thing about phones. It brings those faraway close. "I left unexpectedly. Did you get my message?"

"Yes, when I woke up." She let out a breath. "When would be a good time to talk?"

"Not now. I'm on my way into the training. I'll text you when I can." He must have turned the phone away because she heard him talking with someone. His voice was muffled. "I gotta go, Stace. I'll talk to you later."

There was a click, and the phone went dead.

She held the phone away from her ear and just looked at it. He didn't even wait for her to say bye. "I don't know what I was expecting. Endearments of love, words of joy." She talked out loud. "He's probably done waiting for me. I screwed up one too many times."

She puffed out air and sat there for a while, ignoring her book. "I can't be here all day. I'll go crazy." She called Kristen. Painting would be the perfect activity to keep her busy, so she asked Kristen if she could get started. She got the okay and a text of instructions, put on some paint clothes, and left her house.

Kristen lived on the other side of town. It wasn't far, but it still wasn't like she would be able to run over for a cup of sugar if she ran out. Her friends' lives were moving on, like they should be. Careers and marriage. *I never wanted more than my career—until Tristan. I'd like more with him.* "Great time to realize that."

She pulled up in front of Kristen's house. She lived in the town they grew up, in her mom and grandma's house. Her grandmother had gone into an assisted living facility in Florida a few years ago, and her mother moved down there to get away from the Tennessee winters and be closer to her mother.

Stacey did a quick walk-around before she got started. Kristen had done a lot of work. The two full bathrooms had both been gutted and updated. And the same with the kitchen. The rest of the house had the carpet pulled up, wood floors put down, and now they were just finishing the painting. It looked brand new, and Stacey almost didn't recognize it from the house, which was like a second home to her since middle school. Now Kristen and Jacob would get to fill the walls with their own memories and children.

Wow, that is a strange thought. Her best friend and her brother are going to have babies together.

Stacey laughed, remembering a conversation she and Kristen had when they were in college, after Stacey's breakup. They were both bad-mouthing guys until Kristen came clean and told Stacey that she had a crush on Jacob and would one day have his babies. Stacey remembered saying that that ship had sailed. Jacob no longer had a crush on her. He had moved on.

Little did she know then that one day, she would be here, painting their house so they could start their life together. *I'm glad they're both happy. They deserve it.*

She picked up the paint roller, put on music, and got started.

CHAPTER 36

Texas in April was perfect. Tristan always loved coming here. There was something different about this ranch. It felt real. Maybe it was because Texas and cattle went together. He always thought he wouldn't mind moving here if ever it came up. The older he got, the better it looked.

The training was interesting. They were learning about new advancements in environmental conservation and sustainability and how these can increase the bottom line. He was enjoying himself and learning a lot, but by the time five o'clock came. He was starving. It was a long day with a short break for lunch, which consisted only of sandwiches. He needed something big and hearty. Lots of carbs and protein, and maybe a beer or two. Texas barbecue would be perfect. His mouth started watering.

"Tristan."

He recognized the voice before he turned around. It was Janet. His lungs deflated. He wasn't sure whether he wanted to talk to her.

Janet was a beautiful brunette with a to-die-for body. She loved all things Texas. Rodeos, country music, and cowboys. He was none of the above, but she was his last relationship. They lasted about five months and ended over two years ago. He came here to work one summer season—May through August—to learn the business. The business wasn't the only thing he learned about.

He also learned all about Janet.

They tried a long-distance romance after he went back home, and he tried to talk her into moving to Tennessee. But she loved Texas, and he wasn't ready to leave Tennessee, so they went their separate ways. Now, here she was again, and from what he heard in the training today, she was still single.

He couldn't help but check her out as she got closer. Her long dark hair fell around her shoulders. She wore a form-fitting-button-up shirt, the top two buttons undone, showing off the beginning of what he knew was some amazing cleavage. Her shirt was tucked into her tight dark blue jeans, which showed off the perfect curvature of her body. Her signature brown boots finished the look. She was beautiful. Some things never change.

Her perfect white smile lit up her face, and her bright blue eyes gleamed. "I heard you got here." She caught him in a hug, and he spun her around. Her laughter rang brightly in his ears.

"Janet. It's great to see you." And he was surprised it was true. "I'm heading out for dinner. Thought I'd grab barbecue. You hungry?"

"Yeah, I am. It'll be good to catch up."

He gave her his elbow. "Let's go. You drive. I came here with one of the guys."

"Sounds good." She grabbed his arm, and they left for the best barbecue in this part of Texas.

Dinner was amazing, as usual. Tennessee barbecue might be good, but it sure didn't compare to what they made in Texas. He pushed his plate away and motioned to the server, pointing at their empty mugs, and held up two fingers.

Janet smiled over at him. "So, tell me. Who's the lucky girl that has your heart?"

"Excuse me?" As far as Tristan could tell, he didn't have anything on him anywhere that said Stacey. He hadn't heard from her since this morning, yet he did tell her he'd call her. But here he was instead.

Janet leaned on her elbows. "Tristan, I've been flirting with you all night. You're ignoring my advances. I want to know who she is."

She'd been flirting, and he hadn't noticed. Wow. Who was he? That was easy. He was a guy whose heart was taken, though a bit empty. Stacey's image floated in his mind. Light brown, almost blonde hair, those amazing golden-brown eyes. His jaw clenched. "There is someone, or there was. I had to walk away because she has baggage she needs to sort out." He shrugged and picked up his beer. There was nothing else to say.

"Well, I can tell she still has a hold on you. Maybe you'll hear from her." She finished her beer. "It's late. Let's get out of here."

As Janet drove, Tristan stared out the window. His heart felt empty now that the chaos of the day was finished, and his mind could relax. The focus of the training was the perfect way to occupy his mind and keep from thinking of Stacey and wondering what she was up to. Now, that's all he was doing.

"Hey, do you want to grab some drinks at the bar and talk a bit?" asked Janet as they pulled in front of the hotel.

Tristan glanced her way and noticed the look she gave him. Sultry and hungry. He remembered that look. It used to grab him and hold on, causing him to be at her mercy. But it didn't work this time. "You know, it's been a long day. I think I'll skip it. See you tomorrow. And thanks for the ride."

He walked inside alone and turned on the television. Light brown hair and golden eyes filled his mind again. "I need to call her. I won't be able to sleep if I don't." He dialed the phone, but it went to voicemail.

He checked the clock. *Eleven.*

She was probably in bed and had to work in the morning. He decided to do the same.

The weekend flew by. Saturday was a long day. He spent the day on horseback riding the many acres, checking out the cattle with some of the ranch hands. On Sunday, he toured the facilities and barns, asking specific questions for his uncle.

He had another couple of days of training on Monday morning. The thought irritated him. He'd rather be out getting his hands dirty in a barn or riding a horse than sitting in a room listening to someone speak. He slowly walked to his car and was looking forward to a beer, a nice dinner at the hotel, a hot shower, and bed.

"Hey, cowboy. Want some company?" Janet pulled up in her black convertible.

"What are you doing here on a Sunday?" Tristan leaned in her window. "Nice car. This isn't the one you drove to the restaurant."

"That was my spare. This is my baby."

"I think my uncle may be paying you too much."

"Yeah, whatever. Anyway. Want company?" She raised her eyebrows, waiting for his answer.

"Sure. I'm just going to the hotel restaurant. Want to join me?"

"Meet ya there. I'll get a table." She pulled out.

As he entered the hotel lobby, his phone pinged. It was Stacey. She wanted to talk. He let her know he was eating. They decided to talk around eight o'clock. Plenty of time for him to eat, relax, and get his head on straight.

Janet had two beers waiting for them and a basket of chips with salsa. "Everything good?"

He took a seat and dove right into the chips and downed his beer in one gulp. He was hungry. The beer was cold. "Yep."

"What's her name?" Janet dipped a chip in salsa.

Why does she care? Tristan watched her as she ate. Janet looked good, relaxed, and more mature. They were both very young, immature, and self-centered when they were in their relationship. "Her name's Stacey."

"Is she pretty?"

The server appeared, and they placed their orders.

He ignored her question and changed the subject. He asked her about the ranch and how she felt things were running. They talked shop a bit more until their food appeared, and they were quiet while they ate.

"So, is she pretty?"

Seriously? She needs to let it slide. Tristan raised his hands, palms up. "Why does it matter?" He was getting annoyed. "Yeah, she's pretty. She's gorgeous. She's fun. She's amazing. Why do you want to know?" His gaze was intense.

She raised her hands, palms up. "No reason." She backed off, and things got quiet.

Tristan's mind kept wandering to Stacey. What was she doing? Did she miss him at all? Was she thinking about him? Or was this all one-sided? The more he thought about her, the more he drank.

He needed to get his mind off her. "So, tell me about you. Do you have a special man?" Tristan asked. "You seem so concerned about my love life. What's going on with yours?"

She shook her head and pushed her plate away. "Nope. No one. Nothing. Pretty boring. Has been since you left." She pursed her lips to the side and shrugged.

Did he just hear her correctly? Since he left? "That was two years ago. You've had nothing for two years?"

She smirked. "Now, I didn't say I've had nothing. Just nothing special." Her eyes held his. They looked sad and empty.

He shook his head. *Don't go there again. It's not worth it.* He fought back a yawn and scrubbed his hands over his face. "Look, I'm sorry. It was a long day yesterday; I was at the office early this morning. I'm really looking forward to a good night's sleep." He motioned to the server and handed him the card to pay the bill.

The lobby was empty when they left the restaurant, and they stepped to the side so Tristan could wait for the elevator.

"Thanks for dinner." Janet gave him a hug. She held him tight.

She smelled lightly of flowers. It was the same perfume she had always worn. "Thank my uncle. He paid for it." When they pulled away, their eyes met. He could kiss her and ask her to stay. He knew she would.

It was like Janet read his mind. She leaned toward him, and her lips were on his.

He hesitated and held his breath. *Tristan not a good idea.* He leaned away and opened his eyes. He couldn't do it. He loved Stacey and had to figure out what was going on with them. He didn't want to hurt Janet, but he didn't want to hurt Stacey more. "Janet." He hesitated and stepped back.

Janet squeezed her eyes tighter and sucked her bottom lip in. "I get it. I hope she's worth it." She patted him lightly on the arm and walked away.

"I do, too," Tristan whispered as the elevator opened. When he got out, he called Stacey as he walked down the hall toward his room.

There was no answer. He sighed and threw his phone onto the bed. He hopped in the shower and pictured Stacey's mouth on his, his hands on her, and he relieved himself the only way he could.

CHAPTER 37

S he didn't want to go another day without talking to him. Phone tag was getting old, and Stacey had a nightmare last night that involved Tristan in the arms of another woman. She was scared that if she didn't talk to him soon, that might become a reality.

She dialed his number. It was early, six-thirty, but she hoped he would answer. She was on her way to work and had three busy days before she got Thursday and Friday off for the wedding.

It was now or never.

The phone continued to ring. "Dammit."

She was preparing to push the disconnect button on her steering wheel when a drowsy Tristan answered.

Her heart beat fast. His voice sounded amazing. "Hi, Tristan. It's Stacey." Was that stupid? Wouldn't he know it was her?

"Hey." She heard him clear his throat. "Sorry. Give me a second."

She couldn't tell what he was doing, but when he got back on the phone, he was more awake. "Sorry. I drank some water and just had to wake up a little bit."

Her nerves were going crazy. It seemed like it had been forever since they had last talked. She was so nervous. Just get on with it and say your piece. "I'm sorry it's so early. I'm on my way to work and didn't want to play phone tag anymore."

She paused, but there was no response from him. She focused on her breathing to calm her nerves. *Just talk. You need to straighten things out.* "Look, I don't know when you're coming home, but I want you to know that, for what it's worth, I'm so sorry. I have to let go of the shit that's in my past. I know that. And I miss you so much. I miss us." Her heart was thumping so hard she was sure he could hear it through the phone.

She waited to see if he had anything to say. It was so quiet on his end that she wasn't sure he was even still there. "Tristan, are you there?" She pulled into the parking garage.

"Yeah. I'm still here."

She pulled into a spot and put the car in park. "Say something, please."

She heard him breathe on the other end of the line. "What do you want me to say, Stacey?" His voice sounded drained, finished.

A knife was stuck in her heart. "I don't know." She felt tears welling up in her eyes. "I messed up. I talked to Carla. She told me you didn't have sex."

Tristan's voice boomed through the phone. "No, *I* told you we didn't have sex. *She* made you think we did. Why would you believe her in the first place? You don't even know her, and you believed her. You didn't believe me, and I loved you."

He sounded mad and hurt. She couldn't blame him. She squeezed her eyes tight. She heard the past tense he used, and angry tears threatened to spill from her eyes. She caused this. How stupid could she be? "I know you did. I'm sorry. I should have believed you."

"Yeah, you should have, and I know you're sorry. But those are just words."

"I know they're just words." She felt herself getting angry. Her voice raised. "I can't show you how sorry I am because you aren't here."

Again, all she heard was a loud breath, like a sigh coming through the line.

You need to calm down, Stacey. Breathe. She sucked in a long breath and slowly blew it out. She felt her body relax. "Tristan, look, I don't know when you're coming home, but I want you to be my date for the wedding on Friday. The reception starts at six. Maybe if you get in before then, we can talk. I'll come to you."

The clock on her dash showed her that she needed to get out and get in to work, but she waited. She had to know that he hadn't totally given up.

"My plane gets in Thursday afternoon. I can have my driver drop me off at your house. We can talk then. I won't promise anything, and I'm not sure about the wedding."

She hopped out of her car and headed toward the hospital. A large sigh released from her lungs. "I understand. Thank you." She still had a chance to make things right. "I'll see you on Thursday."

"Yep." He hung up.

She'll take whatever she can get. Her steps were lighter as she walked into the hospital and rode the elevator up to Labor and Delivery. Her smile was wiped from her face as she entered onto a floor of chaos.

He still loved her. He couldn't deny it. He wiped his face with his hands. *Thursday. I have to wait* until *Thursday.*

He was so irritated and tired. He thought that hitting thirty would change things. All the crap of dating would go away, but it hasn't. Relationships are just as hard—harder maybe. The older you are, the more time has passed for your heart to get hurt. He had a newfound respect for people who find their soulmates when they are young.

Thankfully, he knew that today and Tuesday were filled with training. Maybe he'd get lucky and be able to leave on Wednesday instead of staying and shadowing to observe the running of things. His uncle wanted a report, but maybe he could get out of it, and hopefully, when the training's done for the day, he will be able to sneak out and keep Janet from hunting him down. After his dream about them last night. That needs to be a priority.

That dream.

God, it was...wow. In the dream, they didn't separate after the kiss at the elevator. He brought her back to his room, and they had the hottest sex of his memory. In the shower, in the bed, against the wall.

He woke up with the biggest hard-on of his life, and on the phone was Stacey. He felt like she had caught him in the act. Because of that, he couldn't talk to her much because he was scared she would hear his guilt through the phone, then all this mess would start over.

But it was just a dream.

He jumped into the shower and made sure it was as cold as he could stand. Once he was ready, he drove to the office and typed a text for Stacey before he got out of the car, but he hesitated and deleted it. "Only answer her texts. She needs to come to you. She has to prove herself." He blew out his breath and thought about her as he crossed the parking lot.

She was still on his mind when he pulled the door open and entered the lobby of the office and walked right into Janet.

"Good morning, Tristan." Janet gave him her famous toothy smile, which lit up her face.

Tristan's gaze stopped at her lips. He remembered what those lips had done to him last night in that dream. *Enough, Tristan! Focus and breathe.* "Morning." He passed by her quickly, not trusting his body to stand there looking at her. He heard her follow him like he knew she would. "So, what do you have planned today?" He asked.

She walked beside him. He could see her out of the corner of his eyes.

"It looks like I'll be sitting in your training session, then escorting you to your appointments tomorrow." She lifted her brows. "Looks like you're not getting rid of me that easily."

Great. Two days with Janet. He put a smile on his face. Hopefully, a believable one. "Awesome."

"Yep, that's what Don said. It'll also be easier for us to get a hold of each other in case anything else happens and we need to get in touch with you."

Tristan nodded slowly and deeply. *Just what I need. To have Janet able to call me whenever it seemed necessary.*

CHAPTER 38

The chaos Stacey walked into Monday morning continued the entire week. She lost count of how many babies were born, how many mothers had to have emergency c-sections, and how many dads passed out in the delivery room.

All she knew was that the babies born in the hospital this week of April were the cryingest bunch of babies she had at one time in her five years of nursing.

All week, her shifts flew by, and she hardly got time to eat or pee, for that matter. She was so glad she had all the details of the wedding finished because she was of no use to Kristen by the time she got home. She just nodded and agreed, not hearing most of what her best friend was telling her and fell into bed.

By the time her shift was over Wednesday night, she about crawled out to her car.

She wasn't sure how she made it home that night, but she did, and as soon as she got there, she climbed into bed. Her goal was to sleep in Thursday morning, and when she woke up, even though it was her day off, she was going to work her butt off to prepare for the wedding of her two most favorite people.

She fell asleep thinking of Kristen and Jacob being happy.

Then she was shaken awake.

"Stacey, I'm so sorry."

Was Kristen really waking her up? Someone better be dead. She opened her eyes a little bit. "Who's dead?" She mumbled.

"No one. I forgot to order the flowers. I just remembered. What are we going to do?"

Flowers. Kristen was waking her up for flowers. She reached for her phone. Her eyes opened wide when she saw the time.

Seven o'clock.

Kristen woke her up at seven o'clock because she forgot the flowers. She grabbed the pillow next to her and put it over her head, willing Kristen to just go away.

"Stacey. I know. I'm so sorry." Kristen pulled the pillow from her head.

Stacey let out a moan. Knowing she was not going to win, she sat up and tried her best not to glare at her future sister-in-law. "Okay. You make coffee, find a way to get me a cinnamon roll from Des, and I'm going to take a shower and meet you in the kitchen as soon as possible."

Kristen grabbed her in a hug way too hard for her still-sleeping bones to handle. "Thank you, thank you, thank you. You're the best, Stacey!" and she bolted out the door.

Stacey really contemplated dropping back onto her pillow and getting back under her nice warm covers but knew she wouldn't do that to her friend. So instead, she pushed herself out of bed and trudged heavily to the shower.

One very hot shower, two cups of coffee, and, surprisingly, a warm cinnamon bun later, Stacey was awake and calling around to flower shops to find flowers for Kristen. Luckily, they didn't need many, and the tragedy was soon fixed. Flowers would be delivered with boutonnieres and bouquets, by ten a.m. tomorrow.

"I can't believe you woke me up for something that was that simple to deal with." Stacey was on her third cup of coffee and second cinnamon roll. If she kept this up, she wouldn't be able to fit in the already tight dress she bought for the wedding. She looked at the rest of her breakfast and all its ooey gooey goodness sitting on the plate in front of her and contemplated throwing it away.

Her phone pinged.

It was Tristan.

> **I won't be able to be at your house. My plane was delayed. I'll hopefully be home tonight. Do you still want me to come by?**

Stacey felt her shoulders droop as her body deflated. Yeah, she did want him to come by, but it wouldn't be fair, and she couldn't go to him. The girls were all staying here.

**No. I'm sure you'll be
tired, and we're having
a thing for the wedding
anyway. I'll see you at the
reception?**

He didn't answer. Stacey couldn't hide the concern on her face.
"What's wrong?" Kristen asked.

"Tristan's plane's been delayed. He won't be in until late
tonight."

"Stace. Sorry. I knew you wanted to see him and finally have that
talk."

She shrugged. Not a big deal. Just another day to figure out her
feelings. He didn't answer her text. Give him time. Her attention
went back to the cinnamon roll. No need to waste good food.

"So, what do we have left to do?" Stacey asked. Change the subject.

Elizabeth and Jessica both had today and Friday off, so they came
by. Stacey was so thankful for the extra help. She and Kristen would
never have been able to get everything done on their own. Even with
the extra help, the girls took all day to finish everything on the list
and took only a small break for lunch.

Chad and Brady brought pizza and beer to the house for dinner,
and the seven of them ate, then set up the outside tables and chairs
and strung lights from the deck and the trees. Everyone got their
directions and rules for the next day, and then the party began.

They celebrated Jacob and Kristen's relationship, which spanned
years.

Stories of Jacob's obsession with her when he and Chad were freshmen in high school, and she and Stacey were juniors. It took him a while to get over his Kristen obsession, but he finally did soon after he left home for college.

It turned out this was when Kristen started having a crush on him. It then went back and forth for years. On again, off again.

Stacey stood up, quite a few beers in, and tried her hardest not to slur her words. Her emotions were getting to her. Here it goes. "Y'all are my two most favorite people. Everyone knows how much stress you both put on me. Whether you were together or when you broke up, I always picked up the pieces. But what you didn't know is that I always prayed that you would both find each other."

She paused and took a breath. She could feel her emotions getting the best of her. "When Mom and Dad died, things got hard. Jacob, you were a handful. I think Chad would agree."

For once, the joker of the group had nothing to say. He just nodded.

"But that was when I first really noticed how good you two were for each other. Kristen, you supported him in a way I couldn't. He listened to you. You were there and helped get him back on the right path. I know that if Mom and Dad were here today, there's no one else they would want you to be with, Jacob."

Jacob stood up and engulfed his sister in a huge hug. "I love you so much, Stace."

"I love you, too." Her voice was thick with emotion. She held on to her brother. Tomorrow night, he would be leaving their house and officially moving in with Kristen as her husband. Stacey would be alone.

She was sure this was what parents felt like when they watched their children get married and move away. She wiped her tears. "Kristen, you've been my best friend since middle school. Honestly, at times, I thought I was your only friend."

Kristen nodded. "You're the only one my bitchiness never scared away."

Jessica chimed in. "That's because Stacey was the only one you were never bitchy to."

"Probably true." Kristen agreed.

"Anyway. Kristen, we always talked about becoming sisters." Stacey's voice caught. "Then, in college, you said once that you knew you would one day marry Jacob. I never believed you. But I do know that your heart only ever loved him."

She stopped as the tears streamed freely down her face. She took a deep breath and accepted the napkin from Elizabeth. "Last thing I want to say is that I'm so proud of you two. I love you, and one day, I hope to find the forever love that can endure like y'all's can." Even though her heart was full, and she was so happy for her brother and best friend, her heart was also breaking. Could a heart do both of those at the same time? It seemed like it. *I really wish Tristan were here.*

Everyone drank to the couple.

Kristen pulled Stacey off to the side. "Thank you for that." She leaned her forehead against Stacey's. "I love you and am so glad we'll finally really be family. You know tomorrow night, Jacob won't really be gone, right? We will still be here so much you'll be sick of us."

Stacey nodded. She had too many emotions floating around inside her to do anymore speaking.

Kristen grabbed her arms. "Stace, it's time for you to let go of the past and not worry about us. We're going to be fine. You have a guy who will treat you as wonderfully as you deserve to be treated. Don't let him get away. It's time for you to think about yourself. To be selfish. You deserve it."

"I know. You're right. I know all this shit between Tristan and me is my fault. Right now, my goal is to get him to come to the wedding. That's step one. Then I'll make sure he knows how much I need him. How much I love him." She smiled the first real smile she had in days. "Hopefully it's not too late."

"If he loves you, it won't be."

Stacey rolled her eyes. I guess I'll have to wait and see.

It was getting late, and it was time for everyone to leave.

Stacey insisted that Jacob had to leave before midnight. He couldn't see the bride before the wedding. There were some objections from both Jacob and Kristen, but Stacey put her foot down. They needed to keep some traditions, and Jacob was not going to see Kristen until they met at the altar at the justice of the peace tomorrow evening at five-thirty.

Chad and Brady took Jacob to his and Kristen's house. They were going to spend the night there; the girls were staying at Stacey's. The girls all slept in Stacey's room. Stacey and Kristen in the bed, Elizabeth and Jessica on air mattresses on the floor.

While everyone was getting ready for bed, Stacey snuck out and sent Tristan a text.

I'm sure you're home or almost home. I hope I see you at the wedding. We

**need to talk. There's so
much I have to say. 6:00**

She waited for a bit but didn't get a reply.

Her heart fell, but she wouldn't let it get to her. She was sure he had a reason.

"Airports suck." He was on the phone with Adler. "They canceled my flight. The earliest I'll get home is late tonight. And that's hoping there are no issues with the layover in St. Louis." He gave the flight information to Adler, who promised to relay it to their driving service, then he made his way to find something to eat and a place to relax for the day before texting Stacey to let her know.

Twenty-four hours later, his plane taxied into Nashville International Airport. Twenty-four fucking hours he had been either on a plane or in an airport. He finally got to St. Louis only to find out his flight was delayed yet again. He should have just rented a car. The drive from Dallas to Nashville is about twelve hours. From St Louis, it's just over four.

His entire day was shot, and he was exhausted.

He couldn't wait to climb into his bed and sleep.

As soon as the car pulled up to his house, he was out and inside before the driver even had his bags out of the trunk.

"Hey. You finally made it." Adler gave him a strong guy hug, complete with hard pats on the back.

Tristan did not return it. "I'm going to bed." Tristan could barely get the words out. He was so tired.

"I'll be leaving here around one to help Desiree with the cakes. Will I see you at the wedding?" Adler lifted an eyebrow.

"I don't know. I haven't decided yet." He left Adler behind, walked to his room, and barely closed his door before he crashed onto his soft bed.

Chapter 39

Stacey and Kristen were in the woman's restroom at the courthouse. Stacey got the confirmation from Chad that everything was a go. At five thirty, he and Jacob would be down front with the judge, and she and Kristen could walk in.

There was no music, no pastor, no guests. Just the four of them and the judge.

A perfect Kristen wedding.

They finished applying their lipstick and packed all their things back in the bag Stacey had brought with them. Then they stood in front of the mirror.

"Don't do it, Stace." Kristen pointed at her reflection. "Don't you dare cry."

Stacey took a deep breath. "You look beautiful, Kristen." Kristen's skin was a golden tan due to her religious trips to the tanning booth. Her blonde hair was curled slightly to add some waves, but she kept it loose and hanging. Just like Jacob liked it. Her white dress was perfect on her and looked amazing against her golden-tanned skin. The dress was long, yet fitted snugly around all her perfect curves, and the front plunged just low enough to be sexy, and she wore simple white heels.

"Well, Stace, you look amazing as well."

Stacey looked at herself and had to agree. Her dress was just like Kristen's, yet a dark yellow color. With Stacey's light brown hair and tanned skin, the dress really made her eyes pop.

She reached for her bag and pulled out the simple little bouquets they had ordered from the florist. Each one had a white lily and greenery.

Kristen lit up when she saw them. "They're perfect."

"Thank God. I was worried you wouldn't like them. They're very simple, but we only had a couple of days, and they worked with what they had." Sometimes, Kristen can be difficult. Maybe marriage will change her a little. Stacey checked her watch. Five-thirty. "It's time. Ready?"

Kristen's eyes were bulging, and she started to shake.

"My God, Kristen. You look terrified." Stacey turned her away from the mirror. "Look at me." Their eyes focused on each other. "Breathe." Stacey led her through some concentrated breathing. Slowly, in and out. "There. Good. Remember, It's just Jacob."

Kristen smiled. "You're right. I'm getting ready to marry Jacob."

"The exact husband you wished for." Stacey felt tears welling up. "Everything is going to be perfect."

She watched as Kristen's body relaxed and her face lit up. "Let's do this. Take me to my husband."

The girls hugged and left the bathroom.

Chad, Jacob, and the judge were waiting when they walked in.

Stacey and Kristen walked side by side down the short aisle. As she walked, Stacey's eyes never left her brother.

His face was shining. If he was at all nervous or had any doubts, they didn't show. His eyes never left Kristen. His smile filled his face.

The love radiating from both of them would have made the biggest miser believe in true love.

Stacey's heart swelled. This is how things should be. Two people, for better or for worse. Knowing each other's flaws, yet still in love, still together, pledging themselves to each other forever.

Stacey tried to pay attention to the short ceremony, but she couldn't keep her eyes off her brother and best friend.

Chad wrapped his arm around her waist when they were announced husband and wife.

Tears ran down Stacey's face when Jacob was told to kiss his bride.

It was beautiful. It was perfect.

Jacob and Kristen were married. Together forever as one.

Stacey had never felt so proud.

She drove with Chad to her house, and Jacob and Kristen rode together. She sent Elizabeth a text letting her know they were on their way, and she and Chad pulled in first.

She looked around her backyard. "Elizabeth, Jess. Everything is perfect." The tables all had white tablecloths and a small vase of flowers. The food was set up, and Desiree did a great job on the cake and dessert table. Stacey went to thank her and was shocked to see Adler there.

"Hi, Stacey." Adler gave her a small, slightly awkward hug.

Stacey couldn't help but look around. Her heart deflated when she noticed Tristan wasn't there.

"He's not here." Adler read her mind. "He had a shitty time getting home and didn't get to the house until nine this morning. He went right to bed."

Stacey shrugged. "Do you know if he's coming?" Her voice was small.

Adler shook his head. "He didn't say."

Stacey nodded, yet didn't have to worry about it for long because Jacob pulled in.

Jacob and Kristen did just as they were told and waited until all the outside lights were turned on before they got out. They walked down the walkway, edged with lights, hand in hand, all smiles while everyone cheered.

Everyone but Stacey. She cried. Watching her brother and bestie so happy filled her with joy. Not having Tristan here to share it with, put that knife right back in her heart.

"Hey." Elizabeth came over and wrapped her arms around her. "This was perfect. And they are so happy. Good job."

Stacey laughed and wiped the tears from her face. *Get yourself together.* "Thank you, Liz. They are happy. They deserve to be."

Stacey enjoyed the party as everyone started eating and celebrating, and laughter filled the air. Soon Chad changed the music. It was time for the couple's first dance. Stacey stood off to the side with Elizabeth and Brady as Jacob and Kristen took the dance floor. Arm in arm, they danced to their song. They seemed to be so into each other that they didn't notice all the people standing around watching them.

Stacey wiped a silent tear.

Elizabeth wrapped her arm around her. "You know, Stace. They aren't the only ones who deserve to be happy."

Not now. This day isn't about me. He forgot anyway. "It's not about me, Liz. And anyway, I screwed things up. I've got a lot to fix, and I think it could be too late."

Brady leaned over. "Hey, I don't want to step in, but if you really love him and think it's worth fighting for, you need to do whatever is necessary to make things right." He placed a kiss on Elizabeth's cheek.

Elizabeth smiled a broad smile. "He's right. I don't know, Stace. I don't think it's ever too late for love." Elizabeth's gaze fell behind them, and she gestured with her head.

Stacey followed her eyes and turned around.

Her heart stopped.

Walking toward her was Tristan. He was wearing a black suit with a light gray shirt and a gray tie.

She forgot to breathe. She forgot to move. Elizabeth gave her a nudge.

She walked up to him, and butterflies flew wildly around in her stomach. A smile slowly crept across her face. "You made it."

"Yeah, I had an awful night and didn't know if I really wanted to be here."

Stacey's pulse picked up speed the longer she stayed near him. "But you're here. You came."

Tristan reached out and grabbed her hands. "Of course, I'm here. You asked me to come."

She squeezed his hands and stared into his eyes. "I really messed up, and I know I said things and jumped to stupid conclusions, and if I could take it all back, I would, but I can't, so I can just say I'm sorry. You don't have to believe me. I've been a basket case lately, and I'd understand if you walked away. But I need you to know I'll work on my trust issues. I know I can trust you; I know you never deliberately kept anything from me. I was very difficult, and I'm sorry. So sorry." She finally took a breath.

Her eyes searched his. *I love you, Tristan.* Maybe if she thought it enough, he would believe her. "I know I need to prove to you that

I trust you and have faith in us. The only way I can do that is for us to try again." She paused and backed away just a little. "Can we try again?" She winced as she said it. What if he said no?

She would deserve it, but she would still fight for him. She needed him. She wanted him. Her heart beat for him, but for now, her heart was suspended in time, waiting for his answer.

"Yes."

Stacey froze. He said yes. That quickly. "Really?"

A smile grew on his face. "Again, yes."

There was his crease.

Her heart started beating, and she exhaled. She slowly reached out to brush her fingers over his cheek, and her body relaxed. His arms wrapped around her waist, and her body melted.

She looked up into his eyes. Those smoldering, smoky gray eyes, as usual, took her breath away. Her voice came out in a whisper. "I missed you. I missed us. I'm so glad you're here."

Tristan peered down. She was wearing the necklace he had given her. He touched it. "It's perfect with that dress. You look perfect in that dress."

"Thank you," she whispered. "And thank you for showing up. I was scared you wouldn't."

"Thank you for asking me." His hand went to her face.

His touch sent a familiar spark throughout her body. She closed her eyes and leaned into his touch. He was here. With her. A tingle warmed her insides.

He wasn't perfect. She wasn't perfect. It won't always be easy, but a relationship with him was as perfect as it could be. They were great together. His love was all she needed. His love is enough for her, now and always.

She opened her eyes. She had to do whatever she could to get him back. "I'm sorry, Tristan. I'm sorry I let my insecurities from the past come between us. What we have...had...is different. It was real." She was so nervous. She had to get those butterflies to calm down. "I hope we can put our relationship back in the present. I hope we can give us another try."

His hand held her face. "I'd like that." Tristan's thumb brushed gently across her jaw.

A weight lifted from her, and her eyes searched his smoky grays. She had missed those eyes. Her gaze flicked down to his lips. She missed those lips. She missed everything about him.

Her heart skipped. Relax. "Can I kiss you?" She asked him. Not sure how much he wanted.

Their eyes held each other for a minute, then he answered her by leaning down and placing his lips gently on hers.

The butterflies in her stomach swarmed to life. The kiss was warm, sweet, deep, and perfect.

He was exactly what she needed.

EPILOGUE

2 years later

Stacey pushed herself out of bed. It felt like a truck rolled over her. She was exhausted from a long week at the hospital and really had to pee.

She traipsed into the bathroom, and then down to the kitchen.

The aroma of bacon pulled her forward. Her face lit up at the sight that met her eyes. Tristan was making breakfast, French toast and bacon. He made the best French toast and knew it was her favorite.

He looked up from the stove as she entered, as if he could sense her presence. "Hey, gorgeous." He pulled a pan filled with the delicious, doughy and eggy goodness from the oven and placed the bacon on a paper towel to drain.

There was already a glass of orange juice and a banana waiting for her as Stacey took a seat at the table. He was amazing. "What's all this about?" Her face lit up with joy.

Tristan placed a plate of food in front of her and kissed her lips before taking a seat. "Nothing at all. I just want to make sure you know how much I love you. You work hard and deserve this, and it's going to be a busy day. You need to eat."

They ate in silence, and Stacey couldn't keep her eyes off him. They had been married for a little over fifteen months, and every day had been amazing, and it felt like time had stood still.

He looked up, their eyes met, and the crease appeared in his cheek. Butterflies fluttered in her stomach. Even after two years, he still had that effect on her. She left her place at the table and went to sit on his lap.

"What are you doing, Mrs. Calhoun?" He wrapped his arms around her waist.

"Just needing to be near you, my handsome husband." She placed her lips on his, and quickly their kiss intensified.

He moaned as he pulled away from her. "I'd love to do this all day, but you know your brother and Kristen will be here soon. We need to get dressed and look a little decent."

"You're right." She dropped a peck on his cheek. "I can't wait to tell everyone the news."

Tristan's hand went to her belly. In the yoga pants, you could scarcely make out the start of a baby bump.

They've been trying for a while to get pregnant, and it finally happened, but decided to wait until the first trimester was over before they told anyone. "I can't wait to tell Kristen and Jacob. Thank you for letting us tell them first."

"Of course," answered Tristan. "They're your family. My aunt and uncle can wait a little longer. It'll do Aunt Elie good. God, she's going to die."

Stacey chuckled as she started clearing the table. "You're not kidding."

"Here. I've got this." He nudged her away from the sink. "You go get ready."

"Okay, thanks."

He winked at her as she left the kitchen.

Jacob and Kristen were a little late, which was typical. Stacey and Tristan were on the front porch when the car finally pulled into the driveway. Tristan wrapped an arm around her waist. "Are you ready?" His face radiated excitement.

Sometimes Stacey thought he was more excited about this baby than she was. That was okay with her. He was going to be an amazing dad. "Yep. Let's do this."

She walked at a fast pace toward the car, with a wide smile on her face. An adorable little girl with long blonde hair, the spitting image of her mother, came toddling into Stacey's arms. "Hey, precious angel. How's Aunt Stacey's girl?" Stacey twirled Carly around in a circle before landing her perfectly on her hip. Carly's laugh twinkled like wind chimes. Once her laughter stopped, her two little hands pressed against Stacey's face, and she left a slobbery, wet kiss on her cheek. "Wow, thanks."

"Here, let me say hi." Tristan took his niece from Stacey's arms.

Jacob laughed as Stacey wiped her cheek dry. "Hey, sis." He wrapped her in a hug. "You know that was a slobber of love."

"Yeah, little brother. I know." Stacey turned to Kristen, whose stomach was huge. "Hey, bestie." She sang.

Kristen scowled, causing Stacey to throw her head back in laughter as she wrapped her in a strong hug. Kristen was an amazing mother, much to her own surprise, but hated being pregnant. Pregnancy brought out her bitchy side a little more.

"Looks like you're feeling great," Stacey teased.

Kristen placed her hands on her enormous stomach. "Yeah, well, this little guy's in no hurry. He was due yesterday. I'm really over this. I'm hot, my feet are swollen, and I'm so tired."

Jacob wrapped his arms around her, resting his chin on her shoulder. "But you are still the most beautiful woman I've ever laid eyes on." He kissed her cheek.

Kristen's face softened. "Thank you, Jake. I don't know how you see that, but as long as you believe it."

"Oh, Kristen. You're being a little over dramatic. It can't be that bad," said Stacey.

The scowl was back on her face. "Let's just see what you say when you're finally pregnant, and the baby decides not to be on time, has made your stomach blow up like a hot air balloon, your shoes don't fit, *and* you can't walk without everything hurting. Until that happens, just don't talk to me."

"Well," said Tristan. "Those were some encouraging words for your best friend, who will be facing all those issues in about..." he turned to Stacey.

She looked at the sky and counted on her fingers. She held up six. "Six months, give or take a day or two."

Tristan winked at her, and they waited for Jacob and Kristen's reaction.

Jacob picked Carly up in his arms, and his eyes got wide. "What?" He turned to Kristen, then back to his sister. "You're pregnant?"

She nodded.

"Wow!" He wrapped her in a hug. "Congratulations!"

Kristen squealed. "Yes! I'm so excited for you!" Kristen joined in their hug, and Carly got smooshed and let out a little cry.

Stacey laughed and leaned into her beautiful niece. "You are going to have a big year, princess. First, you'll be a big sister, and then you get to be a cousin. Aunt Stacey is having a baby."

Carly pointed to her mom's belly. "Baby there."

Kristen grabbed her daughter's finger and kissed it. "Yes, Car. And there's also a baby in Aunt Stacey's belly."

Carly, being only eighteen months old, didn't really care and wanted to get down. She ran around the yard chasing the birds.

Tristan wrapped his arm around Stacey's waist and gave her a kiss.

Jacob wrapped his around Kristen. "I'm so happy for you two," said Jacob.

"Me too," agreed Kristen. "The best thing is that our kids will be close in age and able to grow up together. Life is perfect."

Stacey's face shone. Kristen was right. Life was perfect. She and Kristen were married to the men of their dreams, and their kids will grow up together.

Life couldn't get any better.

"You're glowing, gorgeous." Tristan brushed some hair off her face. "That look fits you perfectly." He leaned in and kissed her.

Notes to the Reader

Thank you for taking your time and reading *Your Love is Enough*, book 2 of the *More Than Enough* series. I hope you enjoyed reading it as much as I enjoyed writing it. If you enjoyed the story and characters, I would be so grateful to you if you would take the time and leave a review wherever you purchased the book.

I would love to hear from my readers, so please connect with me, on Instagram and Facebook—Donna R. Madden Writer, or email me at author@donnarmadden.com

Or visit my website Donnarmadden.com

Turn the page to read a sample of *You Are Enough* now

You Are Enough-Sample

Chapter 1

—Adler and Leila's story—

I f someone would have told him he'd be sitting at a wedding and pining for a relationship, while he watched so many couples spin dreamily arm in arm with their significant other on the dance floor, he would have scoffed and told them they needed to get their fucking head examined.

Adler Warfield was a typical handsome, charismatic, egotistical rich playboy, and the heir to the biggest meat company in the United States, Warfield Meats. He had never had a problem finding a girl to drape from his arm, or to warm his bed. Ever since he was sixteen and finally talked the beautiful captain of his college prep academy's volleyball team to accompany him to his formal and ended up "getting some" for the first time in the back seat of his jeep, girls had been easy, and sex had been prolific.

Last night was no different. He and Desiree, the woman he had been sort-of seeing, had a typical night of groundbreaking sex. That woman was creative, that's for sure. Now here he was, at the wedding of someone he hardly knew with Desiree. Unfortunately, she was off working, helping the caterer, and cutting the cake, and he was left sitting alone, like so many girls he had left in his wake.

Okay, so he sort of knew the bride. He'd met her at the end of last summer when he and his cousin Tristan were at a convention in Gatlinburg and spent the last weekend hiking and enjoying the area. Tristan had ended up with Stacey, his now girlfriend, and Adler met Elizabeth, today's bride, who was at the time on the outs with her fiancé, today's groom. Elizabeth was one of the few women who didn't fall for Adler's charms. There was a first time for everything.

But now, as he watched Elizabeth and Brady dance in each other's arms with their son cuddled between them, he couldn't deny she was happy. Any idiot could see that. Both her boys adored her, the tiny one with brown curls and his dad. Good for her.

It was a good thing they didn't start a relationship. Adler didn't do kids. Maybe one day, if they're his own, but someone else's baggage? Yeah. Not his thing.

Adler's gaze roamed the tent. It was a perfect May night for an outdoor wedding. The temperature was mild, with a little nip in the air, but ideal for those dressed in formal wear. His gaze stopped on Tristan and Stacey. They were holding each other tight and dancing to the slow song that played over the speakers. Adler's mom might get her lifelong dream of becoming a grandma after all.

Tristan and Stacey were perfect together. He was head over heels in love with her, and Adler was sure she felt the same way. Tristan deserved to be loved and happy. He'd had a hard enough life. His father died when Adler and Tristan were just babies. Tristan and his mom moved onto the grounds of Adler's house. Their moms were sisters, so Tristan and Adler, who were only one month apart in age, ended up growing up more like brothers than cousins. Then

Tristan's mother came down with cancer and passed away, forcing him to move into the main house when he was in sixth grade, and was raised like a son by Adler's parents, Don and Elisha.

Adler let out a sigh and emptied his beer. *I can either sit here like a creeper, watching everyone dance, wishing I had what they had—which is just fucked up—or go pull Des away from the cake table long enough to dance and get my mind back on the here and now. Being with a sexy, hot woman.*

Adler pushed himself up and sauntered to the other side of the tent. He admired Desiree the closer and closer he got. She was hot and trouble, two things that always got his attention.

She'd pinned her auburn hair on top of her head, and it looked elegant along with her spaghetti strap, formfitting maroon dress. It clung perfectly to all her curves and accented her breasts—his favorite.

"Hey. I was studying you as I crossed the room. You look hot tonight," Adler said as he approached.

"You were studying me? What am I, a textbook?" She placed a slice of cake on a plate.

"Maybe. Sometimes you're as hard to crack." He smiled a sexy, crooked smile that met his eyes.

Desiree shook her head. "We'll get some studying done later."

"Sounds like a plan." He picked up a plate with cake on it.

Desiree looked up. "So, you're finally ready to try my cake? I figured you'd be one of the first in line."

"I've heard cake is an excellent substitute for sex, and with what you're doing to me in that dress, I need something to take the edge off."

Desiree laughed and stared at him, her eyes hot and focused.

"Excuse me." The young woman Adler had noticed helping Desiree earlier was at the table with a large empty tray. He stepped out of the way as she filled it with more cake slices.

Her downplayed attractiveness caught his eye. It wasn't the first time he'd seen her. He'd seen her around, knew she worked at the boutique in town and sometimes helped Desiree, but this time, her being there, this close to him, sent a strange sensation into the pit of his stomach.

Up close, Adler could tell she wasn't drop-dead gorgeous like Desiree, but she was cute and very attractive. Her brown hair reflected the light and fell in soft waves over her shoulders. She wore very little makeup and had a spattering of freckles across her nose. They were adorable and made her even more attractive. His gaze lingered there.

When she looked up, their gazes locked, and he noticed her eyes were a unique hazel color that drew him in. A smile ticked up at the edges of his lips. Yeah, she was hot, but in a different way than Desiree. She seemed almost innocent.

She gave him a small smile as she picked up the now full tray and continued her job.

Adler admired her from behind as she walked away. She wore a red dress that fell just below her knees. The sleeves were ruffled and short, barely covering her shoulders, and the bodice was cut in a scooped neckline which showed some tantalizing, yet tasteful, cleavage.

He studied her as he ate his cake. See, he did a lot of studying. Her hips swayed enticingly as she walked. A tighter dress, fitting snugly around those hidden curves, would be interesting. *I bet she's got some curvy hips and a nice ass. Too bad she's hiding it.*

"Why are you zoning out?" Desiree followed Adler's eyes and raised her brow.

He tore his thoughts from across the room and turned his attention back to his date. He shoved the last bite of cake into his mouth. "This is delicious. Do you think there'll be any left?"

Using the cake knife, Desiree slid another piece onto his plate. "Shouldn't be much. It doesn't matter. You won't be needing cake."

He raised his brows.

Desiree laughed and bumped him playfully. "Anyway, Leila's doing a great job of making sure everyone eats. Usually there's so much cake left because no one takes it."

"Leila?" Adler asked as he scooped up a bit of icing from the cake onto his finger and offered it to Desiree, who licked it from his skin. That small movement sent blood straight to his cock and put it at attention.

He placed the finger she'd licked into his own mouth and winked.

"You're too much." She shook her head. "Leila, the girl I've introduced you to at the bakery. The one you were just ogling as she delivered cake across the room."

What? Adler turned all his attention to Desiree. "What are you talking about? I wasn't ogling anyone. I don't ogle. If I want to watch, I watch. I stare. I've even been known, as presented before, to study. But ogle?" He shook his head, wrapping her in his arms. "Now you, I stare at and watch. I study. I've been studying you all night as you've been working. Okay, I might have ogled you a little, trying to picture you skinny dipping in my pool later. I like what I see. I like what I'm imagining, and now I'm wondering if there is anything creative we can do with this extra icing. It's good. I like it."

"I'm glad. It's my secret recipe."

"Hmm, I like secrets. And since it's that amazing, it really would be a shame to waste it."

"I think we can figure out something to do with it."

Damn. This was one of the many things that made Desiree so intriguing to him. She had a dirty mind that rivaled his own and was up for anything.

"Save it, then." He winked. "Now, do you think you can pull yourself away to dance with me? We haven't danced all night."

"I know. I'm almost done here." Just then, Leila came back with an empty tray. "Here Leila, I'll take that from you. I need to clean up anyway. Could you do me a huge favor and occupy my date? He needs to dance."

Leila looked like she had seen a ghost. Her eyes were wide.

He searched her face as she talked with Desiree. She looked endearing and sweet. Innocent even. He usually liked them tattooed, loud-mouthed, and wild—like Desiree. But endearing and sweet, something about those qualities suddenly grabbed his attention.

Change may not be a bad thing.

"Come on." He offered Leila his arm. "Let's dance and let Des finish cleaning up."

"You want to dance with me?" Leila's gaze traveled down his body, then back up without a bit of interest.

Okay, this might be a challenge. Her face sure didn't light up like a woman's usually did when admiring his body. "Yeah, why wouldn't I?" Adler placed her hand on the crook of his arm.

Again, Leila eyed him, then shrugged. Adler led her onto the dance floor.

A new slow song started when they got onto the floor. Adler held her at a safe distance to help her feel more comfortable. "So, Leila,

I know we've sort of met before, but never officially. Nice to meet you."

Leila smiled. "You too. I've always thought Adler was a unique name."

"It is. My parents are unique people. They knew what kind of son they were going to have and named me accordingly."

"What kind of son is that?" Her voice was short and static.

Her body stiffened under his touch.

He backed up and scrutinized her features. Her hair blew slightly in the night breeze as they danced in and out of the crowd. He had an overwhelming desire to touch it and see if it was really as soft as it looked. Her eyes, enticing hazel, glimmered under the lights and held him in their grip. His pulse picked up its tempo, and his suit jacket became constricting. Suddenly it was as if there were only the two of them on the dance floor. He tightened his hand around her waist, and her back straightened under his grip. Time to lay on the Adler charm and get her to relax.

"Well," he cleared his voice and regained his composure, "Adler means eagle, and it just so happens I'm laser focused and can see what I want from miles away. When I go for what I want, like the eagle, I hardly miss." He shot her what he considered his "melt their panties off" smile, which usually caused girls to fall at his feet, but all he got from Leila was more space between them and a raised brow. His mouth became dry. A drink would be great right now.

"Here's what I know about you," she started. "I know you're from a rich family. You enjoy women—lots of women—and you think very highly of yourself."

A smile ticked at the edge of his mouth. Maybe she was a little interested. "You've been asking questions about me?"

A soft laugh came from her chest, and her face lit up, causing her expression to finally relax. She was even more beautiful when she laughed and let herself go a little.

"Don't put your ego into overdrive, Casanova. I haven't asked any questions about you. Desiree talks, and so do some of my friends. You are quite the conversation piece. The girls you dated before Desiree were a bit . . . how can I describe them . . . Brainless? Fake? Easy?"

Damn, that made him sound shallow. He tried to swallow, but his mouth was dry. He really needed that drink. "Hey, be nice. They all had their own special qualities and talents, but did Desiree say we were dating?"

Leila's brows raised, and she put a little more space between them. "No, I just figured with as much time as you two were spending together, it had to be called something."

"So, is that maybe a bit of jealousy I'm detecting from you?" Adler wiggled his brows. Maybe she did think of him, even a little.

Again, she laughed, but this time her head tipped back, exposing her neck. His heart stopped. Her skin was a smooth ivory, and he longed to caress her neck with his lips. To feel the vibration from her throat against his lips as she moaned his name. *Adler, what the hell is going on with you?*

Her smile lit up her face, and her gaze met his. "Not a chance, Adler."

His dark eyes held hers, and he shook his head slightly to clear the thoughts that were taking over. Thoughts of his lips on her skin and the erotic sounds he could imagine coming from her throat. He pulled her closer and tightened his grip, adding in some fancy two-step footwork as he led her around the dance floor.

His mother had forced Tristan and him take a ballroom dance class in high school. She said it would help them with the company dinner parties they had to attend. At the time, he'd hated it. As an adult, it helped to impress women.

Well, usually. Again, not so much today.

But he enjoyed dancing with Leila. They fit together well. She was the perfect height. He'd guess five-foot-seven, which fit his six-foot frame perfectly. He slid his hand down over the arch in her lower back as he continued his trek around the dance floor.

A smile lit up her face. He winked, and his hand slipped lower on her waist. He could feel a soft panty line under the light fabric of her dress. He slowed to a more comfortable speed and gave her a chance to catch her breath. "Why don't you tell me something about yourself, Leila? What brings you here to the wedding?"

Leila tilted her head, holding his gaze as she reached around and raised his hand up a bit and stepped back to put more space between them. "I work with Elizabeth at Main Street Boutique in town. She's my boss." Her eyes traveled around the tent.

Adler smirked. Again, his advances were being ignored, and now he got the feeling that he annoyed her. "Got somewhere to go?" He followed her gaze.

She stopped dancing. "Honestly, yes. I need to get home, so I figured I'd go tell Elizabeth and Brady bye. I'll be working for her while they go on their honeymoon." She pulled out of his arms. "Thanks for the dance and the conversation. It was surprising. I'll talk to you later."

She gave him a small smile and walked away, leaving Adler alone on the dance floor. That was a first. He watched her retreating form and knew he needed to see her again.

"All single women need to meet on the dance floor immediately. All single women." The DJ's voice thundered through the speakers. "Single guys don't go far. You're next."

Adler found himself surrounded by Tristan and his friends, Chad and Jacob. Tristan handed him a beer. Thank God. He was spitting feathers.

"Thanks man." He raised the beer to his lips and downed half the cold liquid immediately. God, that tasted good. He was thirstier than he'd thought. "Where's the girls?" He wasn't used to seeing Tristan alone. Stacey was usually glued to his side. What had happened to them being single guys enjoying all the girls? Oh well. He'll need to get in touch with some of their friends from college.

Tristan pointed with his beer. "Out there. It always amazes me how excited women are about catching the bouquet."

Jacob and Chad started talking with Tristan, but Adler wasn't listening. His attention was across the dance floor. He spotted Leila between Jessica, Stacey, and Stacey's best friend, Kristen, and they were surrounded by women of all ages. Even in a crowd, Leila stood out to him like she was the only woman at the wedding. He couldn't tear his gaze from her.

As quickly as the women gathered, music was played. Elizabeth entered the floor and turned her back on them. Then she tossed the bouquet over her head, and it was like she threw gold. The women jumped toward it, hands flailing in the air. Some of them fell to the ground as they tripped over each other. Limbs sprawled everywhere, screams were heard over the roar of the music, but then Jessica whooped and hollered congratulations.

The mob of women stepped away from a wildly blushing Leila, who was left in the center of the floor holding the white and pink bouquet of roses. The blush put some extra color on her already pretty features, and Adler's heart missed a beat.

"What?" he asked as the guys were being pulled onto the floor. He found himself in the center, joined by Tristan, Jacob, Chad, and other men. None of them were as excited as the women, as they stood there with their hands in their pockets or clasping their beer with both hands, and there was a fight—which no one wanted to win—over who would stand in the front.

Before he knew what happened, Adler was pushed to the front of the mob just as Brady let the garter fly, and it landed right in his hands. There was no fight, no screaming, no one falling on the floor. Just a bunch of men acting like getting touched by the garter would give them cooties—if they still believed in those childhood creatures.

"Well, Adler, have fun." Tristan gave him a hard pat on the arm as Adler was drug over to Leila by the DJ. *What the hell is going on?* It was as if he were in a dream. First, he was alone on the dance floor; now he was with Leila again, but everyone's eyes were on them. He tried to catch her gaze, but she was looking anywhere but at him.

"Okay, everyone," announced the DJ, "It's time for the bachelor to put the garter on the bachelorette." He leaned in close to Adler as if he was going to tell him a secret but whispered into his microphone. "Okay. Now, you're a good-looking guy. She's a pretty lady. We want a show. Don't we?" He yelled the last two words, getting the crowd riled up.

And yes, they got involved. Everyone cheered, and there were a lot of cat calls. Adler was certain he should be embarrassed, but luckily embarrassment wasn't within his range of emotions. Leila, on the other hand, had a blush on her face that matched the pink of the roses in the bouquet, and it was getting redder by the minute.

When he looked over at Tristan and the guys, they were all laughing and jeering.

"Go ahead and kneel in front of her," instructed the DJ. "When the music starts, put that garter on her leg and put it up as far as you can. Keep going until the music stops."

Here he was, on the floor, kneeling in front of Leila. Her blush now matched the red of her dress, making her even more endearing. This wouldn't be bad at all as long as his heart slowed down a bit. He gave her a large, toothy smile. "Well, so much for getting out of here." He brushed his knuckles against her shin, sending a chill up his arm. He cleared his throat. "Want to give them a show?"

She huffed out a breath and stared at the ceiling. "Just get it over with."

He held up his hands. "I can't do anything until the music starts." The music started. He wiggled his brow and turned to the crowd, putting up his hands and letting out a holler. He was going to enjoy this.

"Good grief, just get on with it," said Leila as she shot daggers at him with her eyes.

The music was sexy with a hard beat. He touched her shin again and brushed his hands up her leg, causing his heart to skip. *Damn. It's not the first time you've touched a woman, Warfield.* He took a deep breath, then slipped the garter around her foot and slid it up slowly.

Yeah, this was nice. Her skin was soft and smooth. He dragged his hand slowly up her calf to her knee, and a shiver moved through her body. His pulse picked up speed even more. He was tempted to kiss her knee and finally taste her soft skin that had been tempting him all through their dance, but instead he placed his palm on her inner thigh as the garter traveled past her knee. He breathed in, and his eyes caught hers. She looked shocked. And something else. Maybe she was enjoying this more than she let on. He sure was. He swallowed hard, and his eyes slowly trailed up her leg. God, he was wrong before. She was sexy and hot.

He brushed her thigh with his knuckles and continued creeping the garter up higher until his hands finally dipped beneath her dress. His heart thumped quickly and hard, pumping blood to all parts of his body and causing the crotch of his pants to become a little snug. He gripped her thigh as he moved to adjust the tightness.

Leila took in a sharp breath, and his focus snapped to her face. Her hazel-green eyes sucked him in like they were an endless hole.

His breath caught, and she bit her lower lip, causing his attention to go straight there. He had an immediate need to place his mouth on hers. To finally taste what he had been desiring all night.

The voices and cat calls all around increased.

He cleared his throat. "It's all a show, beauty," he said, his voice thick. This shouldn't be turning him on, but it totally was. Just touching her soft skin sent electricity running through him, not a feeling he was used to. He suddenly realized he was caressing her skin when her legs closed hard on his hand.

"Party's over, Casanova." Leila's eyes were smoldering as if they could burn him up from the inside out. "You've put on your show. Now it's time to remove your hands."

Yeah, she might be over it, but she had to have felt something. There was no denying the unmistakable connection between them. *Pull yourself together.* He winked. "You've got it. I'll remove my hands—for now." He threw his hands in the air, surrendering to her.

She wrenched her leg from his touch, breaking their connection. "Whatever," she said as he stood, raising his hands over his head in victory.

He pulled her up and held her hands in the air while the hoots and hollers continued until the dance music started and everyone filled the floor. The electricity that was unmistakable between them was gone, but his heart was still going mad.

Adler held on to her hand, not ready to fully let her free. "Come on. Stay and dance." Their faces were close. He could smell her perfume, flowers and something he couldn't pinpoint but wouldn't soon forget.

"Like I said, I've gotta go." She pulled away from his grasp.

His hand was suddenly empty and cold. He made a fist, willing the warmth of her touch to remain. *What the hell are you doing? Pull yourself together.* "Well, thanks for letting me put my hands up your dress. I hope it was as good for you as it was for me." Adler chuckled uncomfortably, trying to make light of the situation, but his pulse was still racing, and the heat that had seeped through his fingers when he touched her skin had traveled throughout his body. *Yeah, this was so good for him.*

"Oh, you have no idea." She tipped her head, and for the second time that night, she left him standing alone on the dance floor.

He raised a brow while he watched her retreat and had to resist running after her and begging her to stay. He'd relished the feeling of holding her in his arms and feeling her skin against his fingertips. Soft and right. She was beautiful, but when she smiled and relaxed, that beauty tripled and took his breath away. What was going on with him?

She had a different kind of spunk. She didn't give in to his flirting. Usually when he said that about his name, with that smile, the girls fell at his feet. Leila didn't. She might be a challenge.

His smile filled his face. Oh yeah, she might be. He liked that, and he never backed away from a challenge.

That was just a taste. Grab your copy of *You Are Enough* and watch as Adler fights for something he wants for the first time in his life.

About the Author

Donna R. Madden lives in a small town north of Nashville with her husband of over 30 years, where they've successfully raised three amazing boys who are now out in the world doing their own thing. These days, their fur babies—Briar the dog and King Marcus Henry XXII (aka "Kitty Kitty")—rule the roost and demand all the attention.

When she's not teaching or dreaming up her next romance novel, you'll find Donna with an adult beverage in one hand, and a book in her lap (yes, she's mastered the art of multitasking). Her happy place is anywhere near water—poolside with friends, toes in the sand at the beach, or sitting by a lake or relaxing by a river with the sun in her face and a story in her hand.

Donna believes in happily-ever-afters, both in the pages of her books and in real life. She writes the kind of romance she loves to read—stories filled with heart, heat, and characters you'll want to invite over for wine and girl talk.